LADY VIOLET PAYS A CALL

THE LADY VIOLET MYSTERIES — BOOK SEVEN

GRACE BURROWES

GRACE BURROWES PUBLISHING

Lady Violet Pays a Call

Cover design by Wax Creative, Inc.

Cover art by Cracked Light Studio, Inc.

DEDICATION

This series is dedicated to my nephew, Jackson.

CHAPTER ONE

HUGH

A gentleman who asks the woman he loves to marry him should be devastated when circumstances prevent the lady from speaking her vows. Circumstances, in the person of a wife I had thought long dead, showed up at precisely the moment when Lady Violet Belmaine had agreed to become Madame Hugh St. Sevier.

Le Bon Dieu has a unique sense of humor, *non*? And in my humble person, the Almighty has been provided with endless entertainment. Nonetheless, divine providence has also smiled upon me in my blackest hours. A gentleman does not complain.

My wife Ann and I were the victims of complementary vagaries of war. While I was serving as a medical volunteer during Wellington's campaign on the Iberian Peninsula, Ann's first husband—a young Scotsman—died in battle. She was not on the official rolls as an officer's wife, and thus she was stranded in a foreign land, her options limited to holy matrimony with my humble self or unholy prostitution with half the regiment.

Ann is pragmatic by nature.

After we married, she watched me practice battlefield medicine for less than a year. She then took her chances trailing a band of deserters heading for the coast in hopes of finding passage home. I was told her party had come to a bad end at the hands of a French patrol—no survivors.

That erroneous information was spread by English officers in an effort to stem the never-ending tide of disloyal soldiers. Ann, a few months later, read of my supposed death on the casualty rolls, and thus our paths diverged. Chance alone had me traveling to Perth, Scotland, in the company of Lady Violet Belmaine, my former intended. On the streets of Perth, not a year past, Ann had caught a glimpse of me, and I of her.

At the time, I had resorted to the usual widower's defenses—my eyes had played tricks on me. Scotland, the land of Ann's birth, had played tricks on me. My increasing regard for Lady Violet had inspired my conscience to see what had not been before me.

Those chance sightings might have been the end of matters—many an ill-suited couple has parted ways to start afresh—except that Ann and I had been married long enough and passionately enough that, unbeknownst to me, a child had resulted.

Do not judge us, not unless you have been young, lonely, and far from home in wartime.

Fiona has her mother's flaming red hair, my brown eyes, and a spirit that delights me every time I behold my daughter.

Fiona's mother has a temper, a complicated code of honor, and an unwavering devotion to our child. I admire all three attributes, truly I do. Ann confronted me with the fact of her existence—and Fiona's—as much to prevent Lady Violet from undertaking a bigamous union as to ensure Fiona enjoyed my support and protection.

What I wanted was of no particular moment to Ann, nor should it have been. Were she to ask me about my wishes, I'm not sure I could fashion a coherent reply in French or English, even now.

In her defense, Ann had no notion when she interrupted my

wedding plans that Violet already carried my child—and neither had I. Violet herself had yet to come to that realization. If all goes well, her ladyship should become a mother in less than six months' time. If all goes perfectly, she will become a Scotsman's marchioness before that happy occasion.

What a muddle, as the English would say.

The only honorable course open to me was to set aside my ambitions where Lady Violet was concerned—or to allow her to graciously set *me* aside. I turned my energies to being Fiona's papa and Ann's...

I believe the English term is *housemate*.

We dwell at Belle Terre in rural Kent, a property I inherited. I had been considering selling Belle Terre, but when Ann and I needed a place to sort ourselves out, I reasoned that an estate to which I was not attached, one where I had little loyalty from the staff, was the better choice.

We have been here nearly three months. We are *settling in*. Protracted silences are relieved by short conversations relating mostly to Fiona's activities.

I am not to buy our daughter a pony for at least two years.

I am to speak French to her in the forenoon. I may speak English to her thereafter.

I am to read to her at bedtime, though Fiona is old enough to grasp simple texts herself in English, French, and Gaelic.

Thus do the lord and lady of the manor *settle in* at Belle Terre.

I am permitted to ride out, and because the acreage associated with the property is considerable, I use my time in the saddle to acquaint myself with the land and tenants. The work is uphill there—there too—owing in some part to my lamentable Frenchness.

I have grown heartily weary of speaking to my tenants in slow, loud words of few syllables, but the average Kentish farmer is apparently prone to poor hearing.

My horse's hearing is excellent, and when Charlemagne pricked his ears and stared intently at the path leading up to the manor house, I came alert as well. I was alone in the stable, the lads having gone for their nooning. I was happy to busy myself with removing Charlemagne's saddle and bridle after a morning of loudly admiring Mrs. Deever's new baby—despite the infant's slight case of convergent strabismus—and loudly hoping Mr. Deever's harvest was as impressive as he predicted.

The steps on the path were soft and quick, also light—not a grown man. I had time to both hope and dread that my wife sought me out before Fiona scampered into view.

"Papa, you must come. Mama says. *Vite! Vite!*"

Ann never summoned me, and I never summoned her. *Vite! Vite!* was both encouraging and mildly alarming. "I must first put Charlemagne away, child, then I will come."

"Put him away quickly, Papa. Mr. Grant has need of you. He came to the kitchen to fetch Mrs. Trebish, and she came to fetch Mama in the sewing room, and Mama sent me to fetch you."

Mrs. Trebish, our new housekeeper, had taken her post with fear and trembling at the prospect of working in the home of *a murdering Frenchie.* Only Ann's repeated reassurances that the owner of the household was also a physician who had *served under Wellington* induced Mrs. T to grace us with her presence.

She was civil to me, but much preferred to deal with Ann, whose Scottish origins were also less than ideal in Mrs. T's eyes, but by no means as dubious as my own.

"You should tell Jules to put Charlemagne away, Papa."

"Jules is taking his luncheon."

"Jules!" Fiona enjoyed prodigiously healthy lungs. "*S'il vous plaît, venez* now! Come, please!"

When excited, Fiona mixed up her languages. When absolutely beside herself, which I had observed on only one occasion, she lapsed into her mother's native Gaelic. Charlemagne looked as if he too was about to start babbling in several languages, so great was his dismay at Fiona's agitation.

"Jules is in the servants' hall, Fiona. He cannot hear you."

"Then I will fetch him!" She dashed off, leaving me to remove

Charlemagne's saddle and lead him to his loose box. I did not put away the saddle or bridle, nor did I give the horse the grooming he deserved. The beast seemed happy enough to be reunited with the pile of hay waiting for him in the corner of his stall, and I had cooled him out properly.

I adopted as rapid a pace as dignity would allow when I made my way to the house. My wife had sent for me, albeit at the behest of a neighbor. Considering that Ann generally had no use whatsoever for her husband, I was pleased to heed her summons.

I came into the house using the back entrance intended for servants and tradesmen. This habit horrified all and sundry. Because Belle Terre was a sizable replica of the Parthenon, my abandonment of decorum saved me many pointless steps circling around to a more genteel approach.

I came to my wife in all my dirt and found her in the company of an agitated Dervid Grant. They occupied Ann's private parlor, an elegant space full of light, soft upholstery, and the scent of roses.

Grant was a tenant farmer, using the term loosely. More significantly, he was the father of a bewilderingly large brood, considering that he was still a young man. His presence in Ann's parlor signified dire trouble afoot.

In addition to being newcomers and foreigners, Ann and I were also well set up. Thus, to the likes of Grant, my wife and I were of an alien species from several perspectives.

"Could be twins again," he was saying as he ran a hand through disheveled wheat-blond hair. "The twins were awful. Cassia nearly died, they took so long to be born."

He noted my arrival and nodded at me, then began circling a battered cap in his hands.

"Your wife is in childbed?" I asked.

"She's in agony, sir. Miss Marigold said I was to fetch you."

But of course. Fetch me now that the situation had become dire, when saving mother and child was a much less likely proposition than it might have been a day ago. If all my skill and all my experience yielded only tragedy, the fault would lie with me and not with the midwife who'd so humbly—and belatedly—had me summoned.

"Give me a moment to fetch my husband's medical bags," Ann said, "and I will need to change into an older dress."

"Please hurry," Mr. Grant said, "and I'll just be going."

Ann had made the sensible decision for me, the only possible decision. "Nonsense, Grant," I said. "My gig will be out front in ten minutes, and you will arrive home much more quickly by traveling with us. Have you eaten yet today?"

He looked bewildered, and as if the slightest breeze would send him into a sound nap on Ann's Savonnerie carpet. I knew what that felt like, when exhaustion and worry stole every last wit.

"Go down to the kitchen, Mr. Grant," Ann said, heading for the door. "You must keep up your strength. Please tell Cook to prepare a basket to send along with us, because your children must eat as well."

Grant looked to me for either a second to that motion or a translation into some dialect a tired, terrified male could understand.

"Food," I said. "A sandwich for yourself, a basket for the children. Off you go to the kitchen, and send one of the grooms for the gig."

I did not clap my hands and snap, *Vite! Vite!* as Fiona had done, for that would have been French of me—also uncharacteristically forward. Grant already lacked confidence in my medical skill, and I did not want to add to his fears.

I caught up with Ann on the landing, though she was moving at her usual forced march.

"You will have to see to my hooks," she said, "and do not think of remonstrating with me, Hugh."

"Why would I remonstrate with you?"

I earned myself an inspection at the top of the steps for that perfectly innocent question. "These people cannot pay you," Ann said, "and what they do not pay for, they do not respect. I know that, but a mother's life and the life of her baby are in peril."

"I do not need their money," I said as we traversed the family wing corridor.

"But you deserve their respect."

What I truly longed for was *Ann's* respect. In a distant way, I'd once had it. The surgeons who supported the military were all too useful after a battle, and even between battles, and our work was challenging. We often toiled for days with little rest and did so in the midst of horrendous suffering. In that sense, we'd been respected, also feared, resented, and egregiously under-supported.

"Respect is earned," I said, holding open the door to our suite. "And that will take time. Who is this Miss Marigold?" An older unmarried woman might well be a midwife if her mother or aunt had been a midwife, but I had come across no Miss Marigolds in the local churchyard.

"Miss Marigold Fletcher," Ann said. "Daughter of the late vicar. She and her mother bide in the little stone cottage just down the green from the smithy. The one with the blue salvia in the window boxes and flower beds. You should change out of that waistcoat."

"Right." I was wearing a blue waistcoat embroidered with red and gold lilies, one of my favorites. Pretty and a bit Continental, but not gaudy. A practicing doctor kept a supply of plain black waistcoats, the better to hide the inevitable stains.

We reached the bedroom, and Ann swept the hair off her nape and presented me with her back. As far as the servants knew, we enjoyed the usual pleasures and familiarities of marital partners.

The day we'd arrived at Belle Terre, our trunks had been taken up to the largest bedroom suite. Neither Ann nor I had been willing to announce that husband and wife did not share a bed. I had offered to sleep on the cot in the dressing room, and onto that lumpy, short rack I had consigned myself every night since.

On this occasion, perhaps because I knew time was of the essence, I permitted myself the barest hint of awareness of my wife's person. Ann's looks were too bold to be considered pretty by the English, but I was not English.

Her hair had first drawn my notice, a lush, incendiary red that reached to her hips when unbound. She had the legendary temper of a redhead, and more than once, her first husband had bedded down with the horses rather than face her wrath.

I had admired Ann's spirit then. Now, I was consigned to spending my nights on the *lit de tourment infernale*. In defense of my sanity, I ignored her abundant feminine charms as best I could.

My wife was beyond pretty. She was *attractive*, full of vitality and passion. Her mood was often broody, but she also had a quick, earthy sense of humor that charmed and surprised me. She had the most lovely skin, petal-smooth and pale, and for a moment, I allowed myself to imagine brushing my thumb over her nape.

"You should eat something too," she said. "You haven't had lunch, and babies are no respecters of schedules."

"We'll raid the hamper," I replied, pulling myself from reveries that replaced the brush of my thumb with the brush of my lips. "You haven't had your lunch yet either."

She walked away from me, her dress gaping open. I should not have found the sight fetching, but on a purely animal level, I did. My emotions—and Ann's—were more complicated. Not three months past, I had been all but engaged to Lady Violet, a woman I had taken to my bed, loved sincerely, and would always hold in highest esteem.

But when I'd been a young man trying to find his feet in the military world, I had also loved Ann. I had admired her from a discreet distance since the day she'd shown up in my infirmary to ask if her husband was among the injured.

She had been married at the time. My admiration had thus been of the purely theoretical sort. I aspired to all the honor a gentleman should claim, of course, but more to the point, I was a Frenchman practicing medicine in an English military camp.

I watched my step.

When the officers' wives had proposed that I solve the problem created by the death of Ann's first husband, I had immediately agreed. After a hasty wedding, I simply had not known how to nurture the seedlings of loneliness, genuine respect, and desire into the blossoms of affection and abiding regard. In time, I might have puzzled it out, but Ann's patience had reached its limit after less than a year of marriage.

I could not determine if my desire for Ann was a betrayal of Lady Violet—now engaged to another—or a betrayal of the Ann who'd deserved to be wooed and charmed. Perhaps admitting desire was a betrayal of my *amour propre*, because I deserved a wife who desired and respect me as well, didn't I?

I ruminated on these imponderables while I tidied myself and changed into a black waistcoat. Ann donned a dress of a plain, lightweight brown wool. I did up her hooks, and then we were off down the steps to await the gig.

"I never asked if you wanted me to come along," Ann said, gaze on the sweeping curve of the front drive.

We had fallen into the habit of tucking our questions under casual observations. I despaired to see Ann, once so bold and saucy, all trussed up in manners and caution. I was none too happy in such attire myself.

"Of course I want you with me," I said. "A woman's presence at a lying-in is always a comfort, and any fellow but the husband is a decided awkwardness." For high society, that was changing, as the profession of accoucheur found a foothold with families of rank. Here in the shires, neither physicians nor surgeon-apothecaries typically attended births, though they might consult on difficult cases.

"You like bringing babies into the world," Ann said. "You always have."

She and I had attended a few birthings together, there being midwives among Ann's older female relatives.

"I also like *keeping* babies in the world," I said. "I know of no greater heartache than to watch a tiny life expire. What sort of God does that? Puts a woman through months of physical hardship, raises a couple's hopes, and then replaces joy with tragedy?"

Ann squeezed my hand, the gesture startling me half out of my boots. "We will manage, Hugh. The Grants are sturdy stock, and Miss Fletcher is sensible. She might well be sending for you in an abundance of caution, or just to get Dervid out from underfoot for an hour."

The gig pulled up, and Ann slipped her hand from mine before I could kiss her knuckles or muster any husbandly gallantry. Grant was perched on the boot, along with a pair of hampers, and thus we were chaperoned for the entirety of the journey.

We took turns driving and eating—a skill we'd perfected in Spain—and were soon at the humble establishment that passed for the Grant abode. The cottage was set into a swell of land, gray native stone with a thatched roof. My guess was, an abandoned cow byre had been converted into a dwelling, so low was its ceiling. The chimney was yielding to the onslaught of time, or perhaps a want of proper mortar was at fault.

A drystone wall ringed the yard, and a pair of identical little girls—equally dirty, equally skinny—looked up as we arrived. Scrawny chickens pecked about, and neither child wore shoes.

"Mama's still alive," one girl shouted. "Miss Fletcher said we were to tell ye that. I know you. You're the doctor!"

I liked children, liked their honesty and innocence, and liked very much that they were less prone to judgment than their elders. I did not like that these girls were underfed, under-clothed, and tasked with reporting on the progress in the birthing room.

"I am the physician," I said, hefting the hampers from the back of the vehicle, "and this lady with my medical bag is my wife, Madame St. Sevier."

"*Mrs.* St. Sevier," Ann said when both children seemed puzzled. "Wash your hands, and you may have some luncheon."

The children pelted around to the back of the dwelling, where I hoped a rain barrel or some source of soap and clean water was to be found.

Grant looked at his home as if he both dreaded and longed to cross its threshold. "It doesn't get any easier," he said. "This will be our sixth, God willing, and I'm flat terrified, same as I was with the first."

Ann sent me a look. *Save the lecture on self-restraint for later.*

"If you would tend to the hampers," I said, passing both to Grant, "I will look in on your wife."

A young woman appeared in the doorway. Her brown hair was in a neat bun, her apron was spotless, her hands were clean. Her boots were sturdy, such as sensible ladies wore when tramping country lanes, she exuded a brisk manner without coming across as rude.

I liked her on sight and had the odd thought that Ann probably liked her as well.

"Come in, Doctor, madame," she said, making a shooing motion with her hand. "All your great learning and brilliance won't do us any good standing about in the yard with the chickens, will it? I am Marigold Fletcher, and this birth is not going well."

"Has Mrs. Grant's water broken?" I asked as Ann and I ducked to enter the dwelling. We were hit with the combined stink of boiled cabbage, onions, and sweat.

"Her waters finally broke just as I sent Dervid off to fetch you, but I fear it's too late. Mrs. Grant's strength is ebbing, and labor is not progressing."

"It's never too late," I said, passing Ann my coat and rolling up my cuffs. "As long as there's breath, there's hope." And sometimes, even if the mother's life was forfeit, the child could be saved. I kept that thought to myself. Grant likely feared the challenge of feeding eight mouths instead of seven, but the loss of his wife would be a tragedy too great to contemplate.

On the other side of the only interior door, a woman yelled that Dervid Grant was a dead man, and this time, *she meant it.*

"There's breath," Ann said, preceding me into the other room. "And plenty of it."

"And thus," I said, following after, "there's hope, and plenty of that too."

Miss Fletcher looked dubious, but adopted the cheerful manner considered a tonic to all in medical difficulties. She attempted pleasantries, but Mrs. Grant was soon in the midst of another contraction. Polite rituals gave way to the more compelling business of bringing a new life squalling into the world.

Four hours later, that life—Sixtus Dervid Grant—was swaddled in a beautifully embroidered blanket and rooting greedily at his mama's breast, though of course her milk hadn't come in yet. The situation had wanted mostly a change of position for Mrs. Grant, from bed to birthing stool, so that the sizable infant could better navigate the birth canal. I had made shift with an overturned half barrel and the cushion from the gig's bench.

I handed Ann back up into the gig, the cushion having been restored to its intended use, and felt the usual combination of fatigue and joy that followed a successful birthing.

"You still swear in French," Ann said. "I believe Mrs. Grant thought you were muttering incantations."

"Miss Fletcher knew better." She'd mostly busied herself with keeping the older children occupied, but she'd sent for help when help had been needed, and thank God she had. "Is she the local midwife?" I would have to foster her acquaintance if so.

"Not officially. She's unmarried, but she attended a lot of births with her mother when the late vicar was alive. Why am I so tired?"

"Births are like battles, but with the hope of a much better outcome. The nerves grow exhausted even if the body does not."

The horse was only too happy to head for home, and thus we sped along lanes that ran between verdant summer hedges. The livestock was fattening in deep pastures, and a breeze riffled across ripening fields of grain. We might have been any couple out paying calls for the sheer pleasure of socializing with our neighbors.

Except we weren't. We were interlopers enduring an awkward marital rapprochement, tied together by legalities, duty, and a daughter. As we passed a meadow full of fluffy sheep, I realized that if I was to salvage my marriage, then I would have to look for opportunities to create a wider foundation.

The afternoon's activities were such an opportunity, and I had just mentally rehearsed a recitation of my appreciation for Ann's company in the birthing room when she sat up straighter on the bench beside me.

"How will Miss Fletcher get home?" she asked. "Grant has no vehicle worth the name, and it's some distance to the village even as the crow flies. The lady has been on her feet for two days."

I was tired, but far from physically exhausted. "I will drop you off at Belle Terre and retrieve Miss Fletcher from the Grant domicile. That will also allow me to take another hamper to the Grants." The children were not starving, but neither were they thriving. I had prescribed cod liver oil for two of the younger girls in hopes of treating inchoate rickets.

The baby needed blankets and clean linens. The mother needed regular servings of cow's milk and butter, which were fortunately in good supply, given the season. Red meat was another necessity, as was a stern warning to both mama and papa about the perils of too many births in quick succession.

I could not take Ann's hand because I held the reins, but I needed to somehow express my thanks to her for her aid. She had been a calm, good-humored assistant, and she had not sworn in any language no matter the provocation. She had helped me stay calm, in other words, and thus I could focus on my patient more effectively.

We pulled around to the Belle Terre stable, and I leaped down to assist my wife from the bench.

She alighted and kept her hands resting on my arms. "You did well, Hugh. I was proud of you. Go fetch Miss Fletcher, and I'll see that the Grants get another hamper from us before sunset."

I was proud of you. The words stunned me, as that earlier little squeeze to my hand had stunned me. I fumbled for something to say, something winsome and husbandly, but not too familiar. *I was glad to have you there. You made the situation much easier. I'd forgotten what a wonderful birthing assistant you are.*

What came out of my handsome, well-educated, charming mouth? "I'll see you at dinner."

Ann smiled. "You'll need a bath first."

She strode off with that particularly confident gait of hers, and I wanted to call after her, to squeeze her hand, to lay even a single small rock in a new and broader foundation for our marriage.

"A bath sounds lovely," I called, which earned me a curious look from the horse and no reaction at all from my retreating wife.

~

I came upon Miss Fletcher marching along the lane about a quarter mile from the Grants' abode.

"Miss Fletcher." I brought the horse to a halt. "May I offer you a lift to the village?"

I was an unrelated male to whom she had been introduced only in passing. I was not even English, and I'd dwelled at Belle Terre for only the past few months. Another woman might have hesitated, despite the fact that I drove an open gig and she was doubtless exhausted.

"Merciful ministers of heaven, yes, you may." She climbed nimbly onto the bench before I could assist her. "I thought that child would never deign to join the earthly sphere, monsieur, and it did not occur to me the issue was the mother's position."

"Position and posture," I replied, signaling the horse to trot on. "The urge to push can mean an urge to arch the back, which is counterproductive to the desired outcome, especially when the infant is large. I'm surprised Mrs. Grant herself did not know that."

Miss Fletcher arranged a worn canvas haversack at her feet. "All she knew, by the time you arrived, was that Dervid would never again get within six feet of her. She said the same thing after the twins were born. Young Oswald arrived about a year later."

"The Grants are devoted, then. That is all to the good, considering the effort involved in raising so many children."

Miss Fletcher gave me a sidewise glance. She wore a straw hat, which did less to conceal her features than a poke bonnet would have.

"The Grants are young," she said, though she herself was hardly old. "They are too poor to afford many comforts. I'm sure they decide after the arrival of each child to forgo the activities that lead to conception, but with what pleasures can they replace marital congress? How can they preserve a sense of intimacy if what they impose on themselves is instead frustration?"

A blunt and interesting speech, especially coming from a genteel English spinster. A change of subject was in order.

"Your father was the vicar?"

"Yes, and thus I was not raised in ignorance of life's more vexing conundrums. Thou shalt not kill, unless thou stealeth a spoon. Then one's death can become roaringly good entertainment for an enormous throng. God save the king, but nobody asks God to save the people *from* the king when his profligate regent bankrupts the nation in a time of war."

In London, one did not bruit about such sentiments, because the crown employed spies to lurk in the taverns and report sedition wherever it arose.

We were not in London. "Are you part French?"

"I am good, sturdy Sussex stock by birth, monsieur, but I accompanied my mother on many of her calls to sickrooms and birthing rooms. I also assisted her with her dame school. Mrs. Cooper has allowed me to continue in that capacity, but as you doubtless know, we lack competent medical practitioners in these surrounds."

"Not even a midwife?"

We rolled along between the fields and pastures as Miss Fletcher answered questions that had lurked at the edges of my awareness.

The local surgeon-apothecary had retired without a successor several years ago. The midwife had left the area to dwell with a daughter even before that, leaving the aging Mrs. Fletcher to cope as best she could. The neighborhood was merely genteel—no lofty titles to underwrite the cost of hiring medical talent—and the village was half empty as a result of decades of enclosures. Bad harvests had been painfully frequent in the past two decades.

All over England, the countryside was losing population, and landowners were struggling with falling rents and rising foreign competition for their corn and produce.

"If you could choose," Miss Fletcher said, "to open a surgery in London and have your patients come to you, coin in hand, or to practice here, where your payment might be in eggs you do not need, which would you prefer? You could hold surgery hours in the village on given days, but illness has no calendar. More likely, you would spend years trotting up and down the lanes in all weather to deal with a putrid sore throat here or a colicky baby there. When old age or a carriage accident claimed you, you would have nothing to show for all your hard work."

Was she trying to wave me off? Making conversation? "Should we then leave the families of our squires and yeomen without medical care?"

She took off her straw hat to sweep a lock of hair over her ear, the gesture unselfconscious and feminine. She was... pretty. Not English-rose pretty, but her features were lit with intelligence, even as tired as she was, and she was given to smiling. I noticed this as I might notice that a passing stranger had an uneven gait, or that a baby crying in church sounded tired rather than hungry.

Miss Fletcher turned her face up to the westering sun and closed her eyes. "We pay a pittance," she said, "but we do pay—to ensure that immortal souls have some care in every shire, monsieur. One cannot see the soul, one cannot be assured of its existence save for the bleatings set forth by ancient men in ancient texts. And yet, we pay to keep those souls in good repair, as my mother would say.

"At the same time," she went on, "we leave the Grants and their ilk to fend for themselves when illness strikes. If you asked the struggling farmers of England to pay taxes for the support of a local physician, as opposed to supporting the Regent's debts, the East India Company, or the Church, which do you suppose they'd choose? Which would result in a happier, healthier nation?"

She had an interesting point, particularly in light of the perennial agitation in England to extend suffrage beyond the relatively wealthy few.

"Is this what a vicarage upbringing yields in Merry Olde England?" I asked. "Radical philosophy and political speculation?"

She put her hat back on and left the ribbons trailing. "I am an only child. My mother grew tired of my father's philosophical maunderings, and I was thus exposed to more theorizing than most would deem healthy for a girl. I often accompanied Papa on his calls, and that meant many miles of Plato, Aristotle, the Stoics, Locke, and Adam Smith."

"How did your father die?" That was a physician's question, though Miss Fletcher did not take offense.

"Ague," she said as the gig clattered over the arched bridge that brought the village green into view. "He went off on a winter night to attend a sick parishioner, slipped into a ditch, and got a soaking. Lung fever followed. He was hale and hearty one day and, a fortnight later, making his final arrangements."

"Ditch water is notorious for propagating foul miasmas. I am sorry for your loss, but glad you took to heart his determination to comfort the sick and ailing. Mrs. Grant might well have lost her life or her baby if not for you."

"And if not for you, monsieur. I wasn't sure you'd come." Miss Fletcher took a belated interest in tying her hat's ribbons. "Thank you for that. Death in childbed is horrible. Painful, messy, undignified, and so... despairing. If the mother has other children or a devoted spouse, she's not only dying, her heart is breaking. She feels like a failure before God, nature, and her own family, and that is so unfair."

"Tragic," I said. "One of few times when that word is genuinely applicable."

Miss Fletcher peered at me. "Yes."

We enjoyed a moment of medical understanding, though a sad moment.

I realized as we tooled around the green that I had been guilty of a crime I detested, that of making judgments based on superficialities. Ann and I dwelled at Belle Terre by default. We had other properties, but Belle Terre was commodious, and Fiona seemed to like it.

I dreaded the day when Ann suggested I might be more comfortable establishing my household at one of those other properties, but I accepted that such a day might come. I did not enjoy sleeping in the dressing closet, and in all likelihood, Ann did not enjoy knowing I slumbered there.

The difficulty for me was, no matter where I chose to dwell, I was viewed with suspicion by my English neighbors. I *talked funny*, and people who spoke as I did, people who shared my national heritage, had shot at, killed, and maimed my English neighbors in untold numbers. That those French soldiers had also been shooting *at me* from time to time was of no moment.

Nor was it relevant that the English had been shooting back at my fellow Frenchmen on every occasion.

Miss Fletcher was a warning to me not to grow lazy in my thinking. I had consigned the entire shire to backwardness because of the actions of a few. My neighbors had recently seen me arrested and detained for a crime I had not committed—a tale for another time, as Lady Violet would say—and I had retaliated by tarring the whole community with the brush of ignorance and prejudice.

Miss Fletcher was far from ignorant, and her thinking was so distant from close-minded that she gave even me—a product of revolutionary France—pause.

We pulled up to the stone cottage with the blue salvia in the window boxes. The dwelling was as tidy as Miss Fletcher, with symmetrical white curtains hanging in the windows and more salvia growing along the walkway. The little front yard of grass was bordered by a stone wall, much as the Grants' home was, but the effect was markedly different here.

When I assisted Miss Fletcher from the gig, I learned that she was lighter than she looked. She also weaved a bit when her feet touched terra firma.

"Steady," I said, keeping a hand on her arm. "I hope you helped yourself to something from the hampers, Miss Fletcher."

She shook her head and stepped back. "The children needed the food far more than I did. Thank you for your many kindnesses, monsieur. I hope I'll see you and madame at the trials on Saturday."

I had no interest in trials of any sort. "I beg your pardon?"

"Some old master of foxhounds two centuries ago figured out that if the pack sees some exercise over the summer, they go into hunting season in better condition. We race the swiftest hounds twice a month from Beltane onward. After Michaelmas, we have horse races for the same reason. The result is a cross between a village fete and a race meet, with the occasional informal prizefight behind the smithy. I'm not supposed to know about the prizefights."

Violence, spirits, and contests of speed. English entertainments in a nutshell. My inclination was to decline, but how much longer did I expect my wife to dwell in isolation at Belle Terre? At Ann's insistence, we'd hosted Lady Violet and her beau, Sebastian MacHeath, Marquess of Dunkeld, for a short visit.

We'd had no callers other than the current vicar and his wife. Ann was probably lonely, and not for more of my snoring from the dressing closet.

"I will ask my wife if we are free. What time does the gathering start?"

"Six-ish, by the country clock. I'll look forward to seeing you there." She let herself through a wooden gate painted light blue and then turned to face the street. "Will you look in on Mrs. Grant?"

"Am I welcome to?" In the space of a short drive, I had learned that I could trust Miss Fletcher to answer the question honestly.

"You will make Dervid uncomfortable, because he cannot pay you, but Mrs. Grant will be relieved to see you. She's had other babies, but has never had a chance to question a physician about how to go on with them."

"She needs to *not* have babies for a time. Two years at least."

That indelicate observation prompted Miss Fletcher to study the salvia that had likely been blooming in her yard for weeks. "Tell that to Dervid, why don't you? My mother was never quite equal to lecturing the papas, but somebody clearly needs to."

I was that somebody. Husbands, in my opinion, ought to attend their wives in childbed, even titled husbands. Most of those fellows would doubtless rather take up arms against the whole Grand Armée than endure one hour of a woman's travail—travail the husband at least in part caused.

The baby might be the work of divine providence, but a man decided when his own breeches came off.

I waited by the gig until Miss Fletcher had entered her house, then resumed my seat on the bench. As I turned the vehicle, I got a nod and touch of the hat brim from our local magistrate, Thaddeus Freeman. He and I had played a few games of interesting chess while he'd detained me in his home—detained me illegally, as it turned out.

He'd had his reasons. I nodded in return, my hands being on the reins. I did not precisely like Freeman, but I respected him. He, too, had served on the Peninsula, and he, too, was a man with regrets.

I passed again over the arched bridge and took the lane toward Belle Terre. Ann would probably enjoy a call from Miss Fletcher. They were both blazingly smart, independent, and physically and intellectually vigorous women.

Perhaps I should have invited Miss Fletcher to tea? But no, that was for Ann to do, if she pleased to do it. When I reached Belle Terre, I handed the gig off to a stable boy and approached the house with visions of a warm soaking bath quickening my steps. I was half submerged in that bath, drowsing at my leisure, when it occurred to me that *I* liked Miss Fletcher.

I liked women generally, but on the strength of our conversation and my observations of her in the birthing room, I liked *her*.

I had not yet decided whether my liking was a good thing or a troublesome thing when I rose from the water and began toweling myself dry. I was thus in a state of complete undress and caught entirely unaware when my wife walked into the bedroom.

CHAPTER TWO

ANN

I had not seen my husband in his natural state since we'd shared a tent in Spain. Even then, between poor lighting and the modesty of a couple joined by pragmatic considerations rather than sentiment, I had rarely seen Hugh St. Sevier fully unclad.

At some point after our reunion, I had become aware that Hugh had matured into a spectacular masculine specimen. He was slightly above six feet with athletic proportions. In Spain, he'd been gaunt, chronically tired, and driven by a need to perfect his medical skills. Restlessness had plagued him even in sleep, and his wardrobe had suffered the vagaries of military life.

The years had been kind to him. His damp chestnut hair was now tousled from his bath, and he wore it a tad longer than English fashion preferred. He was trim, though his leanness had become well muscled. In Spain, the other women had deemed him lanky, a very young man outgrowing the last vestiges of an adolescent frame.

That frame was attractive now when clothed. The man as God made him was utterly breathtaking. I frankly gawked, while he toweled himself off as casually as if we'd been a couple of many contented years.

The room was redolent of the honeysuckle scent I'd associated with Hugh even in Spain, and the sunbeams slanting through the window revealed every plane, hollow, and curve of his physique. An ache I'd been ignoring for weeks roared to life low in my body.

As I fetched his dressing gown from the wardrobe, I reminded myself that Hugh had chosen to sleep in the dressing closet rather than share a five-acre bed with me.

"Can't have you taking a chill." The most inane thing I could have said. A North Sea winter gale would have been challenged to chill Hugh St. Sevier, so vigorous was he. A memory rose, of snuggling up to my new husband and reveling in the sense of warmth and safety his presence in bed had yielded.

I missed that warmth.

And the sense of safety.

He stepped from the tub, pitched the towel onto the cedar chest, and allowed me to help him into his dressing gown. Even that casual toss of balled-up linen conveyed grace and power. I forgave myself for smoothing the dressing gown over Hugh's shoulders. I had yet to forgive myself for marrying him in the first place—or for abandoning him.

"Miss Fletcher had just begun her return journey to the village when I caught up with her," Hugh said, easing his damp hair from the dressing gown's collar. "She was appreciative of a ride and suggested we might attend some dog races on the village green this Saturday."

"Dog races?" He wanted to talk about *dog races*, while I wanted to kick myself for fetching the dressing gown. I must have sounded befuddled, because after Hugh had belted that dressing gown, he faced me.

"We are married," he said gently. "We share a home, and you have certainly seen me *sans vêtements* before. I have the usual assortment of parts, and this passing display is of no moment."

Hugh St. Sevier had the usual parts, but in unusually generous allotments of grace, strength, and beauty. His impressive masculine attributes notwithstanding, what had first drawn me to him were his lovely brown eyes. Hugh gazed upon all of creation with kindness and understanding, and frequently with humor too.

Because of those eyes, were he my physician, I would comfortably entrust to him all my bodily woes, no matter how personal. He was my husband, though, and I barely knew how to hold a conversation with him.

"Tell me about the dog races." I busied myself laying out an ensemble for supper, a ridiculous exercise necessitated by the ridiculous life Hugh and I found ourselves sharing.

"Miss Fletcher describes the occasion as a combination village fête and race meet." He used a comb to bring order to his damp locks, though he was going about it all wrong.

"Don't comb from the top," I said. "Start at the back, at the bottom, else you will make all the tangles worse."

I had managing tendencies in the words of my dear granny. Hugh's slight smile as he passed me the comb said he and Gran agreed on that point.

"Sit," I said, gesturing to the vanity stool. "I have no desire to watch our neighbors drink themselves stuporous under a summer moon."

I had no desire to comb my husband's hair either, not that I would admit of, but assistance with a toilette was a courtesy spouses performed for each other. In Spain, Hugh had laced me up any number of times—he did not favor tight corsets, bless him—and I had tied his cravats just as often.

We had *tried*, in as much as a young couple in our circumstances could try. I eased the comb through the last inch of his hair, then worked higher, encountering a few knots.

"I will only attend if you accompany me," he said, "and we need not stay long. These people have neither doctor nor herbwoman nor midwife, Ann."

Somewhere in that statement lay a question—a request. "You are willing to step into all of those roles?" Did I want him to again fall prey to his medical passions? Going without sleep? Missing meals? Exposing himself to all manner of illness?

Hugh was a rarity among England's medical men, in that he had both apprenticed to a surgeon-apothecary and studied medicine at university in Edinburgh. His professional expertise had grown rapidly on the battlefields, where corpses and severely wounded patients had been on hand in an abundance no member of the Royal College could imagine.

Between battles, when Hugh wasn't dealing with the myriad disease plaguing a typical military camp, he'd wandered the countryside collecting herbs and conversing with the local healers and midwives. At the time, I'd accused him of using any excuse to avoid our quarters, but he was in truth simply devoted to his vocation.

"When it comes to medicine," he said, "I have a wealth of information, gained in a hard school. Mrs. Grant might have eventually concluded her travail successfully, but an infant cannot manage indefinitely in the birth canal. What was wanted was knowledge, knowledge I have."

Lady Violet, whom I desperately longed to hate but actually liked in my unguarded moments, had told me that Hugh yearned to resume his doctoring, focusing particularly on children and expectant mothers.

"Her ladyship suggested I should aid you to re-establish yourself as a medical practitioner," I said, drawing the comb through Hugh's now-untangled locks. "I did not envision that my assistance would include attendance at dog races, but if that's a step forward, I will take it with you."

Only when Hugh's gaze met mine in the mirror did I recall that he and I never discussed her ladyship. Lady Violet was due to have Hugh's child several months hence and had secured a proposal of marriage from no less than a Scottish marquess. The marquess, another veteran of the Peninsula, was fully aware of her ladyship's situation and willing to raise the child as his own.

Hugh and I did not discuss her ladyship or her impending marriage to the marquess.

We did not discuss the child.

We did not, now that I thought about it, discuss the future in any regard.

Hugh rose, and wearing only his fussy blue French dressing gown, he nonetheless looked imposing.

"You are willing to attend this gathering with me?"

"I am. Shall we take Fiona?"

He wrinkled his splendid nose. "We shall be very much on display. While Fiona's charms are limitless, the evening will be easier if we attend without her."

He would be on display. I was determined to be the unremarkable, pleasant helpmeet he had doubtless hoped he'd married all those years ago.

"Fiona will worry." She fretted anytime her papa, a wonderful new feature in her life, was in the village for any length of time. That Hugh had been accused of heinous crimes and detained for days by the local magistrate had made Fiona understandably anxious.

A bleakness came into my husband's eyes. "I will promise to look in on her when we return from our outing."

Hugh looked in on our daughter frequently. He took Fiona up before him on his horse, and though she was too big for such nonsense, he carried her piggyback in the churchyard, and read her stories before bed most nights. After only a few weeks' acquaintance, they spoke French with an ease and rapidity I had trouble following, but then, Hugh knew very few words of Gaelic, which was Fiona's preferred language with me.

English was our linguistic neutral territory, just as in the house, the library was neutral territory. We could all occupy that room at once without much awkwardness. I did not intrude on the estate office, and Hugh rarely set foot in my parlor. The nursery suite was Fiona's retreat, and belowstairs was for the staff.

We were as neatly organized as a military camp, but with none of the sense of purpose or *esprit de corps*.

"You could go without me," I said, returning to the wardrobe and pretending to debate my choice of shawl.

"*Non*." He disappeared into the dressing closet. I might have followed him to argue—I was loath to join one of St. Ivo's rustic bacchanals—but I did not dare risk catching my husband unclothed again.

"Why *non*?"

"Because you are my wife, and if you appear to trust me, the ladies will trust me." Some muttering in French followed. "We have a potential ally in Miss Fletcher, and I'm sure Vicar and Mrs. Cooper will extend us a cordial welcome. A village gathering is a step forward, Ann, as you say, and I would like you to take it with me."

Forward toward what? I should have had Hugh undo my hooks before he'd disappeared into the dressing closet, but I wasn't about to ask him for that assistance now.

"You promise we won't stay late?" I asked.

"We leave the moment you tell me we must go. I will be solicitous of your welfare and sweetly devoted for the duration of the outing. Where is my fleur-de-lis cravat pin?"

"You're wearing that to dinner tonight?" A bit fancy, but nobody did a bit fancy with more dash than my husband.

"I shall wear it Saturday, to indicate that I am aware of my nationality, lest anybody think I have forgotten it."

"That pin belonged to your father."

Hugh sauntered out of the dressing closet, attired for supper minus his coat and with a starched length of unknotted linen draped about his neck.

"I wear Papa's pin for courage." He smiled crookedly. "If you must know the truth, these people are a challenge to me."

Because I took up the ends of his cravat, I saw that his smile did not quite reach his eyes. "You mean that. They worry you."

"They detained me illegally, Ann. Charged me and bound me over for the quarter sessions, all for crimes I did not commit. Yes, they worry me. Whether or not I provide medical services to my neighbors, I cannot allow them to limit me and my family to churchyard civilities. Befriending them is the prudent course, for Fiona's sake as well as ours. These English squires and their ladies would prefer that we remain on the margins, but that is no way to be neighbors."

Hugh's admissions were a moment of rare honesty between us. He was disclosing some ambitions regarding our future, humble though those ambitions might be. I yearned to lean into him, to put my arms around him and reassure us both that miscarried English justice would never part us again.

Instead, I tied his cravat in the cascading coachman's knot that showed off the linen's lacy borders to excellent advantage. I held his coat for him, and he was soon the picture of masculine pulchritude, ready for a fine meal made arduous by the fact that he and I had run out of small talk before the end of our honey month.

"We'll put in an appearance at these dog races," I said, "but only that. I'm not used to the heat of an English summer."

"You traveled the length and breadth of Spain in heat far worse than anything England offers."

I shoved him toward the door. "I am not used to the heat of an English summer, monsieur. Do not argue with me."

He bowed. "I beg your pardon. English summers are oppressive, I quite agree. I'm off to hear Fiona's report for the day. I'll see you at supper." He was out the door in the next instant.

I sat upon the five-acre bed, feeling unaccountably winded. I would have to ring for my maid to undo my hooks—an opportunity missed, blast it to perdition—and I would somehow have to find the courage to attend the damned dog races with my husband.

Our neighbors loomed as a challenge for Hugh, but the prospect of our Saturday outing filled me with the next thing to terror.

~

My husband sought acceptance by the local society, as a medical professional if not as a neighbor. My duty as a loyal spouse was to support those ambitions. Hugh was too skilled a doctor and too deserving of some happiness for me to do otherwise.

I thus resigned myself to paying a call on the vicarage, the only establishment where I had earned the right to make such an imposition. Mrs. Cooper had dragged her husband out to Belle Terre on a duty visit, an awkward fifteen minutes of weather-and-crops while both visitors discreetly inspected Belle Terre's exquisite appointments. For the last five minutes of the visit, I had allowed my daughter to join us in the formal parlor, where she'd shown off her good manners, much to my relief.

I walked along the lane in the direction of the village, mentally correcting myself: Fiona was *our* daughter, not *my* daughter. When Hugh referred to her as *his* daughter, his voice overflowed with such affection and wonder that I could not take offense. Generosity of spirit was harder to muster when Fiona spoke so glowingly of *my papa*, but referred to *my mama* as she would any old commonplace.

"Madame St. Sevier, good day."

A man on horseback had drawn even with me, and I had not noticed his approach. Such lack of awareness could have been fatal in Spain.

"Mr. Freeman, good day." Thaddeus Freeman was the king's man, the party responsible for wrecking what little standing Hugh had had with his neighbors. Freeman had much to atone for, and thus I felt at liberty to press him for information. "Will you, as the local arbiter of truth and justice, preside over the upcoming dog races?"

His features acquired a stoic cast, and they were handsome features. Freeman wore his blond hair a trifle long, and he'd lost most of the use of his left hand during the war, the hand with which he'd painted glorious murals and landscapes. He was nonetheless a fine specimen of a Saxon squire, tall, rangy, and—despite his terrible blundering in Hugh's situation—fiendishly clever. He'd been one of Wellington's best code breakers, and the French had put a price on his head early in the war.

"I am no longer the magistrate," he said. "May I walk with you? Tacitus has had his gallop, and I'm returning a book to the lending library."

"Suit yourself."

He dismounted, leaving the reins looped over the neck of the sizable gray gelding. The beast toddled along behind his owner as docilely as an old mutt.

"The hound races," Freeman said, "—the local huntsmen take offense if we call them dog races—are a source of controversy. Until a few years ago, we also had hare-coursing. The former vicar and his wife objected to blood sport in view of the church, and we were left with the hound races to entertain us of a summer evening. You missed the horse races, but those will start up again as harvest concludes."

"What sort of controversy could a lot of panting canines cause?"

He'd adjusted his stride to my pace, as a gentleman would. I well knew that courtesies on a public lane did not prove that a fellow also held title to gentlemanly honor.

"The usual problems arise where an activity combines money, liquor, and pride," Freeman said. "The wagering is discreet, lest the authorities meddle, but tempers flare, and the pugilistic displays that go on behind the smithy can become less than good-natured, particularly when the wrong fellow's dog—hound—loses, and the publican has done too brisk a business with the ale and spirits."

"Sounds like life in a military camp. Brawling, stupid wagers, and even stupider pride." Soldiers at least had the excuse that they frequently faced death. Short tempers and inebriation were to be expected. What excuse did my neighbors have?

"You have summed up the matter exactly," Freeman said. "I did not sell my commission just to be subjected to the same foolishness in the name of socializing that I endured in the name of soldiering, but St. Ivo's must have its traditions."

I did not want Freeman agreeing with me about anything, but he clearly viewed the hound races with distaste.

"And the displays of pugilism?"

"Rank farce, most of the time. Every squire's son and gamekeeper thinks himself an exponent of the fancy. They end up with black eyes, split lips, and bruised knuckles, which become so many more excuses to overimbibe, and *that* only fuels more differences of opinion. Truth be told, I hate the damned hound races, but Nigel Bellamy, our new magistrate, has asked that I attend in the interests of keeping the peace."

The lane was half sunken between two pastures, the stone walls overgrown with brambles and honeysuckle. Orange and yellow lilies climbed the banks, lacy white cow parsley grew immediately beside the roadway, and bright pink knapweed added an occasional flourish.

"I want country life to be like this lane," I said. "Peaceful and, in an ordinary way, beautiful. Miss Fletcher suggested to my husband that we attend Saturday's gathering, but the occasion sounds like everything awful about village society."

The horse *clip-clopped* along as if content to listen, and chaffinches twittered in the hedges. I sensed Freeman choosing his words even more carefully than usual.

"Leave early, and the evening should be pleasant enough."

"Who patches up the losing pugilists?" Hugh would never turn his back on an injured party.

"I intervene before the violence gets out of hand. Rutherford looks after the split lips and black eyes."

Johann Rutherford ran the local dry-goods store. He was a stout, gregarious German who sold patent remedies among other sundries. He was heartily cordial to Hugh and me in the churchyard, but then, he appeared to be heartily cordial to all of creation.

"Will Selene Faraday have your escort at the races?" I asked.

Selene and Freeman shared a passion for chess, and Freeman had expressed his admiration for the young lady in other regards as well.

His gaze turned stoic again. "Miss Faraday has removed to Edinburgh for the nonce, making a visit to some auntie or godmother. Her letters to her sisters are full of literary salons, literary dinners, and fascinating lectures on Madagascar's bird species."

"Are you a lover scorned, Mr. Freeman?" The notion did not please me as much as it should. Freeman had made tremendous sacrifices for his country, such that even I, a lowly infantry wife, had heard of the mounting reward for his capture or execution.

"I am a friend entirely forgotten," he said. "Selene—Miss Faraday—can do better than a glorified farmer with one good hand. I wish her the best."

This was not Freeman's first disappointment in love. He'd apparently courted a local widow, and she'd broken it off rather than allow the matter to end in matrimony. The village consensus was that he'd had a narrow escape that time—the widow was kicking her impoverished heels on the Continent—but he genuinely esteemed Selene.

"On your worst day," I said, "do you ever wish you were back at war?"

He smiled, and handsome became astonishingly winsome. "Never. Not for a moment. You remind me that a raucous Saturday night in St. Ivo's is a mere passing annoyance. Thank you for that. How are matters progressing with you and St. Sevier? I heard he delivered the Grants' baby."

In a nation that could not reliably move mail ten miles overland, news in the countryside traveled faster than pigeons.

"Monsieur and I delivered that child when Miss Fletcher requested our aid. Mother and baby appear to be doing well, though some charitable neighborliness on the occasion of a lying-in is always appreciated."

Shoes for the Grant children would be appreciated. A joint of beef, half a cheese, a loaf of bread, a tub of butter. I had sent over that much and more, but a large family made locusts look abstemious by comparison.

"Perhaps a new baby will keep Dervid home from the village festivities," Freeman said. "He's a hard worker, but drink puts the temper on him, and he cannot afford to wager away what few coins he has."

"Does he turn that temper on his family?"

We crossed the bridge that arched over a low stream just at the edge of the village. The music of the burbling water added to the sense of sleepy bucolic repose. The green itself made a cheerful picture, bookended by beds of red and blue salvia that ran along the shops, houses, and yards and shaded by a pair of enormous oaks.

A lovely setting, though every village, no matter how pretty, had its unhappy families.

"If Dervid is less than gentlemanly with his wife and children, madame, there's little enough I can do about it."

The same helplessness that every officer retreated behind when faced with violence among the enlisted men. "If Grant's short temper is the result of overwork or lack of means, you could remedy those ills."

"A man has his pride."

So, for pity's sake, did a woman. "A man with a healthy sense of pride does not wreak violence on his family."

The church sat at the far end of the green, a tidy little house of worship with a venerable bell tower that supposedly dated from Viking days. If Dervid Grant was abusive to his wife and children, the church would do nothing about it, the neighbors would do nothing about it, and the magistrate would do nothing about it. Hugh might tell me not to interfere, and I would be faced with a dilemma.

"St. Sevier has a temper," Freeman observed, ever so casually. "He'd take on any officer, argue in three languages, and tattle to Wellington himself if he thought medical priorities were being ignored."

He'd also, on occasion, argued with me in three languages, or two and a half.

"In my experience," I said, "the British army operated on the theory that its foot soldiers should be more terrified of their commanding officers than of the enemy. Wellington prevailed on the Peninsula in part because he did not tolerate harsh discipline to the rank and file, and he expected his officers to comport themselves like gentlemen. St. Sevier agreed with His Grace. Flogging a man half to death did nothing for his fighting abilities, and very likely inclined him and anybody witnessing the flogging to desertion."

The horse came to a halt before the lending library, which occupied what might once have been the vicarage summer kitchen. The structure was stone with a thatched roof, a window in each wall, and pots of forget-me-nots on the steps leading to its single door. I had yet to patronize the library, but I added that to the list of semi-social outings I could make to further Hugh's settling-in campaign.

"Which brings us back to St. Sevier's temper," Freeman said.

"My husband's disposition is the next thing to angelic, Mr. Freeman, and my dealings with him are none of your concern."

Freeman should have been offended by my tone, as I was offended by his innuendo. Instead, his gaze was curious, and perhaps —had he no sense at all?—amused.

"Are you always this contrary?"

He did not have the first inkling how contrary I could be. "I have had to learn a certain firmness with the male of the species."

"Your husband was referred to as the irascible French doctor who saved lives while nearly getting himself killed. He was regarded among the officers as part demon-possessed and part angel of mercy. He got more than one officer relieved of command, as I heard it."

I knew how the enlisted men had regarded Hugh. They'd mistrusted him, and after marrying me, that mistrust had become resentment. When injured, though, they'd invariably begged to be taken to *the Frenchie doctor*.

"What does St. Sevier's passion for healing have to do with

anything, Mr. Freeman? If the fine bigots and gossips of St. Ivo's will allow him to, he will deliver their babies, treat their gouty toes, and set their broken bones."

"I know he will," Freeman said, taking a book from his saddlebag. He slipped off the horse's bridle, patted the animal's neck, and waved in the direction of the green. This was apparently a signal for the beast to wander across the lane and enjoy a grassy snack. "But I also know your situation with St. Sevier is less than ideal. If he should ever prove too difficult, you may apply to me to remind him of the respect a husband owes his wife."

My imagination was prodigiously adept at forecasting tragedies. This was partly the Scot in me—we had endured tragedies without number, many of them at the hands of the English—and partly a result of my personal history.

I could never, in years of trying, envision that Hugh St. Sevier would mistreat me, and why on earth would Freeman offer to intervene in my situation but leave Mrs. Grant without a champion?

"You mean well," I said, "but you insult my husband, and that, I will not have. Until Saturday, Mr. Freeman."

He touched a finger to his hat brim and allowed me a dignified exit. I made for the vicarage and was graciously received by Mrs. Cooper, who of course inquired whether I'd had any correspondence from that *delightful* Lady Violet and her handsome marquess.

I took the requisite cups of tea and decided to stop by the lending library on my way home and to drop in at the dry-goods store as well. I needed no books—Belle Terre had an embarrassment of literary riches—and I certainly needed none of Mr. Rutherford's quackery.

But I needed to support my husband, so I schooled myself to such approximations of friendliness as I was capable of and spent the rest of morning toddling about the village shops. All the while, though, I was plagued by nagging questions.

Hugh and I had engaged in shouting matches that had doubtless been overheard from Gibraltar to John O'Groats. I had been far too young for the challenges of widowhood, much less immediate remarriage to a near stranger in a military camp.

Thaddeus Freeman had warned me against my husband's temper. Whatever Freeman's numerous and egregious faults, he had a certain integrity. What did he know about Hugh St. Sevier that I did not know?

Was I entitled to learn that answer, when I myself was keeping secrets from my husband and hoped to take those secrets with me to the grave?

CHAPTER THREE

HUGH

When Ann came down the Belle Terre's main staircase late Saturday afternoon, I was struck again by my wife's sheer feminine perfection. Desire hummed happily around the edges of my awareness, for in Ann's lovely form and exquisite features, the Creator had fashioned a special woman.

In Mayfair drawing rooms, Ann's complexion would be the envy of every woman who beheld her, even as those same women would murmur that red was *such* an unfortunate hair color. Ann's hair had been the first of her features to catch my notice—that, and her contralto singing voice.

When I'd later come upon her and her first husband in the midst of a blazing row, her facility with a scold had also made an impression. One did not have to be fluent in Gaelic to appreciate a virtuosic berating in that language.

My wife was passionate, or she had been. Dressed for an outing to the village green, she was every inch the genteel lady too. She wore an emerald walking dress trimmed with lavender, though such was her inherent dignity that she might well have been wearing ermine robes. As I bowed over her hand, I realized that my appreciation for Ann had lately been lacking a certain postscript.

Violet Belmaine was both ladylike and passionate, but I no longer automatically compared the two women. Ann was not different from Violet. Ann was simply Ann, and Violet was simply Violet. I wished Violet well, I prayed for her happiness, and should Lord Dunkeld displease his prospective wife, I would take the marquess to task at the first indication from her ladyship that my meddling was needed.

I prayed nightly for the good health of her ladyship and the baby, though I tried to think of the child as... hers. Not mine. Not mine in the paternal sense. Mine to love in the privacy of my heart. Mine to fret over and take pride in from afar, but not *mine.*

As regards her ladyship and my wife, my heart had come around some fundamental corner, such that Violet was more a fixture of past joys than present regrets or longings. Or perhaps, weeks spent taking meals with Ann, watching her devotion to Fiona, and listening to her humming over a bit of mending or flower arranging had brought me around that corner.

I also had memories of shared intimacy with Ann, old, sometimes awkward memories, but precious nonetheless.

"Will I do?" she asked, smoothing a gloved hand over her skirts.

"Splendidly. Will I?" I executed a slow pirouette and endured her perusal with some trepidation. Ann was kind, but also relentlessly honest.

"The season is late for roses," she said, touching the blossom on my lapel. "Where did you find this one?"

"Behind the stable at the edge of the woods. A volunteer from discarded prunings, would be my guess. Shall we be off?"

I offered my arm, and even in so small a gesture, the tattered nature of our marriage was in evidence. Ann hesitated, then wrapped her hand about my sleeve. Not for the first time, I wondered if her wariness about touching me was a symptom of antipathy toward me or the result of some misfortune during our separation.

She had been a prisoner of war, after a fashion, and she'd given birth. Childbed made many a woman rethink her enthusiasm for sexual congress, as well it should. I shuddered to contemplate Ann's treatment by the *guerrillas* who'd taken her captive and the French and British military authorities through whose hands she'd also passed.

When and whether we discussed that chapter of her life was up to her.

"Thaddeus Freeman claims these hound races are a subject of controversy," Ann said when I'd handed her up into the gig. "The men start drinking and brawling, and the wagering can get out of hand."

When had she and Freeman had that discussion? "We will depart the moment you tell me we should leave, Ann. My objective is to do a bit of socializing and allow the neighbors to inspect us. This is not an assembly, where we would be expected to dance, and not a church social, where speeches and prayers clutter up an otherwise uninspired meal."

"A place to start," she said, gaze on the rolling pastures bathed in slanting sunbeams. "I have longed for a place to start."

Whatever did that mean? Following that thought came another. *Why don't you ask her?*

"When you and Fiona dwelled in Scotland, were you living with family?"

"Family dwelled with us. I occupied the Perthshire farm, which is technically yours as a result of our marriage. I wondered when the London lawyers would see me turned out. My cousins did the farming and sent off the annual rent, and when the solicitors returned it, I considered that you might have willed that property back to me and thus to my family. I promised myself I would get the whole matter sorted later, before Fiona came of age."

On my great list of matters that Ann and I had to sort, the Perthshire property had not figured at all. To Ann, her farm was likely near the top.

"Were you happy there?"

"Fiona was. That child would go barefoot from Beltane to Michaelmas if I allowed it. I was mostly worried that some cow or horse would step on her toes."

Her first husband had died of sepsis after a similar mishap. "I can deed the property to your cousins, if you like, or leave it in trust for you or Fiona." I had revised my will such that Ann and Fiona would be very comfortably provided for. Ann was Scottish, though, and had spent more time in Spain than in England. Did she want that farm as insurance against the day when our marriage finished unraveling?

"Let's leave legal discussion for another time, Hugh. The evening is too pretty, and I am too nervous, to think of such matters now."

The horse trotted along, and I considered that I had asked one marginally challenging question. Ann had replied honestly—Fiona loved the farm, Ann loved Fiona. I decided to attempt to double my earnings.

"Why nervous, Ann?"

"I do not care for crowds. In Scotland, I knew everybody and was related to half the village. Here..."

"Right," I said. "They are strangers, and English strangers. I will make a bargain with you. If you do not abandon me to the company of these strangers, I will keep similar watch over you. Are we agreed?" I had meant the offer in jest, but Ann was too perceptive not to sense the real misgiving beneath my good cheer.

"*They* wronged *you*, Hugh, not the other way 'round."

"All that aside, this is an English village, and I am more the outsider than you are. Besides, I like showing off my pretty wife."

My flattery fell flat. Ann was pretty, and she was my wife, which left the showing-off part as the reason her slight smile disappeared.

"And I will show off my handsome husband," she said, rather grimly. "Squire Freeman is apparently disappointed in love. Selene Faraday has gone to Edinburgh, where all is culture and learning."

"He needs a wife and children to confound him."

"Confound?"

"Love is a code not easily deciphered. A wife and children would fascinate him. He is happiest when faced with hard puzzles." Lady Violet also delighted in puzzles. Who stole the widow's brooch? Where had an errant bridegroom got off to? Why was an estate suffering endless petty vandalism?

I, by contrast, wanted a settled, orderly life in which to woo my wife and delight in my daughter. I would not miss the puzzles and intrigues that seemed to abound in Lady Violet's presence. Sorting culprits and clues had preserved her ladyship from an inchoate bout of melancholia. *My* interest had been in Violet, not in the culprits or the clues.

"Children might confound a father," Ann said, "but for the mother, they are a rather different proposition."

"Was Fiona's birth difficult?"

"She did not want to be born, according to the midwife. I took months to recover." Ann became fascinated with the horse's muscular quarters as we trotted along. "I wished you could have been with me."

The next time, I will be. Except... we had miles and miles of ground to traverse before siblings for Fiona were even a remote possibility.

"I am sorry I wasn't there, and if I haven't said it before, Ann, I am grateful to you for bringing Fiona into this world and into my life."

Had I not chosen to make that declaration when both of my hands were on the reins, and the village green coming into view, I might have attempted to punctuate my words with a kiss to Ann's cheek. Because my timing was lamentably off, I was left to gaze at the same horse's backside that so absorbed Ann's attention.

"Fiona adores you," Ann said. "That's... that's good, I think."

A ringing endorsement of my skills as a father that was not. "But?"

"But whoever said it's better to have loved and lost than never to have loved at all wasn't going about the loving properly. For Fiona to lose you would… We cannot allow that, Hugh. Whatever happens between us, Fiona must not suffer for it."

"I would never intentionally visit suffering on you or Fiona."

And just like that, our first foray into a real discussion concluded with Ann feeling doubtless as frustrated and bewildered as I did. *Whatever happens between us* acknowledged chasms and precipices I would frankly rather ignore.

I found a place to tie up the horse at the edge of the churchyard and assisted Ann to alight.

"Don't forget the hamper," she said. "I brought pies for the dessert table."

I had not even known that such a gathering would have a dessert table. I fetched the hamper and wondered when, if ever, I would feel competent, at home, and at ease, much less all three, in the company of my wife.

We crossed the road and navigated the rope lanes that formed the raceway. I surveyed the crowded green for a friendly face—for any familiar face. Freeman stood on the steps of the posting inn in conversation with the vicar's wife. Miss Thetis Faraday, sister to the scholarly Selene, was similarly engaged with Mr. Cooper, the vicar. Johann Rutherford beamed good cheer in all directions from the door of his dry-goods shop, and a cluster of men stood smoking cigars outside the smithy.

My gaze landed on Dervid Grant, a tankard of ale in his hand as he slouched against one of the enormous oaks shading the green.

"Grant should not be here," I said.

"Maybe Mrs. Grant wanted him out of the house," Ann replied. "There's Miss Fletcher, and she will want to know how the mother and baby are faring."

I had ascertained earlier in the day that Mrs. Grant's milk had come in, an occasion for both relief and significant pain. She'd known what steps to take for the pain and what steps not to take. Patent remedies, spirits, laudanum, and the like would result in a colicky baby, assuming Mrs. Grant could afford such indulgences.

Miss Fletcher was among the throng inspecting the hounds who occupied a row of what appeared to be lambing pens in the center of the green. I passed over the hamper to Mrs. Faraday, the top pie wrangler, and accompanied Ann to greet Miss Fletcher.

"The pups are eager to run," Miss Fletcher said when the civilities had been observed. "Old Hector knows the drill, and the youngsters take their cues from him. Plato will be the rabbit hound, though in years long past, he was the favorite."

I liked dogs, but hardly knew a harrier from a spaniel. Old Hector, though, apparently adored Miss Fletcher. He was a sizable foxhound, sturdier than many of the other canines present, and he eagerly licked at Miss Fletcher's bare fingers.

"He's the favorite now?" Ann asked. "Looks a bit heavy for extended bursts of speed."

"Hector has a good deep chest, and he is wise," Miss Fletcher replied. "He paces the pack until they begin to flag, and then he simply outruns them. But you're right, he's not as lightly built as, say, young Richmond."

"I do not understand the English," I said. "They name their canines and equines after gods and philosophers or dukes and heroes, while naming their children John, Susan, and Orville."

Miss Fletcher and Ann both looked at me in some confusion, then Miss Fletcher smiled. "You jest so subtly, monsieur, that your humor nearly passed me by. I, for one, am happy to be named after a flower, while my mother—"

A shout went up from the steps of the posting inn as the publican created a racket by banging on a metal triangle with a soup ladle.

"The first heat will start shortly," Miss Fletcher said, bustling along the lambing pens. "We'll want to get a spot place at the finish line. Have you placed your bets?"

"We'll just watch for now," Ann said as the crowd shifted to gather along the rope lanes so the thickest knot of people formed at the base of one of the oaks. As we moved, partly following Miss

Fletcher and partly as a result of the crowd moving us, Ann's grip on my arm became quite firm.

"I'll meet you at the gig if we get separated," I said.

Ann's reply was to take a snug hold of my hand. "I will not lose you."

Those few words held a hint of the old Ann, the one who'd marched across Spain, made short rations suffice, and faced widowhood and worse without flinching.

We stood side by side in the jostling crowd as the rabbit hound was released—the beast who'd run ahead and stir all the others into giving chase, apparently. As the first group of competitors made their circuit, the noise on the green grew deafening, particularly considering how humble the entertainment was. The expressions on my neighbors' faces suggested we were watching the St. Leger Stakes with vast fortunes riding on the outcome, not Old Hector and Richmond flapping and bounding their way around the St. Ivo's village green.

Neither Hector nor Richmond prevailed, as it happened. A younger animal, Lionheart, crossed the finish line a length ahead of the other five contenders. Dervid Grant picked him up in his arms and got a thorough face-licking in return.

Which explained Grant's presence in the village.

Somebody started up a *hip-hip-hooray* chorus. General merriment ensued—as well as general grumbling—along with an exodus in the direction of the publican's barrels, brought outside for the occasion. Some rotund fellow eager for his post-race libation jostled into Ann and offered a beery apology.

I was left holding hands with my wife, an agreeable development, until Ann leaned near. "I must leave, Hugh. Please take me home now."

"But, Ann..." We had just arrived.

"You *promised*."

The physician in me gave the husband a swift kick *dans son derrière.* Ann was pale, anxious, and having difficulty drawing a breath.

"Inhale normally," I said, slipping an arm around her waist. "Don't gulp the air. Try to remain calm. We are but a few steps from the gig, and I can carry you if need be."

"I'm sorry," Ann muttered wheezily. "Hugh, I'm sorry."

Sorry for what? "Crowds are unpleasant," I replied, using my best calm-physician voice. "The evening is warm. Would you like to sit for a moment on the church steps, or shall we depart?"

"Home," Ann said. "Please, home."

I hoisted her over the ropes of the racing lane and deposited her on the bench of the gig. Her color had improved, and her inhalations were quieter by the time I'd unhitched the horse and joined her in the vehicle.

As we rounded the green, we passed the posting inn, where a circle of revelers had formed around two men who were loudly disputing the race results.

"The wrong dog won, apparently," Ann said, her voice rasping as if she'd been crying.

The victor had been slight, but small dogs could be fast. "What set you off?" I asked.

"I don't like crowds."

My wife, whom I regarded as an honest woman, had just handed me a polite falsehood. "What's the real reason, Ann? If we are to go on as a couple, we must be truthful with each other. I don't care for crowds, and I hate the sound of thunder."

"The artillery," she said. "I'm none too fond of thunder either. But in this case… it was just the crowd, Hugh. I told you I don't care for crowds. I'm sorry."

We drove the rest of the way to Belle Terre in silence as the sun sank toward the western horizon. I did not like that Ann was withholding information from me, and I positively loathed her repeated apologies.

What precisely was she apologizing for?

We nonetheless observed our usual routine later that night, with Ann climbing beneath the covers of the four-poster and me retiring to the lumpy rack that now passed for my bed.

~

"No laws protect an animal from abuse," Thaddeus Freeman said, "so I told Nigel Bellamy to arrest Donnie Vaughn for disorderly conduct, though I doubt our new magistrate will heed my guidance. I gave Richmond into Miss Fletcher's temporary keeping, because the beating Vaughn gave him left him in wretched shape."

Freeman had ambushed me in the churchyard, and because I was remaining at Ann's side like the proverbial loyal hound, she heard this exchange. Freeman had kept his voice down, though, and waited until Ann and I were nearly at our gig before accosting us. The unfortunate canine was apparently a sensitive topic.

"What has this to do with me?" I asked.

Ann, looking prim and lovely in a blue merino walking dress, answered the question. "Mr. Freeman wants you to look in on the dog."

"I am a physician, not a veterinarian."

"We have neither in these surrounds," Freeman countered, "and the hound is suffering."

Ann gazed at me with a quiet sense of entreaty. She would not castigate me for refusing to examine a dog, but I would lose yet still more standing in her eyes if I declined Freeman's request.

"What is this hound to you, Freeman?"

"A mute beast, helpless to defend himself against his owner's drunken violence. I am not the magistrate any longer, but I still have pretensions to gentlemanliness. Miss Fletcher will be devastated if the dog dies, and she and her mother have been through enough."

Ann's hand rested on my arm as lightly as sunshine.

"Madame and I will call upon Miss Fletcher and her mother," I said, "but Richmond will still have an idiot for an owner if he survives. What can be done about that?"

Freeman tipped his hat to Thetis Faraday. His expression was genuinely cordial, his smile friendly. I was reminded that Freeman was intimately acquainted with code work and ciphers. Did he hide the truth of his emotions as effectively as he'd hidden Wellington's orders?

"I agree with my husband," Ann said. "The race was fairly close. Richmond is a young hound, and the old favorite also lost. This implies the winner was a surprise all around. For Richmond's owner to pummel the beast will only make the poor dog less able to run in subsequent contests."

"Vaughn was drunk when he took after the hound. He loves that dog, but he lost a fair amount of money on the race, as did several others."

"While Dervid Grant," I said, "who desperately needs the funds, came into some luck for a change. I will have a look at the unfortunate beast, Freeman, but don't bruit that about."

I handed Ann up into the gig and would have gone around to the other side to join her on the bench, but Freeman had more to say.

"Vaughn was understandably upset, and so is Old Hector's owner."

"Both men lost money," I retorted. "This is exactly how wagering works. Perhaps you can explain that to your neighbors, Freeman, for I am reduced to treating their beasts."

"Dreyfuss is a steady sort," Freeman said. "He would never treat Old Hector ill, and he admitted neither Richmond nor Hector were running at their best."

I wanted nothing so much as to leave the blasted village and go for a long ride in my enormous, overgrown woods. The squires and their families were no longer making free with that part of my estate, though I did find the occasional farmwife or stray boy on my bridle paths. The poorest families had my permission to harvest what bounty they could from the woods—short of poaching, of course—and yet, it was getting too late for berries and still too early for nuts.

I'd have the woods to myself, and my conscience.

"Dreyfuss knows better than to make public accusations," Freeman went on, "but he suspects the race was fixed. Hector should have been in fine form, but he was slow off the mark. Richmond might have given Hector a run for his money, but Richmond came in third."

I did not care about any of this.

"Does Dervid Grant own Lionheart?" Ann asked.

"He does. Arden Donohue won a fair sum on the dog too."

The Donohues were also among the very poorest of the parish, eking out an existence one step ahead of starvation. I was treating the younger Grant daughters for rickets with regular doses of cod liver oil, and they—despite protesting the means—were slowly improving.

Ann gave Freeman the sort of inspection that should have made him squirm. "What aren't you saying, Mr. Freeman? You excel at the sort of deep stratagems that put my husband in the thick of trouble, and I will not allow you to do so ever again."

Her tone had been civil, but had I been Freeman, I would have taken a few prudent steps back. That Ann would remonstrate with Freeman surprised me. This was the same woman who'd gone to pieces the previous evening simply because of a lively crowd.

Or had something else provoked Ann's fit of panic?

"I am being overly cautious," Freeman said, "thinking like a magistrate when that burden is no longer mine to carry, but Nigel Bellamy has asked me to keep an eye on the situation."

"You enjoyed being magistrate," I said, climbing into the gig and taking up the reins. "Liked all the petty squabbles and competing interests that go with keeping the rural peace. Answer my wife's question. What's afoot, Freeman?"

"If the race was rigged," Freeman said, "suspicion will fall on those who benefited the most."

Ann's gloved hands were fisted in her lap. "When a wealthy

man's young hound prevails," she said, "that is good luck. A poor man won, and another poor man benefited—among others—so we must accuse them of foul play. Need I remind you, Squire, who exactly was poaching in my husband's woods?"

The woods were not my woods, they were *our* woods—Ann's and mine—but my wife had made the obvious point.

Freeman gave a short shrill whistle, and a gray gelding lipping grass near the smithy raised his head, then began to amble in our direction.

"The race was very likely not rigged," Freeman said. "Hector is getting on. Maybe Richmond is too young to have as much bottom as his owner accords him. Lionheart had a lucky night and will likely not be able to repeat his performance. Vaughn is demanding a rematch, and Dreyfuss is up for it."

"But Richmond is out of the running," Ann said.

"Dreyfuss has agreed to split any winnings with Vaughn if the rematch is held and Hector prevails."

"A dog race cannot be rigged," I said. "It's not as if jockeys sit atop each dog, subtly impeding its speed or allowing it to get trapped behind a slower competitor. The hounds ran freely."

Freeman's horse came up to him and nuzzled his arm.

"Can you tell if a dog has been drugged, St. Sevier?"

I was torn between intrigue and insult. Now I was not only a veterinarian, but also some sort of diviner of canine mysteries.

"Perhaps, if the symptoms mirror those presenting in humans, but only while the poison is active. Twelve hours later, the toxin might well be out of the patient's—dog's—system and impossible to detect."

"What would make a hound slightly slower than usual?" Freeman asked.

"I am a *doctor*," I said in my slowest, most distinct English. "I treat *humans* and have no idea what might marginally impede a canine's gross motor locomotion." Somnifera was the first drug that came to mind, also known as winter cherry, which I knew to be effective on horses. Had we an herbwoman, I might have consulted her regarding other possibilities.

"If my husband," Ann said, "who enjoys an embarrassment of medical training, has no idea how to drug a dog, why would you think Dervid Grant has that knowledge?"

"Grant's father was a gamekeeper who took to drink. No telling what his son picked up from the old man, and Grant is in desperate need of funds, as is Donohue for that matter. I will thank you for looking in on the hound, and please give my regards to Miss Fletcher and her mother."

He took up his girth a few holes, swung into the saddle, and offered Ann a nod in parting.

"I don't like him," Ann said. "His abominable treatment of you aside, I do not like that man. He has a knowing air, and what is there to know in St. Ivo's, for pity's sake?"

I knew something. I knew that whatever else was true, Ann was protective of me. She was protective of the Grants and the Donohues, too, and was willing to speak up on their behalf. That was another glimmer of the old Ann, the Ann who'd ordered me to take naps and eat regularly, the Ann who'd been intrepid enough to attempt a journey to the coast of Spain without benefit of my escort.

"I respect Freeman," I said, "but I am not pleased with the direction of his thoughts."

I gave the horse leave to walk on and resigned myself to calling upon Miss Fletcher, her mother, and the damned dog.

CHAPTER FOUR

ANN

My sense of smell became bothersomely acute when I'd carried Fiona. Frying bacon had been intolerably offensive, and I had known from the odor of a horse's droppings if he'd been at clover or grass.

Some of that acumen had stayed with me. I was still none too fond of bacon, and I had no patience whatsoever with the scent of drunken men. Be he a bandit, some village lad careening into me at the hound races, or one of Wellington's strutting officers, a man in his cups was an olfactory abomination.

That stink had been all around me the previous evening.

I could even detect gin on the breath, which was supposedly impossible. At divine services, I endured proximity to half a village still sweating off the previous night's excesses. My husband, by contrast, carried the fragrance of honeysuckle and summer meadows on his person.

"Why is the dry-goods store open?" I asked as Hugh steered the gig away from the church. "One is not to transact business on the Sabbath."

Hugh drove with the sort of effortless style that made for happy horses and smooth journeys. He was not flashy. Only when in a temper—or in a passion—would Hugh St. Sevier set aside the self-possession that he'd probably learned along with the English language and human anatomy.

"Rutherford will likely take no money from his customers today," Hugh said, "and thus he's not technically doing business. He will put all purchases on credit, and given the state of the congregation this morning, I suspect the patent remedies will sell out."

"This displeases you."

"If one does not wish to have a sore head, then one should not overimbibe."

Hugh enjoyed a very firm grasp of logic. "And if one wants to simply enjoy an evening socializing on the green, and one gets a little carried away, is one to have no relief the next morning?"

And I enjoyed playing devil's advocate. I'd forgotten that about myself, had left my barrister tendencies behind some hedge in Spain.

"Patent remedies," Hugh retorted, "are mostly a drop of this and a dash of that in a base of cheap spirits and honey, Ann. Their efficacy is doubtful, and some of them become habit-forming. That is all well and good for assuring the shopkeeper's secure old age, but hardly a healthy state of affairs for the patient."

Hugh was expressing a medically informed opinion, but I felt as if he were scolding me. "Shall we drop in on the Fletchers now, or put it off until later in the day?"

"You have changed the subject, madame. In an earlier life, you would have argued with me."

In an earlier life, I had married him, thinking that a solution to many problems.

Hugh's gaze was on the lane, which allowed me to admire a handsome profile that would age well. He'd been attractive as a younger man too, brimming with vitality and curiosity, eager to perfect his science. He'd been equal parts enthusiastic and considerate as a lover

—a novelty for me—and, most devastating of all, he'd been affectionate both in and out of bed.

When he'd recalled that he'd had a wife.

"I will not argue with you," I said. "I will state that to endure needless, endless suffering simply to avoid dependence on some cheap elixir is an exercise in stupidity. Many a man and woman bears the day's woes more easily for having a pint or a wee dram by the fire in the evening. Who are you to judge which suffering is deserved and which merits relief?"

He glanced over at me, not with annoyance, which I anticipated, but with curiosity. "Valid point. If suffering is inevitable and relief available, why withhold the relief? But what if the relief simply leads to a different kind of suffering? Laudanum is effective at keeping a patient quiet or putting a megrim to sleep, but what of the headache and fatigue caused by the laudanum itself? The irritability and volatility when it wears off? In some, those symptoms lead to a craving for yet still more of the drug."

The day was pretty, and I was having a conversation—not stilted small talk—with my husband. I took heart from that and applied my mind to the question.

"What if the relief doesn't lead to a different kind of suffering, monsieur? Have you ever had a megrim?"

"I have not, but Lady Violet..."

Her again. She haunted us both, for different reasons, and yet, I had the sense that we haunted her too. "She has megrims?"

"Yes, and Dunkeld can tell when one is coming on just by looking at her. As a physician, his skill fascinates me, but as a man who was intent on impressing a lady... I apologize. This cannot be a comfortable topic for you."

"Nor for you. You have to be worried for her, Hugh. I am worried for her, and for the marquess, and the baby." The last thing I'd wanted when I'd intruded into Hugh's life was to send an innocent woman's plans into the ditch. I had not known she carried Hugh's child when I'd made that choice.

The marquess's proposal had been timely indeed.

"Let's look in on the Fletchers," Hugh said. "If the dog has been drugged, the longer I wait to examine him, the less likely I am to detect any evidence of mischief."

"Now who is changing the subject?"

Hugh drove along in silence until he halted the gig outside the Fletchers' cottage. The house was tidy, but not quite in good repair. A few weeds peeked from the gutters, and both chimneys could have used some pointing and parging. The flowers—blue salvia on this end of the green—going a trifle seedy at the end of summer looked of a piece with the cottage.

"I do worry," Hugh said as he assisted me to alight. "About Violet. She lost two babies, one of them stillborn at six months, which is very hard on a woman. Dunkeld's offer of marriage is noble, and I know from experience that marrying a woman for whom the union is expedient can be difficult for all concerned. I worry for the marquess, too, whom I'm not sure I even like."

"You respect him." And I respected my husband's honesty, even though it intimidated me. "And you worry for their child, who will also be your child."

Hugh stepped away and busied himself securing a rein to a hitching ring in the stone wall fronting the Fletchers' little yard.

"The child will want for nothing," he said, "and I am to have some sort of role in his or her life, but yes, I worry for the child." He returned to my side and stood looking down at me, his expression pensive. "Will you tell me, Ann, why the hound races upset you?"

I had noticed Hugh St. Sevier's eyes before I had noticed anything else about him. Before I was charmed by the French accent, the marvelous physique, the encyclopedic medical knowledge.

Military life could harden the tenderest heart, but amid all that violence and privation, Hugh's gaze had borne a world of compassion for his fellow creatures. I could not afford to test the extent to which that compassion extended to me.

"I detest crowds," I said, "especially drunken crowds, and these people are all but strangers to me, and they have earned my distrust. I was caught unaware by the revelry. It won't happen again."

He took my hand, and when I thought he would place it on his arm, escort-fashion, he instead stroked his fingers over my knuckles. We wore gloves—thank heavens—but the intimacy of the gesture ambushed me all over again.

"I worry for Violet, the marquess, and the baby," Hugh said, "and I have even learned to worry a little bit for myself. Our neighbors, as you refer to them, are not wholly selfless and saintly. But I worry for you, too, Ann, and I abhor that you do not trust me."

He held open the gate, and I preceded him through, though I did not wait for him before I rapped smartly on the Fletchers' door. Trust took time, and if I ever did repose my whole confidence in Hugh St. Sevier, we might both bitterly regret my choice.

The hound was in a bad way.

Miss Fletcher conducted us to the walled garden behind the cottage, and Hugh immediately began his examination. Richmond lay on a folded-up horse blanket, and the poor wretch barely looked up when Hugh and I emerged from the house.

My husband spoke to the dog in French, about how a fellow did not deserve such a hiding for giving his best efforts, and if ever that fellow was to learn to abhor races, then beating him for participating in one would convey the lesson quite well. English pedagogy at its finest.

"I can catch only a little of that," Miss Fletcher muttered to me as we waited on the opposite end of the stone terrace. "Until Monsieur St. Sevier took up residence at Belle Terre, I'd never heard a native speaker use French for everyday conversation. It's a different proposition from parroting a primer at my mother's knee."

"The words don't matter to the patient," I replied. "The language doesn't matter. The caring matters. If St. Sevier is to poke and press, Richmond must trust him."

"Monsieur St. Sevier used the same tone of voice on Mrs. Grant. She stopped cursing immediately. Mama would have known that—how to talk to a mother in childbed."

Miss Fletcher's observation implied self-criticism, because she, who had never given birth, and ought not in the usual course to be attending births, had been unable to stifle Mrs. Grant's profanity.

"My mother was a midwife," I said, "as was her mother. I could not have inspired Mrs. Grant's better manners either, Miss Fletcher. My husband has a gift. Somebody else has a gift when it comes to gardening."

The Fletchers' backyard was not the usual overplanted floral confection attached to most genteel village homes. Basil, tarragon, and mint grew in pots, as did other spices. A riot of late roses climbed an arched wooden frame. Summer vegetables marched in neat rows, with beans flourishing along wire trellises near the wall. Most of the other plants looked medicinal to me.

Marigolds, for itching and swelling of the skin.

Lady's-mantle, for female problems and also for treating wounds.

Elderflower, a disinfectant and anti-inflammatory that could aid with the pains of rheumatism.

Feverfew...

My mother would have delighted in this garden. The scent was brisk and herbaceous rather than floral.

"Marigold, you did not tell me we had visitors." A diminutive older woman, leaning heavily on a cane, shuffled through the back door. Her spectacles glinted like mirrors in the sunlight, and so hunched was she that her knitted shawl fell nearly to her knees, more like a horse's caparison than an item of domestic apparel. "Very bad of you, my girl. I was not asleep."

"Mrs. Fletcher," I said, dipping a curtsey. "Good day." We had been introduced a few weeks ago in the churchyard. I had not seen the lady at services since.

"Madame St. Sevier came with her husband to look in on Richmond," Marigold Fletcher said. "The poor beast has barely moved since Mr. Freeman brought him here last night."

Hugh rose and joined us. "Movement probably hurts Richmond like the very devil. Mrs. Fletcher, good day." He offered her a polite bow.

"I'd like to take my cane to that dreadful Donnie Vaughn," Mrs. Fletcher said. "He always was a sore loser and a slow top. His mother was the brains in that family, and she brought a fair bit of cash to the union too. I intend to see that this hound runs away before his convalescence is complete."

"Mama, that is not funny."

Mrs. Fletcher thumped her cane on the flagstone terraces. "Nor is beating a helpless creature at all amusing. 'A righteous man regardeth the life of his beast, but the tender mercies of the wicked are cruel.' Proverbs 12:10."

She was stooped, skinny, and gray-haired, and all the more fierce because of her limitations. "Where will Richmond run to?" I asked.

"That's for me and Richmond to know, madame. If you ask me, somebody ought to turn Donnie Vaughn over to the press gangs."

The press gangs had been disbanded several years ago.

"What I can ask of you," Hugh said, "is more quiet rest for Richmond. I found no broken bones, thank the good God. I expect that Vaughn, drunk as he was, landed only a few kicks. Richmond should have been able to dodge blows aimed at his head, though his ribs are quite sore. He also has a bruise on his left hip that will make moving painful for a time. The laceration on his shoulder could have used a few stitches, but it's clean, and I doubt Richmond will be vain about a scar."

"Poor lad," Mrs. Fletcher said. "I recall from some pamphlet or other that tincture of hawthorn might help the hip. Never did much for me, but I'm not a dog."

"Mama reads everything," Miss Fletcher said, a shade too

brightly. "She is the reason we have a lending library in St. Ivo's and a dame school."

"What is the point of teaching a child her letters if she has nothing to read?" Mrs. Fletcher replied. "The Bible is not exactly riveting fare for children, nor for many adults either truth be known."

Despite her tart words, Mrs. Fletcher was leaning on her cane more and more heavily. I was about to suggest that we take the discussion inside when Hugh gestured to a pair of wrought-iron chairs.

"Shall we enjoy the fresh air while we continue this conversation? I can tell you that as a boy, I was much more inclined toward adventure stories than the exhortations of the prophets."

Mrs. Fletcher led a halting procession to the chairs and allowed Hugh to assist her into one. He, Miss Fletcher, and I remained on our feet, as if attending a royal reception, where only the monarch was entitled to sit.

"What shall we do if Mr. Vaughn comes around demanding to repossess his hound?" Miss Fletcher asked. "He can be quite emphatic about his opinions."

That possibility had been bothering me as well. Richmond had not moved from his horse blanket, and his breathing was that of a beast already returned to his slumbers.

"This modest, sunny garden," Hugh said, "is just the right size to allow Richmond to move about when he's feeling better. He can amuse himself here without getting overtaxed. Not too many steps either, which is what his hip needs."

I had the sense my husband was improvising, finding an excuse for the hound to tarry with the ladies.

"Mr. Vaughn is to be charged with disorderly conduct," I said. "He can't possibly call upon you until Nigel Bellamy has held his parlor session tomorrow. We will convey to Mr. Bellamy that Richmond must not be moved for the nonce, and I would also count it a mercy if we could send you over some bones for the beast to gnaw on."

"We have no dogs of any kind at Belle Terre," Hugh said. "And

Cook can make only so much soup for such a small family. We are awash in bones, and Richmond has earned a reward, *non*?"

A small family we might be, but our staff was large and hungry. I was nonetheless delighted that Hugh would support my fabrication.

"I'm sure Richmond would delight in a juicy bone," Miss Fletcher said, twitching her mother's shawl. "But Donnie Vaughn will want his hound back, and he is accustomed to getting what he wants."

"He cannot expect Richmond to run next week," I said, "so why be hasty about moving the patient?"

"The next races won't be for a fortnight," Miss Fletcher said. "That's how we always do it."

"Dreyfuss wants a rematch between Old Hector and Lionheart," I replied. "I know not if others will be in the field. Dreyfuss has agreed to split any winnings with Vaughn."

Miss Fletcher frowned. "Why a rematch? Lionheart is young and very much on his game. He beat an older hound and a heavier hound, while Lionheart is built for speed. He has the hip and shoulder angles, doesn't he, Mama? Mama's papa was the quintessential country squire, mad for hounds and horses."

Mrs. Fletcher cleared her throat. "We'll take good care of Richmond, and to blazes with these foolish men and their foolish pursuits. 'Wine is a mocker, strong drink a brawler, And whoever is led astray by it is not wise.' Proverbs 20:1."

We took our leave upon that admonition, and to my surprise, I had enjoyed the visit. "Mrs. Fletcher is very different from Mrs. Cooper, isn't she?"

Hugh handed me up into the gig, took the place beside me, and sat for a moment before asking the horse to walk on.

"Mrs. Cooper seems to consider her remit to manage Vicar Cooper," Hugh said, "and she does that quite well. I gather when Mrs. Fletcher dwelled at the vicarage, she took the whole congregation in hand."

"A woman with managing tendencies?"

Hugh clucked to the horse. "A woman who appears to have arthritis, and yet, she did not interrogate me as most beldames will, about this or that remedy. Her gait is uneven, suggesting her hips pain her, or perhaps a gouty toe, and yet, she mentioned none of this to the only university-trained physician within twenty miles."

"You itch to treat her?"

"To offer her relief from pain. Rutherford is merely a part-time purveyor of elixirs and sundries, not a medical man. I have no idea of his medical credentials, if any he has. I will have to ask him about using hawthorn to treat arthritis in humans, but willow bark tea is bound to help with rheumatism. Ginger tea might as well."

"Not laudanum?"

He slanted me a husbandly look as we passed the smithy. "If laudanum helped appreciably, I would prescribe it, even knowing that some patients can become dependent upon it. Arthritis rarely cures itself. Nonetheless, in my experience, laudanum is not all that effective for rheumatism or back problems. I tested the latter on calvary officers, who almost always ended up with sore backs, and many of them said... I am boring you."

No, he was not. "Lady Violet was right."

Hugh found it necessary to watch Miss Fletcher's progress across the green. She seemed to be heading for the dry-goods shop, and at a good clip.

"About what was her ladyship correct?" he asked.

"You are passionate about healing and should be given every opportunity to practice your vocation. How was the hound?"

"Sluggish," Hugh said as we tooled over the arched bridge. "He'll recover, though in old age, approaching storms might remind him of Vaughn's violence."

"Vaughn should never be allowed to own another dog."

"The man was drunk and disappointed, Ann. Do we condemn him for all eternity for one stupid act for which he is remorseful?"

Now I found it needful to study the orange and yellow lilies growing in the ditches. "He beat *a dog*, Hugh, an animal who could not fight back, who had no one to take up for him, and he did this where others could see him at it. That does not speak of one mean, stupid act. That is evidence of a mean, stupid man." And while I abhorred inebriates as a class, the mean drunk held a special place of loathing in my heart.

The mean, lascivious drunk haunted my nightmares and deserved to rot in hell.

We rolled along in silence, and I wished I had not spoken so honestly. Belle Terre looking grand and lonely on its rise came into view when another question occurred to me.

"Should Richmond have been sluggish?"

Hugh steered the gig around to the back of the house rather than park out front. "I am not a veterinarian, but I suspect he should not have been *that* sluggish. A hard race, a lot of excitement, a beating... Those would all take a toll, but Richmond ought to have been more alert in fresh surroundings and around strangers."

I thought back to our call upon the Fletchers. "He barely looked up when we came along, didn't thump his tail or woof. He seemed friendly enough before the race."

Hugh drew the horse to a halt in the stable yard. "And he went right back to sleep when I finished with my examination, but if he suffered a boot to the head, he might also be showing the effects of that injury."

I kept silent until a stable boy had taken the gig around to the carriage house, and Hugh and I were walking toward the house.

"What will you tell Freeman and the magistrate?" I asked.

"Nothing. Freeman wants to see the races end, apparently, and my evidence is far from conclusive. I am not—why must I restate the obvious?—a veterinarian, nor do I wish to become one by default. Have we any soupbones?"

Maybe all husbands and wives became adept at changing the subject. "We will, and those bones will have plenty of meat on them." Not for the sake of the dog.

We reached the back terrace, and Fiona pelted out of the house to lash her arms around Hugh's waist.

"*Tu es à la maison*, Papa! I missed you so, and you said we could go riding *si les temps est ensoleillé*. The day is quite sunny, is it not? Tell him, Mama. The weather is *parfait pour l'équitation*."

I was quite competent in the saddle, and yet, I had not once ridden out with my husband. I was reluctant to intrude on Fiona's time with her father, and—more to the point—Hugh hadn't invited me to hack out with him.

"Your father must change into riding attire," I said as Hugh swung Fiona onto his back. "The day is very nice, and when you come home, we can have a picnic for our nooning."

My suggestion met with general agreement, though was Hugh happy to fall in with my plan because he sought leisure time with his family, or because he knew that with Fiona on hand, I would trouble him no further about the ailing hound?

Because if the dog had been drugged, then the only physician in the shire was a logical party to have known how to do that—but not the only logical party. I returned to the house and went to the library, where I sat down with pencil and paper and started a list.

~

Not until the blankets had been spread at the foot of the garden and Hugh came down beside me did I recall that he and I had shared an occasional picnic as newlyweds.

Privacy in a military camp had been hard to come by. On rare occasions when weather, an empty infirmary, and foolish optimism had converged, I'd inveigled my husband into sneaking out of camp with me and enjoying a sandwich and some fruit in the countryside.

We'd taken risks venturing forth alone, but risk in time of war becomes a relative matter.

"Charlemagne shied at a squirrel," Fiona said, kneeling before the hamper and rearranging the contents. "He was terrified because squirrels are little and fast."

"Were you terrified?" I asked, though knowing Fiona—and Charlemagne—I suspected the horse had done little more than flick an ear.

"*Non*. Papa would not let me fall. *Nous avons des carottes*!" She brandished a large orange specimen. "May I feed Charlemagne the carrot? *C'était un bon garçon, Papa*. Good boys should be rewarded."

"He was a good boy," Hugh said. "Feed him the carrot, but no running in the stable."

She was on her feet in an instant. "But I may run *to* the stable, *non*?"

"*Oui*," I said. "But you will wash your hands again at the groom's pump before you eat."

She was off, waving her carrot and calling to the horse.

"Such energy," Hugh said, flopping to his back. "Such limitless, extremely verbal, polyglot energy."

I rummaged in the hamper and found a loaf of bread cut lengthwise with brie smeared thickly between the halves. Cook had also included a crock of blueberries and cold sliced ham. Our wine was a cool, fruity Riesling, a perfect complement to the informal meal and the sunny afternoon. For Fiona, we had a bottle of lemonade.

"Did Charlemagne spook?" I asked, taking a sip of the wine directly from the bottle.

"He raised his head swiftly, as horses do when trying to focus on a distant object. Am I truly forbidden to get the child her own pony?"

"Ponies are problematic," I said, tearing off a hunk of the bread and brie. "The child grows, the pony does not, and two years on, we will need a different pony. Then what do we do with the old stalwart? In most families, he would be passed down to the next smaller child, but in ours..."

Hugh lay on his back, his feet crossed at the ankle, his hands linked on his flat belly. He was the picture of an adult male in casual repose, but his gaze was alert.

"We can try for another child, Ann. That decision is yours."

I stared at the bread in my hand. "When did that decision become mine?"

Hugh sat up, tailor-fashion. Abruptly, we were knee to knee, alone on a blanket and in the middle of another difficult moment. "The choice is yours, madame, because I am not a barbarian. I am your husband and a man in good health who once found marriage to you congenial in many regards. Somewhere between those facts lies a way forward for us, if you choose to take it."

"I have trapped you," I said, "again, but I will not trap you further with another child. We agreed to spend the summer together, for Fiona's sake, to take some time to adjust to being married again, but I hardly know how to be a wife to you, Hugh."

His expression turned quizzical. "Then how would you like me to be your husband?"

Not like this, with Hugh intent on joining the local squires, while I... panicked on the village green.

"I esteem you," I said. "That hasn't changed. I left you in Spain because I thought that was for the best, and I have regretted my decision many times."

Hugh twisted off a bite of the bread I held and popped it into his mouth. "Do you regret that decision enough to try being my wife again?"

He had not said that he esteemed *me.* I was no innocent. I knew that Hugh need not even like me to serve as the father of a sibling for Fiona, and that notion made the wine roil in my belly.

"I am trying," I said, "and I appreciate your patience, but—"

I fell silent as a figure rode into the stable yard twenty yards off.

"I know that gray," Hugh said, dusting his hands. "The wicked fairy has come to call."

Thaddeus Freeman swung from the saddle and waved off the groom.

"Must we break bread with that man?" I muttered. "Fiona is afraid of him."

"I am none too fond of him myself, but yes, we will break bread with him, someday. He does not appear to be in a social mood today."

When was he ever? Freeman was attractive, in a blond, English gentry sort of way, but I dreaded the sight of him.

"Madame." Freeman bowed a few yards short of our blanket. "Monsieur."

Hugh helped me to my feet and kept hold of my hand. "Freeman. Your gelding is making free with my lawn."

"That horse is bottomless," Freeman replied. "Less for the gardeners to scythe. I won't stay long, but I was out and about and thought I'd ask what your examination of the hound revealed."

Did he have no small talk? But then, I wanted him gone, the sooner the better.

"Nothing conclusive," Hugh said. "The dog is in pain and knows better than to make the situation worse by trying to chase rabbits he will not catch."

Oh, that was subtle.

"Any sign the beast was drugged?"

"Why, yes, Freeman." Hugh adopted his most clinical tone. "Richmond complained of blurred vision, his speech was slurred and his gait unsteady. He could not recall who sat upon the throne of Great Britain, nor who was in line to inherit the crown, and he was less than certain about the specifics of the Fourth Commandment."

Keep the Sabbath holy. My husband was in fine form, considering the nature of Freeman's errand.

"You are not a veterinarian, I know," Freeman said. "But you also left the churchyard before the worst of the talk started."

The bad fairy indeed. "What talk?" I asked.

"Ugly talk, about fixed races, cheats, and old-fashioned justice. If Bellamy has to arrest Grant or Donohue, those families will not survive."

"They will survive," I said, "if I have to house them at Belle Terre. Your rubbishing gentry neighbors must learn that they cannot turn to bullying and intimidation whenever life hands them an outcome they do not like. Wagering involves chance, and they chanced to bet on the wrong hound." My Perthshire burr had become more evident with that proclamation.

"I am not your enemy, madame," Freeman said. "If Richmond was drugged, and Donohue and Grant had nothing to do with it, then the sooner we find the true culprit, the safer those families will be."

"What do we know about the dry goods merchant Rutherford?" I asked.

Both men looked at me as if I'd announced a plot to blow up the Palace of Westminster.

"Rutherford is new to the area," I went on. "He has access to soporifics, and if his business is not doing well, then he has a motive to bet on an underdog."

"Why do you think his business isn't doing well?" Hugh asked.

"He's informally open on Sundays, which is forbidden by both secular and church authorities. He's forever sweeping his front steps, which are spotless, and if his potions worked, Mrs. Fletcher would not be in such pain." Then too, the man was just too cheerful.

"You've given this some thought," Freeman said. "May I ask why, if there's no evidence to support the accusations of race-fixing?"

I wanted to shake my finger in Freeman's handsome face, but that would mean turning loose of Hugh's hand.

"Because my husband, as the most learned medical authority in the shire, also understands how to use sedatives and poisons. Monsieur has all the London connections necessary to supply the same, if foraging in the woods doesn't yield a suitable drug. Moreover, our neighbors are lethally suspicious of St. Sevier simply because of his French birth. They would still welcome an excuse to be rid of him."

"That is all water quite over the dam," Freeman said. "I have admitted that my tactics were questionable, and I have apologized for bending the rules. Do you really think somebody would rig a race to cast suspicion on the shire's only physician?"

I remained silent rather than disgrace my husband with profanity on the Sabbath.

Hugh gazed past Freeman's shoulder to the stable yard. Fiona had come out of the barn and spied the gray cropping grass. She disappeared right back into the barn.

"Madame has a point," Hugh said. "I am known to be concerned for the poorest families and to have refused to enclose the land they live on. If somebody wanted to serve me a bad turn, attacking those families would do it. To do so while Mrs. Grant is recovering from childbirth is particularly heinous, because you are right, Freeman. For Dervid Grant to be incarcerated now would cause his wife and children great hardship. The Donohues fare little better."

"Vicar and Mrs. Cooper detest the dog races," I said. "For obvious reasons. The betting, the inebriation, the brawling."

"The animal cruelty," Hugh added, "if the wrong man's hound loses."

"I'm none too fond of these races myself," Freeman said. "Will you suspect me of drugging the hound?"

"Yes," I said, "if suspicions have become mandatory. You are just devious enough to drug Richmond, then turn around and ask my husband to examine a patient who can offer no real evidence of anything. You excel at appearing conscientious."

"Ann...?" Hugh was not remonstrating with me. He was concerned.

And I was again very nearly in hysterics, though at least my provocation was simple enough to identify.

"Mr. Freeman's appearance is so repugnant to Fiona," I said, "that she's right now hiding in the barn when she ought to be picnicking with her parents. The sight of *his horse* was enough to terrify her. I will be very surprised if she's not afflicted with nightmares for the next week. Excuse me, please, because I must coax her out of whatever hayloft or grain bin she's cowering in. If you want to be useful, Mr. Freeman, you will obtain a list of who won or lost a substantial sum as a result of Lionheart's victory—who *in addition to Grant and Donohue*—and convey it to us in writing."

I dropped Hugh's hand and stalked off to the barn, all the while congratulating myself for refraining from profanity and violence, though Freeman deserved both.

CHAPTER FIVE

HUGH

I watched Ann march across the lawn, skirts swishing. Part of me worried at the degree of her upset. Another part purely admired the picture she made—a husband's privilege, *non*? Before Freeman's arrival, she'd taken a sip of wine directly from the bottle, and that had sparked a memory of another picnic, another bottle of wine, and a very pleasant interlude in the Spanish countryside.

I had forgotten those pleasant interludes, but proximity to Ann was reminding me of them. Had she forgotten them as well?

"What shall you do with the hound?" I asked Freeman as he, too, observed Ann's departure.

"Richmond? What do you suggest?"

"He is the victim of an undeserved beating, but he is also Vaughn's property. English law takes a man's relationship to his property very seriously."

Ann disappeared into the barn, and Freeman turned his gaze on me. "While the law provides no protection whatsoever for the beasts, wives, and children who become that man's chattel. I do not, contrary to what you might think, miss the magistrate's post. I wish Nigel Bellamy was more willing to take matters in hand."

Nigel Bellamy had also served under Wellington and had come home from the war not quite sound of spirits. His mind was sharp, but he had largely withdrawn from society. Freeman had appointed himself the eyes and ears of the king's man, apparently, and that bothered me.

"Our agreement was that you would step down from the magistrate's post," I said, "not that you would find a supernumerary to do the dull parts while you continue to poke about in the underbrush at will."

"Why don't you take over the poking?" Freeman retorted. "Most of us in St. Ivo's surrounds are barely hanging on here. We survive in part only because we enjoy proximity to London and can get London prices for our goods. An outsider might see clearly what I am too willing to overlook."

"You also survive because I do not enclose my common land, nor do I forbid a reasonable amount of foraging in my woods. What has any of this to do with Richmond's situation?"

The hound, to use Fiona's phrase, was a good boy. He had tolerated my intrusion into his peace and even tried to offer a few feeble licks to my hand.

"What did your examination reveal, St. Sevier? And please do not indulge in another scold. Your wife will remain in the barn until I decamp, and I've no wish to annoy her further."

Valid point. "The dog might have been drugged," I said, "but there's no way to separate the effects of exertion and a beating from the effects of a sedative. Lethargy, lack of appetite, dull spirits, and so forth would be expected in either case. I am more concerned that Vaughn will regain possession of the beast. The Fletcher ladies asked what they should do in the event he makes that attempt."

"They live a quiet life," Freeman said, "but Miss Fletcher has a way with an upset soul. She is an angel of patience with her mother, and that is no small feat. She also coaxed Mrs. Heaver to allow other ladies to volunteer at the lending library, when Mrs. Heaver would have hoarded the whole collection like a biddy roosting on her eggs."

"I, too, have found Miss Fletcher to be a civic-spirited, cheerful lady, but that does not mean you can foist that dog on her. Vaughn would turn his resentment on a pair of women who did not deserve his enmity."

"I don't suppose you want the dog?" Freeman asked.

"He belongs to Vaughn, but I do have a suggestion. Have Nigel Bellamy keep the beast in lieu of levying a fine."

Freeman eyed the remains of the interrupted picnic. "You make that suggestion because Bellamy needs the company, not because Vaughn is likely to beat the dog again."

"I make the suggestion for both reasons. Nigel, like most of his neighbors, has not asked to consult with me in a medical capacity, but he's clearly suffering something like melancholia. Richmond needs a safe home, and the two injured fellows might benefit one another."

"The malady isn't melancholia," Freeman said, gaze now fixed on the gray, who was ingesting grass at a great rate. "Nigel isn't weepy and morose. He's simply... not entirely present."

"Was he ever?" From a diagnostic perspective, that mattered. War, like pregnancy, could exacerbate underlying tendencies, or it could bring its own unique harms to the sufferer.

"Nigel was always quiet, overshadowed by a blustering father and a charming younger brother, but he wasn't withdrawn to this extent. Something happened, probably while he was in the hands of the French or the bandits who delivered him to the French. The dispatches never mentioned him by name, but I know he had a rough time of it."

"He was an officer," I said. "He should have received reasonable treatment." Where was Ann, and was she truly hiding until Freeman's departure?

"To the Bonapartists among the Spanish *guerrillas*, an officer's uniform meant nothing, St. Sevier. You know that."

"I do know that, but as for any definitive findings regarding Richmond, I cannot help you. With rest and care, the dog will heal, though a stern lecture from you is not sufficient punishment for Vaughn's bad temper."

"Vaughn is an alderman. Shall we arrest him for chastising a slow hound?"

"Weren't you considering charges of disturbing the peace?"

Freeman raised his arm and circled his hand. The gesture caught the eye of the grazing horse, who ceased his deprivations upon the grass and ambled toward the picnic blanket.

"I can merely suggest. Nobody will testify against Vaughn, and the charges will be dismissed. I wish to hell nobody had ever thought to hold the damned races. The horse races are just as bad, but one expects that with a horse race. I don't suppose your gelding is inclined to speed?"

"Charlemagne is too dignified to involve himself in such doings." He would also pout if he lost, and three-quarter ton of pouting equine was not to be borne.

"He's a hell of a fine animal, St. Sevier, though he can't hold a candle to my Tacitus."

The gray's ears pricked at the mention of his name. He was a handsome creature, rangy and lean like his owner, but with the soft eyes of the well-cared-for domestic equine. Those eyes were cast longingly at the picnic basket, from whence the delicate equine nose doubtless detected the scent of carrots.

"Who holds the bets for the hound races?" I asked.

"Anderson, the publican. He stays sober, or that's the theory, and he's accustomed to handling money and keeping accounts. I'll have a look at his books."

"Is he honest?"

Freeman took the girth up a hole and ran the stirrup irons down the leathers. "Amos Anderson runs a struggling posting inn. I would say that, yes, he is honest, as all the fine souls in St. Ivo's are honest, but as you are too well aware, I myself have no consistent claim to the virtue of veracity."

"I have forgiven you your little stratagems." I hadn't, or not in any studied sense, but I was ready to put the past behind me and attempt a fresh start with Freeman.

"Thank you," Freeman said, patting his horse. "That still leaves me very much in your wife's bad books."

"I cannot help you in that quarter. Madame is a law unto herself in some regards." Also a puzzle to her own husband most days.

Freeman sent a glance I could not decipher in the direction of the stables. "I will look over the betting book, but I wish no rematch had been agreed to. Anderson might have made that suggestion—he does a roaring good business on race days, far better than market days even—but all the merchants around the green like the races."

"While Mr. Cooper does not."

"Cooper, as vicar, chooses his sermons. In the grand scheme of sins, a little wagering, drinking, and brawling might preserve the community from far worse transgressions."

That was the same argument used to justify dueling. Allow men their little—lethal—displays of violence, and they would be much better behaved as a result. A brush with death or the thought of a brush with death would inspire all and sundry to greater politesse and prudence.

Given the frequency with which lives were lost on the field of honor, and the continued evidence of masculine imprudence on every hand, the argument was contemptibly ludicrous.

"I will call on Nigel Bellamy," I said, "and inform him of my findings regarding Richmond."

"I'm not taking that dog, St. Sevier. I have enough mouths to feed, and I don't want Donnie Vaughn bringing suit to reclaim his property."

Ann would have taken in that hapless canine in an instant, Donnie Vaughn be damned. At the same time, I was not to allow Fiona to become attached to a pony she'd soon outgrow. A complicated person, my wife, far more complicated than I'd realized when I'd agreed to marry her.

Freeman swung into the saddle, which should have been an awkward undertaking for a man who had lost most of the use of one hand, but he managed well enough. Perhaps he'd lost fine motor control of his left hand, but still had strength in his grip.

"For Tacitus," I said, taking a carrot from the hamper and tossing it to Freeman. The horse, to his credit, did not shy at oncoming missiles, and Freeman deftly caught the carrot with his left hand.

Interesting. How much of Freeman's injury was in his hand, and how much in his mind?

"I will ride across the lawn if you don't mind," Freeman said. "One does not want to upset the womenfolk unnecessarily by passing through the stable yard."

"The ladies will not be upset to see the back of you," I replied. "Ann has a temper, and you have offended her. Give it time." Ann was also fair and compassionate, or had been as a younger woman.

Freeman shoved the carrot into a pocket. "She had a hard time of it in Spain. One makes allowances. You should too."

On that cryptic observation, he trotted off across the lawn, clattered over a corner of the terrace, and disappeared from view.

I returned to the blanket, where I was determined to wait for my ladies. The day was still fair, and we had a meal to consume. I tried a sip of the wine and found it picnic-quality, while the bread and brie were quite good.

I wanted to yell to Ann and Fiona that it was safe to come out, but that would imply that both females were afraid. I instead munched on bread and cheese and pondered Freeman's last remark.

Ann had followed the drum, as some infantry wives did. The military obliged up to a point by allowing them rations in exchange for labor—assisting in the infirmary, helping with meal preparation, laundry, or housekeeping. Many a battle had seen the ladies defending the baggage train at gunpoint, and successfully so.

Ann had fared better than most, in that when her soldier-boy husband had died, she'd been offered marriage to a wealthy volunteer in the person of myself. Her duties had become lighter, and she'd risen in status. Rapid remarriage was expected under such circumstances and, given Ann's youth and good looks, had been her best option.

So Freeman wasn't referring to the time Ann had spent as my wife when he'd alluded to Ann having a hard time in Spain. He knew something of what had befallen her afterward, when she'd struck out for the coast. What did he know, and how did he know it?

I had eaten about a quarter of the baguette when Ann and Fiona emerged from the stables hand in hand. They appeared quite in charity with each other, though as we consumed our meal, I had the sense that their goodwill did not extend to me.

Bellamy held his parlor sessions after the noon meal on Monday, and thus Monday morning found me retrieving Richmond from the Fletchers and conveying him in the gig to the Bellamy estate.

Bellamy *père* had taken his missus for a summer repairing lease by the sea. By agreement, that holiday marked the beginning of the Bellamy heir's management of the estate. I had not crossed paths directly with Nigel Bellamy in Spain, though I had known of him. Officers taken prisoner were the subject of much talk and many prayers. He had doubtless known of me as well—Frenchmen volunteering to patch up English soldiers had been a rarity. In truth, I'd patched up nearly as many Frenchmen and Germans as I had British troops.

How was I to patch up my marriage? Since yesterday's picnic, I'd been pondering whether to again bring up the subject of a sibling for Fiona. That approach leaped over many thornier issues. I could simply take my wife to bed, lavish marital pleasure upon her, and all would be...

More complicated? *Plus confus?* Sebastian, Marquess of Dunkeld, might be sympathetic to my situation, but he was presently occupied with wooing Lady Violet.

Who carried my child. Ann was doubtless right to insist that she and I handle our marital rapprochement cautiously, but that did not make my lumpy cot any more comfortable.

"What if Bellamy won't keep the hound?" Ann asked quietly.

I'd had to lift the beast into the gig, and he lay curled at our feet, though his eyes were open. He was apparently a placid soul when not at the races, and Miss Fletcher had made much of him at the moment of parting.

"I suppose he can bide with the Fletchers temporarily," I said. "Unless you'd like to take him in?"

"I would," Ann said, "but we both know that will simply give John Bull another excuse to resent you. You will be labeled a reiver of dogs."

"John Bull, as you call our neighbors, might well be relieved that Donnie Vaughn can no longer abuse the beast."

"Of course they will be relieved. You will have solved a problem of conscience for them—no upright Englishman likes to see a canine abused, but no villager would willingly call an alderman to account."

"Shall we remove to Berkshire, Ann? My sense is that we are up against more caution here than genuine ill will, but the situation is still vexing."

The day was a little too hot for comfort, with a closeness to the air that presaged rain in the afternoon. No breeze sent the wildflowers along the road swaying, and the sheep were abed in the grass beneath any obliging shade tree.

"You probably have the right of it," Ann said, "but a Scot learns caution toward the English too. Fiona did not have nightmares last night. I was wrong about that."

And my wife, whatever her other failings, would always admit when she was wrong. "After I read Fiona her story, she asked why Freeman had come to call."

Ann peered at me. "She didn't mention him to me. What did you tell her?"

"That Freeman is trying to make friends, and he is sorry for arresting me." I hoped that was true.

"For *detaining* you, illegally. You did not bring up the hound races?"

"She would worry." She was her mother's daughter in that regard, though Lady Violet was also one to take on concerns that belonged to others.

"I worry," Ann said. "You mentioned that we might have more children."

Ann had ambushed me in the middle of a sunny, rural lane, and yet, we had privacy, we had limited time to finish the discussion, and the topic wanted airing. She had chosen her moment shrewdly.

"I did mention that very idea," I said as the turn came into view that would lead to the Bellamy manor house.

Richmond sat up, bracing himself against Ann's leg.

"I esteem you mightily, Hugh St. Sevier, and you are proving to be a devoted and caring father."

I should have been pleased at those declarations. I was, in fact, disappointed, and braced for worse.

"But?" I asked, guiding the horse onto the Bellamys' drive.

"But we barely know each other," Ann said. "And some steps cannot be undone once taken. Fiona binds us together, and she will soon be half grown. When she's of age, our connection as husband and wife becomes more distant. A new baby would start that race all over again."

I slowed the horse to the walk, which the growing heat of the day required. My wife was being logical, and all I sought was a secluded bend in the road in which to kiss her cheek.

"I did not marry you with children in mind, Ann."

"What did you have in mind?"

Ann was right about this much—we barely knew each other. "I have had measles, chicken pox, and mumps, rather later than is normal. All of those diseases can affect a man's ability to sire children." And that possibility was not presented to medical students as a potential hazard of the profession. I had been inoculated against smallpox, thank God, because that, too, was believed to affect a man's fecundity.

"I have had those same ailments," Ann said, "as well as scarlatina and a few putrid sore throats. I seem to have good lungs, though."

"I had not known that. Will you tell me sometime of Fiona's ailments and injuries?"

"Of course."

The Bellamy home came into view, a handsome edifice of gray fieldstone set on a slight rise. The house had a subtly grim air, despite the summer day, despite the tidy façade. Nobody had taken the trouble to put out pots of flowers. No geese or ducks ambled about on the lawn. Not so much as a cat sunned itself on the drive.

"About the dog," Ann said.

What about our marriage? "Yes?"

"We must put it to Mr. Bellamy that the ladies do not have room for a lively young hound."

"They don't," I said, "though if Miss Fletcher hares all over the countryside calling on the halt and the ailing, Richmond would get plenty of exercise."

"Miss Fletcher's responsibility is to her mother, Hugh."

And a wife's responsibility was to her husband—also his to her. "Bellamy might well take to the notion of keeping the dog."

But would Ann again raise the topic of more children? She and I were not well acquainted, true, but what—if anything—did she want to do about that?

~

Nigel Bellamy received us cordially after I'd seen Richmond given into the keeping of the stable lads. Bellamy was tallish, dark-haired, and more pale than the usual Englishmen, owing, I supposed, to a penchant for remaining indoors. I would put his age at slightly north of thirty, though in spirit, he struck me as approaching his threescore and ten.

"You brought along the hound, Richmond," Bellamy said when Ann had done the tea tray honors at our host's invitation.

"We did," I replied. "Freeman asked me to examine the dog, who as far as I can see has suffered a sound beating, but shows no clear evidence of being drugged."

Bellamy considered his tea, which he took plain. "None?" His attire, like his family parlor, was entirely unremarkable. Appropriate, with no touches of personality or individuality. His parlor reminded me of the receiving rooms set up by the fancy physicians who kept consulting offices in London's Marylebone neighborhood. All was bland, pleasant, and built to withstand appreciable wear. The curtains were nonetheless closed, probably the better to preserve the upholstery from the ravages of the sun.

"I found nothing conclusive," I said.

"Anything inconclusive?"

"Perhaps." I summarized my findings, such as they were. "I would rather not see Vaughn regain possession of the hound. I propose that you confiscate Richmond in lieu of a fine."

"One confiscates contraband, Monsieur St. Sevier. One does not confiscate pets."

Ann had been unusually quiet, but then, perhaps she was thinking of our conversation in the gig. A conversation that had failed to reach any satisfactory conclusion.

"One can also confiscate goods in lieu of a fine," Ann said, "though the usual recourse is to auction the goods. I believe my husband's hope is that you can keep the hound as a surety against Mr. Vaughn's continued good behavior."

Bellamy made a face at his tea. "Donnie Vaughn is incapable of good behavior for more than the forty days of Lent. He's not a bad sort, but drink gets the better of him."

"Which means, if you made sobriety an element of Vaughn's required good behavior, Richmond would never again be his to beat."

Ann's observation earned her a direct perusal from Bellamy, and something passed between them that I did not comprehend.

"Very well," Bellamy said. "The hound may reside in my stable. God knows my father is fond of his canines."

Now Ann regarded me, and I well knew what expectation she was conveying.

"He will need the hospitality of the manor itself for a time," I said. "Room to pad about quietly, but no temptation to leap after a stable cat or play tag with the mares."

"I cannot have fleas in this house," Bellamy retorted. "The housemaids would mutiny."

Ann topped up Bellamy's tea. "The Fletchers bathed the dog in a peppermint and lavender solution. Fleas will not be a problem."

Ann's sense of smell had always been acute. I had merely noted the scent of peppermint in passing among the other scents in the Fletchers' garden. She had detected that it had come from the dog and why.

"I suppose I have no choice but to acquire the hound." Bellamy's expression was resigned, though I gathered that our maneuvering had not offended him. "Do you play chess, monsieur?"

"I do. Freeman trounces me three games out of four."

"He trounces me three games out of four as well, so you and I ought to be evenly matched. Other than Freeman's recent missteps, have you enjoyed your summer in St. Ivo's?"

I took refuge in good manners. "Our daughter enjoys Belle Terre's grounds, and the weather has been pleasant."

"And what of you, madame?" Bellamy asked. "Does St. Ivo's meet with your approval? One hears that the hound races did not hold your attention for long."

One apparently had reliable spies. I suspected Bellamy's younger sister Elizabeth might have passed along that gossip.

"I do not tolerate the heat of English summers easily," Ann replied, "and to be honest, a half-drunken mob sits ill with me. I had not anticipated the size of the gathering or its boisterousness. Those factors combined suggested a strategic retreat was in order, and my husband was kind enough to oblige me."

I managed not to gape at Ann's disclosure, though she had confided more to Bellamy than she had to me. A drunken mob had gathered on the occasion of her... betrothal to me, to resort to euphemism, and I had not realized that St. Ivo's boisterous inebriates would stir that memory.

"My feelings exactly," Bellamy said. "An inebriated crowd should give everybody pause. I'd like to shut the damned races down, but they seem to have a life of their own. I suppose if the king's man had bestirred himself to look in on the proceedings, some of the mischief might have been held in check."

Another unexpected disclosure. I should go about the neighborhood dispensing feckless hounds, and I might soon learn all of St. Ivo's secrets.

"Will you attend this Saturday," Ann asked, "at the rematch between Lionheart and Old Hector? I am trying to get up my courage for that outing, though we will again arrive early and depart before the sun sets."

I had wanted to avoid the rematch, but if Ann asked for my escort, she would have it. I suspected this was her version of getting back on the horse, but it wasn't a request I would ever make of her.

She did not owe me or my professional aspirations a return to the rubbishing hound races—something else we would need to discuss. I finished my tea and made reference to the possibility of thunderstorms.

Ann rose on that cue, and to my surprise, Bellamy himself accompanied us to the front door. Some awkwardness ensued sorting out hat, bonnet, walking stick, and parasol, but we left on a note of reserved good cheer and an invitation to me to drop around *some time* for a game of chess.

Ann was sitting beside me in the gig, and we were trotting for home before she spoke. "You were right, Hugh. Richmond and Mr. Bellamy will be good for each other."

"Would you like a dog?" A puppy. Why hadn't I thought of that sooner?

"Must you provide your womenfolk with beasts, monsieur? A pony for Fiona, a dog for me?"

As a young husband, I would have heard such a retort as the start of an argument. *I was only asking a question. I was trying to be considerate. Why must you criticize everything I say, do, fail to do, or imply?*

Then Ann and I would go at each other, with the final round fought in the dialect of fuming silences and angry footfalls. If I was very lucky, Ann might reach for me in the night, and come morning, our version of harmony would be restored.

Now, I had a better sense of what my wife wasn't saying. "I would love to give you something that brings you joy. If I cannot shower Fiona with ponies, might you allow me to find a mare for you? You were a natural in the saddle, and we have a lovely property. I'd like to enjoy it with you."

She turned away from me, as if fascinated by the panting sheep collected in the grass under the nearest oak.

"You bring me joy, Hugh St. Sevier. To put Richmond into Bellamy's keeping brings me joy. A mare would be much appreciated. Nothing fancy, mind you. I won't be following the hounds."

"And for Fiona?"

"She can ride up before me, as well as before you. If my mare is quiet, Fiona can start taking lessons on Mama's horse once the mare and I have become acquainted."

A concession, thank the good God. A significant but subtle concession. "You never needed a quiet mount before."

Ann took off her bonnet and brushed at the wispy curls clinging to her nape. "I need a quiet mount now, Hugh. I am not the girl I was. Will you take me to the rematch on Saturday?"

"Why? You were uncomfortable on our last outing, and I would not see you upset for all the champagne in France."

She arranged her bonnet on her lap, ribbons curled in the crown.

"We will arrive early and keep careful watch. If anybody has an opportunity to drug a dog, we will see it."

So much for getting back on the horse. "This is not our fight, Ann."

"It's no fight at all if you leave it to the Grants and Donohues to defend themselves. Besides, I told Mr. Bellamy the truth. Crowds make me nervous, particularly if strong drink is on hand, and I will not have Fiona's mother labeled a hysterical ninnyhammer."

"My *wife* could never be a hysterical ninnyhammer." Though she had clearly been upset. Perhaps she did need a dog, or both a dog and a mare. Cats had always appealed to me as well. Quiet, like Ann, and setting great store by relentless self-possession.

I was mentally turning Belle Terre into a menagerie when the first distant rumble of thunder sounded, more of a sensation than a noise. We made it home without getting wet, but by the time we reached the house, the trees were swaying madly, and the sky had turned a bilious gray.

"You have a caller," Mrs. Trebish said, as she took Ann's parasol. "The oldest Purvis boy. He's waiting for you in the formal parlor. Wouldn't take no tray, says his call is a matter of urgency."

Ann passed over her bonnet, smoothed my hair with her fingers, and led the way down the corridor.

"The Purvises own the smithy," she said. "Five boys, and Mrs. Purvis hales from Jersey. Her family sent her here as a child during the nonsense in France."

Only Ann could refer to decades of violence as *nonsense*. "How do you know these things?"

"I take tea with Mrs. T once a week, supposedly to review menus and expenses."

She paused outside the parlor door, gave my hair a final pat, and then stepped back. I opened the door, and she preceded me through it.

"Mr. Purvis," she said. "Good day. Welcome to Belle Terre."

The oldest Purvis "boy" was a towering heap of muscle and self-consciousness. He was red-haired, green-eyed, and on built on a scale with Belle Terre's soaring ceilings and endless corridors. His attire, however, was the rough garb suited to the forge, and he brought with him the scents of horses and hard work.

"I'm here about my littlest brother," he said. "Beg pardon. Good day. Ma sent me. Benedict can't move his arm. She said please come. I mean, won't you please have a look at him? If that wouldn't be too much bother? He's just a wee mite, and he won't say what's amiss. The lad hates to cry, but he's *whimpering*, and Pa is nearly mad with worry… Please come."

"You are Hadley," Ann said. "Is that correct?"

"Hadley Arthur Purvis, after my grandda. Folk call me Hap because of my initials and because I'm cheerful—happy."

"Benedict probably got up to some mischief he oughtn't," Ann said, "and little children heal quickly. Monsieur must fetch his medical kit, but he will be happy to see what can be done for young Benedict."

Some of the awful worry seemed to drain out of Hadley. "Benedict means blessing. He's Ma's favorite. She calls him her unexpected blessing. He looks like me."

And between oldest and youngest siblings, there was clearly a bond. "Madame, will you come with me on this call?" I asked. "I will have the closed carriage brought around, lest we get a soaking."

"Of course I will come. Mr. Purvis, you will have some sustenance while we wait for the carriage. Excuse us for a moment."

Ann took a decorous leave of our guest and waited until she and I were in our apartment before she commented further.

"You do not need me tagging along for this, Hugh."

Oh yes I do. "I do not know these people. I did not know St. Ivo's blacksmith has five boys, much less that their mother is *une Jèrriais*. The family will be reassured by your presence."

"Will you be reassured by my presence?"

"Of course."

She disappeared into the dressing closet. "Then I will come. Put on a black waistcoat, sir, and be quick about it."

I did as my wife directed, though with each passing day, the woman left me more bewildered. She was in full support of my medical aspirations, did an excellent job running our household, and was a devoted mother to our child.

That version of Ann needed no husband meddling with her plans, but I hoped that the Ann who'd asked for my escort to the village gathering might have some use for me.

CHAPTER SIX

ANN

"You are Benedict?" Hugh asked a red-faced little sprite curled in his mother's lap.

Mother and child occupied a rocking chair in a cozy, tidy parlor. A braided rug covered most of the floor, dried lavender scented the air, and a painting of a whitewashed manor on a windswept shore hung over the mantel. Mr. Purvis, a more imposing specimen than even Hadley, loomed in the doorway with another small boy tucked against his side. Father and son wore identical expressions of concern, though the father's hand on his son's dark hair was gentle.

Benedict mumbled an affirmative to Hugh's question. The child was not crying at the moment, but clearly, masculine dignity alone prevented him from that indulgence before strangers. He clutched the edge of his mother's shawl with his right hand, working the material between his thumb and forefinger.

"I am St. Sevier," my husband replied, kneeling to address the boy at eye level. "I am a doctor, and I particularly enjoy fixing up little boys who've perhaps taken a tumble from a tree. Show me your teeth, Benedict."

Benedict looked puzzled, but obliged with a ferocious grin.

"You suck your thumb?" Hugh asked.

Both mother and child nodded.

"The left thumb, I presume, is your favorite, but you are not sucking that thumb now. Has your wondrously delicious left thumb acquired a sour taste?"

What on earth was Hugh going on about? Mrs. Purvis's expression suggested she had the same question. She was a sturdy, dark-haired woman with pretty features and worried eyes.

Benedict shook his head. His left thumb was apparently as delicious as ever.

"Then might I suggest,"—Hugh rose and pulled a hassock over next to Mrs. Purvis's rocking chair—"that your elbow refuses to oblige your desire to bend it?"

"You talk funny."

Hugh sat upon the hassock and appeared to ponder Benedict's observation. "Do you refer to *mon accent français*, or to my medical diagnosis of your ailing arm?"

"You sound like Mama, but you also talk fancy."

"Your mother hails from an island very close to the coast of France, and her first language was probably Jèrriais. This is a very old tongue, spoken by queens and kings in days gone by."

"She speaks the Jèrriais to Papa when he's been naughty."

This earned Benedict a passing brush of his mother's fingers over his bangs. "I'll speak it to you, Benedict Purvis, if you are not respectful of Monsieur St. Sevier."

A look passed between Mr. and Mrs. Purvis, a dash of humor with a mutual exchange of parental fortification. That glance made my heart ache, for it spoke of years shared raising lively children, worrying over them, praying nightly for their welfare, and scolding them while trying not to laugh at their antics.

Hugh and I had missed sharing those years, or sharing many of them.

"My hands will have a little talk with your arm now," Hugh said, "but I promise I will not make the pain worse. Can you allow this?"

Benedict left off twiddling his mother's shawl to consider the request. "It hurts dreadful, monsieur. You'll be careful?"

"*Absolument.* I will exercise the greatest delicacy in my inquiries."

Benedict held out a sturdy little arm. "It hurts even if I just make a fist."

"Don't worry about that now," Mr. Purvis rumbled from the doorway. "Many a lad breaks his arm, and it heals good as new." Mr. Purvis hailed from the Scottish Lowlands based on his vowels and intonation. Peeblesshire was my first guest.

Hugh slowly explored Benedict's wrist, then his forearm. When he got to the elbow, he went very gingerly. "The arm is not broken, though a hairline fracture is remotely possible. The elbow has been partly disarranged, a subluxation, as the physicians say. I suspect a ligament is caught between the bones of the joint. In small children, the ligaments are more flexible than in adults, and mishaps such as Benedict has suffered can occur all too easily."

"Can ye fix it?" Mr. Purvis asked.

Hugh gazed directly at Benedict. "The solution requires the patient to be very brave, I'm afraid, and very loud."

"I'm loud," Benedict said, sitting up on his mother's lap.

"You're brave too," Mr. Purvis said. "Too damned brave sometimes. The Lord saved the most troublesome for last, after Missus and I had acquired plenty of experience and bravery of our own."

"The louder the better," Hugh went on. "Madame, if you would oblige me?" He held out a hand, indicating I was to join him on his hassock. I managed, though I had no idea what he was up to.

"I will take your arm like so, Benedict," he said, possessing himself of my limb, "and move it thus." He straightened my arm, then bent it upward at the elbow, turning my hand as he did. "We will count—in French—and on three, my young friend, you will yell so loudly that your mama's people on the Isle of Jersey can hear you. *Oui*? Everybody else, hold your ears. The roar will be *deafening*. A true Highland battle cry."

I dutifully put my hands over my ears, as did Mr. Purvis and his other son. Mrs. Purvis kept a prudent hold of her youngest.

"On three, then," Hugh said, cradling Benedict's elbow in one hand and grasping his little paw with the other. "*Un, deux, trois...*"

When he reached *three*, he maneuvered Benedict's arm as demonstrated, and Benedict let loose with a yell that doubtless reverberated across the village green.

"That," said Hugh gravely, "was a very fine bellow. Much louder than I expected, and now you must listen to me."

"That hurt," Benedict said, rubbing his elbow and making a face.

"And soon it will feel better, but you must curb your activities for a time."

"Does that mean I have to stay in the house?" Prisoners sentenced to transportation used the same tone to describe their unjust fate.

"*Non*. Here is the situation. God made children flexible. This is wonderful for bouncing around on ponies, scrambling over walls, or leaping about in the haymow. When unexpected force or torsion—twisting—is put on a child's joints, though, those joints are more likely to be dislocated. If your oldest brother were to swing you about by your hands, for example, your elbow might pop out of alignment again. If your mama were to help you up from the floor by grabbing your right hand, then that elbow might end up hurting as your left one has. The force needed is not great, but if the angle is just so, we have the sore elbow again."

"I think this happened to one of my cousins," Mrs. Purvis said. "She was quite small, and we were playing a game, running with our hands joined. She was on the end of the line, the smallest of the lot, and we swung her around a turn. She was screaming in the next instant."

"Was she as loud as me?"

"As loud as I," Mrs. Purvis said, again smoothing her hand over Benedict's bangs. "I daresay she was. Though not as brave."

Benedict hopped off his mother's lap. "I'm not to climb trees?"

The little imp would be climbing everything but trees if Hugh said yes. "You are to be careful," I said. "Sudden force to your hand or wrist, anything that twists or pulls, and we'll be hearing your mighty bellow again."

"Listen to madame," Hugh said. "When you are a little older, your joints will be more reliable. For the next year or so, you must have a care. My ears will not take the strain of another of your roars."

"Can I go now?"

Mr. Purvis ambled into the room. "Aye, lad, but mind the doctor, or you'll never be fit for the forge."

That was probably the most dire threat in Mr. Purvis's arsenal. Benedict paused at the door and speared his father with a very serious look.

"I will be careful, Papa. I *promise*."

Mr. Purvis settled his bulk into an enormous armchair, while Benedict and his brother raced off down the corridor.

I wanted very much to hug my husband, kiss his cheek, and roar, *Well done!* Instead, I moved from the hassock to the nearest unclaimed chair.

~

"He'll be about as careful as a Channel storm," Mr. Purvis said. "Five boys will make an old man of me."

"Benedict is most like you," Mrs. Purvis replied, "though five boys is a trial sometimes. We love them dearly, but the mending alone keeps me busy."

"The noise," Mr. Purvis muttered, scrubbing a hand over his face. "God in heaven, the noise. Why the great yell, Doctor?"

"Because," Hugh said, "the joint can sometimes slip back into place with an audible click or pop, and that can disconcert the patient or his parent. They hear that pop and think something has been broken rather than repaired. Besides, children like to yell, so it distracts them from an acutely painful maneuver."

Mr. Purvis pointed a great finger at Hugh. "This man, he knows things that a papa should know. Ava, my darling, be a love and brew us a pot while I learn all of yon healer's secrets. You are blessed with a daughter, if I recall correctly?"

Mrs. Purvis slipped from the room, and Hugh settled on the sofa.

"We have a daughter," he said. "A different sort of challenge. I sometimes wish Fiona would yell or stomp about and break things, but she's quiet, and that leaves a papa to wonder."

It did? I would not have guessed that Fiona puzzled her father. "You always seem so comfortable with her, and she adores you."

"Oh, Benedict adores me too, madame," Mr. Purvis said, as above our heads, thunder rumbled that had nothing to do with a summer storm. "Adoring and obeying... These are not in the same lexicon with most children, nor would we want them to be. I have seven younger sisters. I adore them all, and I became very good at following orders, but a man can only take so much of being obedient. Fractious horses are a joy compared to what my sisters put me through. Benedict is the runt of this herd for now, and he has to make up in swagger what he lacks in stature. His turn will come, when Hap is feeling his years and Benedict is yet in his prime. I hope I live to see that."

I had seen Mr. Purvis from a distance, idling outside his smithy, or watching as somebody jogged a horse along the green for his inspection. I had never once considered him as a father, a fellow displaced Scot, or a husband. He brought his brood to Sunday services, where he and Mrs. Purvis were usually preoccupied quelling rebellion among their offspring rather than communing with the Lord or their neighbors.

"He could well dislocate the elbow again," Hugh said, "but he will outgrow the tendency. These injuries are far less common once the children reach school age."

Mrs. Purvis returned, and her husband rose to take the tray from her. They exchanged a few words too softly for me to hear, while the thunder from the next floor went quiet.

"I cannot thank you enough for coming," Mrs. Purvis said as she resumed her place in the rocking chair. "Benedict is too bold for his own good, but this mishap rendered him silent and willing to simply cuddle in my lap. Neither occurrence has happened since he was able to walk. I was terrified."

"Avie, the lad'll be fine."

Mrs. Purvis paused in setting out the tea cups. "You were terrified too, Noah Purvis."

"Guilty as charged. When a storm brews, the lads are like the horses. They get all wound up, and I did not have my eye on them. Business is always slow after one of those damned hound races, so I used today to tidy up in the smithy, to sharpen this and oil that. The boys were messing about in the stable, and then I heard Bennie yelling."

"He was crying," Mrs. Purvis said. "How do you take your tea, madame?"

"A dash and a dollop," I said, though too late I realized that the sugar bowl held only a few lumps of sugar.

"Plain for me," Hugh said. "You do not care for the hound races, Mr. Purvis?"

"Cannot abide them. Nobody ought to be running a canine that hard in the summer heat. The owners keep the beasts penned up for days in advance, hoping the dogs will be bursting with energy at race time. The beasts get all wound up, run like mad, and then remain tied to a tree for hours while their owners and supporters drink away the evening. Damned lot of nonsense, beggin' the ladies' pardon. What's more, on race nights, I'm supposed to keep the forge open until midnight, if it please my neighbors."

Mrs. Purvis passed her husband a cup of tea, the porcelain incongruously delicate in his enormous hands.

"The squires," she said, "are in the village for some entertainment, so why shouldn't Noah put a new set of shoes on somebody's gelding and save the owner another trip? Just because it's Saturday evening, and Noah works himself to the bone six days a week, that doesn't mean the forge should be closed."

"Close up shop anyway," I replied. "It isn't as if there's another blacksmith who will stay open at all hours to accommodate them."

"Madame is right," Hugh said. "The gelding will still need a new set of shoes on Monday if you aren't available on Saturday night. A forge is a dangerous place to make a living, and working tired is a recipe for injury."

"He's wily, he is, this French doctor," Mr. Purvis informed nobody in particular. He took out a flask and dribbled some of the contents into his tea. "Care for a nip, sir?"

"Best not," Mrs. Purvis said. "Noah brews his own mash and gets to putting a little of this and a little of that in it. He has potions that will knock a plow horse on its arse."

Noah stirred his tea with a delicate silver spoon. "Exactly where you want that plow horse if you're tasked with relieving the poor beastie of his balls. I'm the closest thing in these parts to a horse doctor, and I need every advantage."

He took a dainty sip of his tea while discussing castration and moonshine. I rather liked Noah Purvis, and only a little of that was because he was Scottish.

"Can you lend us a boy or two to play with Fiona?" I asked. "She's a little older than Benedict, but I'm sure he could keep up with her."

"I can lend you five," Mrs. Purvis said, "and throw in their father, though be warned—he eats as much as all the boys put together."

"Hap's gaining on me," Mr. Purvis replied equably, "and Finley will be the biggest of the lot, if his brothers don't kill him. Robbie likes his books, but he's fond of his tucker too. Don't ask me about Webster. He's a changeling. If you packed me off to Belle Terre, you'd miss me, Ava. Admit it."

"Come winter, I might notice your absence."

He blew her a kiss and winked. Hugh looked fascinated, also a little puzzled.

"Have some shortbread," Mrs. Purvis said, holding out a plate to me. "I make it daily, and somehow it magically disappears before it's even cooled."

"Fairies," Mr. Purvis observed, peering into his tea cup. "Ye canna turn your back for a moment. They are forever moving my tools aboot too. Benedict swears the fairies unmake his bed the instant he tidies up his covers."

I took a piece of shortbread and bit off a corner. "I can see why the fairies might be tempted to steal your shortbread. It's very good."

"Everything Ava makes is delicious," Mr. Purvis said. "She should have been a fancy cook, but instead threw in her lot with me. I am a vastly lucky man."

"I am a frequently flattered woman," Mrs. Purvis replied. "Flattery has never yet darned a sock, Noah Purvis."

"Teach Bennie to darn," Mr. Purvis replied, gesturing with a square of shortbread. "Tell him it will improve his eye for sewing up wounds on horses, and we might keep him quiet with it for a day or two."

Mrs. Purvis helped herself to some shortbread. "And you will wear the results?"

"Proudly, until I get a blister, and then I will come to you for sympathy, dearest darling."

"For sympathy and supper," Mrs. Purvis said. "My greatest ambition in life is to cosset and feed a passel of delicate males. Don't have five boys, madame. Not unless you can also have five girls to keep them in line and darn their socks."

"What I think we do have," Hugh said, "is an end to today's cloudburst. The storm seems to be moving off, and so Ann and I must away as well."

That change of subject was a bit abrupt, especially for Hugh, but then, the call had not started out as a social occasion.

"I'll walk you to the livery," Mr. Purvis said, rising. "We can haggle over your fees with a skill and passion the English can only marvel at. Where did you get that fine chestnut gelding, by the way? I'd swear he has some Iberian blood in him, though on a fellow that size, such refinement is unexpected."

"Horses," Mrs. Purvis said as Hugh collected his medical bag and followed Mr. Purvis from the room. "Noah loves his family, but if anything happened to us, he'd find his solace among the beasts. He cannot stand to see an animal mistreated, and if what we've heard about Donnie Vaughn's handling of his hound is true, Noah will be having a wee chat with Vaughn. Were you serious about the loan of a playmate for your daughter?"

"Yes. Fiona is an only child and far from home."

Mrs. Purvis dunked her shortbread in her tea. "I thought you lived at Belle Terre. Somebody should. That much house ought not to go to waste."

She had a point. "We're sorting out where we will live. Monsieur and I were separated for years due to a misunderstanding, but..." But what?

"You are trying to patch it up now? Have more children. You'll be so tired, you'll have no time for anything but muddling on, and pretty soon, it's twenty years and five boys later, and you would not trade their father for all the darned socks in England."

If only it were so simple. "Nor he, you."

She nodded, a secret marital joy lighting her eyes. "Monsieur isn't the problem, is he?"

"You are very direct, Mrs. Purvis." For which I liked her.

"With my lot, direct and loud are the only effective strategies. When Noah and I argue, we often resort to our native languages. We think the boys won't understand us as easily, but they have a diabolical talent for mimicry. They imitate us so exactly, complete with flounces and glowers, that we end up overcome with laughter. Laughter is another good strategy. I will always love Noah, because he can make me laugh."

"Him and the fairies?"

"Ye canna turn your back for a moment," Mrs. Purvis rejoined, repeating her husband's inflections exactly. "If you do not think it presuming of me, madame, I would like you to call again. I am desperate for some intelligent female conversation."

"I'd like that," I said, though the admission felt risky. "I can bring some mending to work on while we guard a plate of shortbread."

"Must you?"

We parted on a smile, and I had the oddest urge to hug Ava Purvis. Her comment—*Monsieur isn't the problem, is he?*—gave me much to think about. Seeing Hugh with Benedict reminded me that my husband was good with children generally. He did not regard them as unformed adults. He regarded them as *people* who faced a particular set of challenges in a world run by adults.

He was a good father, and he'd become an even better father with time.

And yet, Fiona puzzled him. Doubtless, I puzzled him too.

I was still pondering that disclosure when Mr. Purvis bowed over my hand as graciously as any courtier. "My thanks again for coming. We do fret something powerful over those boys."

"To be of use to an ailing child is a privilege," Hugh said, handing me up into the coach. "You will keep an eye out on my behalf?"

"I have a few ideas," Purvis said. "We can discuss them on Saturday evening."

Hugh climbed into the coach after me and joined me on the forward-facing bench.

"What scheme are you and Noah Purvis hatching up?" I asked.

"I am to have no masculine secrets from you?" He set his hat on the opposite seat and took my hand. "I haven't done that reduction of the elbow for years. I doubted the boy had a fracture, but I was concerned. A reduction can make a fracture worse."

"How would you have known the difference?"

"I might have dosed the child with laudanum and done a more thorough examination, but given Benedict's lively nature, the elbow was the most likely problem."

Hugh had changed the subject, but I also knew this discussion of a medical case to be part of his method of concluding a course of treatment—a stitching up of the incision.

"You aren't keen on giving children laudanum, are you?"

"I'm not keen on giving anybody laudanum. I wonder what Purvis uses on those plow horses..."

The coach rattled over the arched bridge and onto the wet lanes as a nasty idea rattled into my head.

"Noah Purvis knows how to drug animals," I said slowly, "and he has no use for the hound races. He was on hand Saturday evening, and nobody would suspect him of wrongdoing. Maybe he thought if Vaughn lost his temper, or the wrong dog won and half the village lost money, people would rethink the whole undertaking."

"Your reasoning is convoluted," Hugh said at length, "but Purvis is shrewd and mindful of his good standing in the eyes of the community. Do you suspect him of rigging the race?"

"I don't want to suspect anybody."

I *wanted* the whole business to be a mere passing item of pointless gossip, but my wish was not to be gratified.

"That list is not complete," Thaddeus Freeman said. "Those are only the bets held by the publican. Anderson takes five percent of every wager, and some people prefer to keep their bets private rather than pay his tithe."

Hugh passed me a paper that had two dozen names on it, as well as figures representing sums won or lost. We were on Belle Terre's back terrace—Hugh reading in the afternoon sunshine while I worked at my embroidery—and I suspected Fiona spied on us from the nursery. Her governess had been told to keep book-lessons to a minimum over the summer, focusing on nature walks, drawing, music, and reading for pleasure.

That left ample time for a small child to eavesdrop on her parents.

"Don't the ladies wager?" I asked, for not a one of the names was female.

"They doubtless do," Freeman said, shading his eyes to watch his horse—the same gray—grazing upon our lawn. "But if they don't want husbands or sons learning of their wagers, they'd keep the bets between themselves. The Coopers likely abstain. Purvis has decided views on race wagering, but even the poorest families place a few coppers on an underdog occasionally. Mrs. Fletcher used to bet a coin or two, and she had a good eye for a winner."

The Donohues and Grants had profited handsomely from Lionheart's win. The biggest losers were Winthrop Dreyfuss—Old Hector's owner—and Donnie Vaughn. Both of them were down two pounds, while several other yeomen and squires had lost more than a pound. Dervid Grant, by contrast, had come away nearly five pounds richer, a fortune to a man in his circumstances. Arden Donohue had won nearly half that sum, and Mr. Rutherford had benefited to the tune of ten shillings. Oddly enough, Noah Purvis was also among the winners, though his earnings were among the most modest.

"Who decides which dogs compete?" Hugh asked, gesturing for Freeman to take a seat on the bench at a right angle to ours.

"Anybody who has the entry fee can compete," Freeman said, flipping out the tails of his riding coat and settling on the bench. "The heats fill up as entries are received. Anderson does that part too—earning his fee, to hear him tell it—and he limits each heat to six or eight hounds."

Mr. Anderson made money off the betting, the entries, and the sales of liquor and food on race nights. I made a mental note to inquire regarding who might wish Anderson ill.

"Then Dervid Grant had no way of knowing that Lionheart would run against Old Hector?" I asked.

I resented Freeman for calling, because the afternoon was lovely, the sun's heat tempered by a breeze. Summer would soon wane, and autumn, my favorite season, would be upon us. Hugh and I had agreed to spend the summer together, but so far, we'd resolved nothing. As the week had progressed, I'd pondered Ava Purvis's observation, that Hugh was not the problem.

If not Hugh, then who or what was? I had demanded that my husband and I become reacquainted before making any decisions, but did I expect to complete that process in a mere handful of weeks?

Perhaps I wasn't being honest with myself. I assuredly wasn't being honest with my husband, but how much truth was necessary or desirable in a strained marriage?

Freeman absently rubbed at his left hand. "Anderson lets it be known when the races will be open for entries—a date and time certain, usually at noon on a market day. If Grant was on hand on that occasion, he'd have seen Dreyfuss, owner of the defending champion, sign up among the first few. It doesn't particularly matter that Lionheart beat Old Hector. Lionheart would have been a long shot against any field. He's smallish and has little experience as a runner."

"Anderson is handling the betting on the rematch?" I asked, studying the list. The penmanship was crabbed, though legible.

"The semiofficial betting. We could have used St. Sevier's medical skills at the completely unofficial displays of pugilism behind the smithy last week."

"If grown men," Hugh said, "are inclined to pound on one other for no purpose save to indulge their pride, they can deal with their own split lips, black eyes, and loose teeth. My place will be beside my lovely wife."

"Then Purvis's horse-doctoring will have to do," Freeman said. "He's no great fan of brawling either, but then, he's raising five boys. Brawls likely happen as frequently at his house as does grace before a meal. Purvis is big enough that when he says a match is over, it's over." Freeman rubbed his hand again, soft leather against soft leather.

It occurred to me that most men would have removed their riding gloves upon dismounting—Freeman had removed his hat—but he'd kept his gloves on despite the afternoon's heat.

"Does your hand hurt?" I asked.

"Changing weather bothers it, and we've had a stretch of fine days, though now the heat is building again. Winter storms are the worst for bringing on the aches and pains, but considering what some endured during the war, a sore hand is nothing."

Hugh brushed a glance in my direction. "Ann, if you would be so good as to bring Fiona down from her aerie, she can join us on a walk along the bridle paths. The day is too lovely for a child to spend indoors."

I excused myself, though I paused on the stairway to the nursery to spy on my husband. Freeman's left glove was off, and Hugh was examining a seriously scarred appendage that looked to be missing the tip of the smallest finger. I thought back to my many encounters with Thaddeus Freeman. In most, he'd been wearing gloves, or he'd kept his hands behind his back.

That the former magistrate might be ashamed annoyed me. I wanted to have nothing in common with him, and most especially not that.

That Hugh would spare Freeman's pride, by contrast, touched me. Freeman had bungled nigh unforgivably where Hugh was concerned and would never have asked for my husband's professional assistance. Hugh had offered, though—I knew he had—and Freeman had swallowed his pride to allow the aid of a competent physician.

My husband was a good, honorable, decent man. I was at risk for falling in love with him—falling back in love—and I did not know what to do about that.

When we attended the rematch on Saturday evening, Hugh stuck close to me, and we kept mostly to the fringes of the crowd. I was nervous, but determined to maintain my composure. The rematch was scheduled for later in the evening, after a few other heats, and thus we tarried longer than was prudent.

Lionheart won by two lengths, but more to the point, the entire village lost. When the brawling started, Hugh carried me bodily to our gig, put the reins in my hands, and directed me to make all haste back to Belle Terre.

I had abandoned my husband once before, I wasn't about to abandon him again. I drove the gig into the alley behind the church, grabbed Hugh's medical kit from beneath the seat, and—heart beating like a war drum—waded back into the melee.

CHAPTER SEVEN

HUGH

The good citizens of St. Ivo's were better at brawling than any infantry regiment or French mob I'd seen—and I'd seen my share of both. A proper melee involved fists, feet, excesses of libation, and more profanity than serious violence. With the nastier crowds, furniture occasionally suffered, and sore heads and bruised knuckles were to be expected, though the fight remained basically fair—every man for himself.

Unity of purpose arose spontaneously as soon as the authorities arrived. Then the objective became a swift and uneventful exit from the scene for as many as possible.

St. Ivo's denizens barreled past proper brawling and into the ugly variety in less than ten minutes. I sent Ann home to Belle Terre with no ceremony whatsoever when it became apparent that a royal donnybrook was in progress.

Ugly brawls involved makeshift truncheons, knives, fire, and unfair odds. Dervid Grant was nowhere in evidence—thank the Deity—but Donnie Vaughn and some henchmen had Arden

Donohue by the arms and were menacing him with a lit torch. Burns left scarring, and more to the point, they became infected and thus life-threatening, if they didn't kill outright.

"Hadley Purvis!" I yelled. That sizable fellow was standing on the steps of the inn, sipping his ale and looking bewildered. "Bring me your drink!"

He obliged, bless the boy. Perhaps his father wasn't the only male in the household adept at taking orders. I snatched the ale from him, waded over to the scene of Vaughn's thuggery, and doused the torch with Hadley's drink. Hadley had come along, which was probably why Vaughn and his cronies were inspired to turn loose of Donohue.

"There's fighting," I said, "and then there's utter stupidity. Go home before I lay information against you for assault."

Vaughn looked as if, in the sodden morass that passed for his mind, he contemplated using the steaming torch as a club—on me. I watched his eyes, for in his present condition, he lacked the cunning to strike before betraying his intentions.

Part of me was spoiling for a fight—any fight—but the other part of me, the husband and father and physician—knew my medical skills would be needed, and I hadn't the luxury of indulging in violence.

"C'mon," one of Vaughn's less inebriated friends said, taking him by the arm. "My missus doesn't have no sympathy for scrappin'."

Somewhere across the green, glass broke, suggesting the brawl was turning into a riot. A dog ran between me and Hadley, another dog started barking, and one woman began shrieking at another to "keep your rutting boy away from my Sally Ann."

"I don't like this," Hadley said. "I don't like this at all, monsieur. The fire in the forge is never out, and—"

A loud report cut through the noise of the crowd, followed by a second loud report. Across the green, Mr. Cooper stood on the church steps, a long-barreled pistol smoking in his hand.

"I haven't the authority to read you lot the riot act," Cooper bellowed in his best fire-and-brimstone voice, "but I will certainly spend the rest of the evening in prayer for my buffle-headed congregation. Go home, and I had better see every one of you at services tomorrow."

Mrs. Cooper was nowhere in evidence, but *Ann* stood to the vicar's left.

"Go home," Noah Purvis bellowed from the doorway of his forge. "And I'll have no more fightin' behind me smithy either. The horses need their rest and so, by God, do I." He shook a hammer at the crowd, and the area before his door cleared immediately.

Anderson had prudently moved his barrels of ale from the green into the inn, and a slow drift began in the direction of the inn's steps. Other villagers made for the livery, and still others were left sitting on the green, rubbing sore heads, knees, or shoulders, beneath flickering torchlights.

The scene looked eerily like a battlefield, with moans wafting on the evening air and the green an expanse of trampled grass. Discarded tankards, a lady's shawl, a child's top, and other detritus lay amid the wreckage, and the ropes marking out the raceway sagged between poles or coiled limply on the ground.

"Monsieur!" Miss Marigold Fletcher came up on my right. "Monsieur, your wife asked me to fetch you. Somebody gave Mrs. Cooper a clout on the head, and she's bleeding something fierce."

Why hadn't Ann left when I'd put her in the gig? "I'm coming," I said. "Hadley, if you would please organize a detail of the more sensible survivors and tidy up the green. Look after the hounds—they will need water, at least—and tell Anderson to close up within the hour."

"You want me to tell Mr. Anderson to close the inn?"

"I do, and if he won't listen to you, he will listen to your father or to your mother—or to me. Enough ale and moonshine has been consumed for one night." More than enough.

Hadley picked up the empty tankard I'd discarded. "He'll listen to me. I have four younger brothers, and I know how to make a fellow pay attention." He strode off, putting me very much in mind of his father.

I made my way around to the vicarage, though I was stopped twice by men who'd got the worst of a fistfight. I told them both to meet me at the vicarage, but that Mrs. Cooper's head wound was my first concern.

Mention that the vicar's elderly wife had been among the wounded had the desired sobering effect, and I hoped my prospective patients spread the word. St. Ivo's had lost its collective mind—and over the outcome of a stupid dog race.

When I reached the vicarage, Ann passed me my medical bag. "I thought you might need this, monsieur." Her chin was up, a sign that the lady was on her mettle or spoiling for a fight.

"Thank you," I said, taking the bag. "What good is a physician without his tools? I was too focused on getting you away from the village. You are unhurt?"

"I am unhurt. Mrs. Cooper's a proper mess. Somebody dealt her a drubbing."

Somebody had dealt her a single blow, severe enough to have broken the skin, and head wounds bled copiously. The sight of her bright red blood staining her usually tidy white hair, while her husband sat beside her, looking old and angry, made my heart turn over.

Violence on a battlefield was to be expected, but violence such as this... I was disgusted and sad and weary in my soul, but I opened my bag and examined my patient. I had said I wanted to practice medicine, that I had a calling.

More fool I.

"It looks worse than it is," Mrs. Cooper said. "I have a hard head, and I was simply in the wrong place at the wrong time."

"You didn't see who did this?" Mr. Cooper asked.

"Judging from the location of the injury, the blow came from behind," I said as Ann brought a lamp closer, the better to illuminate the wound. I cleaned the injury as best I could and took preliminary measures to rule out a concussion.

"You did not lose consciousness," I said, "which is encouraging, but any blow to the head can become complicated. For the next twenty-four hours, I want you to limit your rest to catnaps. An hour or so at a time, and then tomorrow night, you can sleep as you normally would. The wound does not need stitches, but infection is always a risk. Douse it regularly with the strongest spirits you have and use a honey poultice for the next three days. Otherwise, keep the gash dry until it closes."

Mr. Cooper blinked at me as if I'd rendered my instructions in Old Norse.

"We're out of honey," Mrs. Cooper observed, one of those incongruously sensible remarks that patients sometimes make to prove they are in possession of all their faculties.

"I'll send some over from Belle Terre," Ann said. "We have barrels of it. Sugar works as well as honey, but it's messier."

"We're out of sugar too," Mrs. Cooper said. "And I am nearly out of patience with this village, Mr. Cooper. If Madame St. Sevier hadn't told you to get your pistol, that lot would still be wreaking mayhem right outside our door."

Ann had told him to fetch his pistol?

"Gunfire is loud," Ann said. "As much as I abhor firearms, loud was needful. I believe you have more patients waiting for you on the porch."

We turned the vicarage porch into a makeshift infirmary, with Miss Fletcher assisting to keep the patients quiet. Most injuries were minor, but I set one broken arm and stitched up a nasty gash on Johann Rutherford's arm. Frau Rutherford had a black eye, though all I could prescribe for that was ice and sympathy. One fellow had to be carried in from the green because a well-placed kick had dislocated his knee.

Filthy tactics, to go for thy neighbor's knee.

By the time I handed Ann into the gig, the moon was well up, and I was exhausted.

"I'll drive," Ann said, taking up the reins. "You have done enough for one night."

"You ensure that my medical bag is with me at all times, don't you?"

"If you want to practice medicine, that seems the wisest course. I never dreamed..." She fell silent as she guided the horse through the turn onto the lane that led in the direction of Belle Terre. "This fracas was not about Lionheart winning another race, Hugh, or not just about that. Miss Fletcher told me that the hounds were kept penned in the livery until the races started. People did the usual inspection of the contenders, but nobody was alone with the dogs. Lionheart ran a fair match."

"What do you think is afoot here?"

"Vaughn was ready to kill Donohue," Ann said. "We've both seen soldiers pillaging and looting when a siege has broken. Vaughn had that look in his eye, and the Donohues are among the families who'd have had nowhere to go if you'd enclosed your common land."

"Vaughn was drunk." And Ann spoke the truth. Vaughn might not have *meant* to kill Donohue, but when clothing caught fire, the victim's usual instinct was to run, which was the worst possible response.

"For all that Vaughn is supposedly a prosperous squire and village father," Ann said, "he behaves like a halfwit. He's drunk far more often than he should be, and having lost a substantial sum last week, he was apparently betting again this week. His neighbors either can't or won't intervene. I'm glad you were there to alleviate what suffering you could, but, Hugh, this village is in trouble."

I was too tired to think, too shocked. A pleasant rural outing had turned into... ugliness. In London, riots were a periodic hazard. In the north, with all the labor unrest, one knew to expect marches, machine-breaking, and other signs of discontent. The yeomanry were regularly called out to threaten their starving neighbors with arrest or worse.

But England was not France, and the French example of where civil violence could lead was a strong cautionary tale to Britain's beleaguered citizenry.

"We can remove to Berkshire at any time, Ann. That property is humbler than Belle Terre, but in Berkshire, nobody will bludgeon the vicar's wife."

"You are needed here, Hugh."

"I was useful." *Something* was needed. I saw again in my mind's eye Vaughn and his friends taunting Arden Donohue. Nobody had come to Donohue's aid. Hadley Purvis had been willing to act, but he hadn't known what to do until I'd given him orders.

Ann drove the gig easily, a skill she'd learned in wartime. In Spain, she'd also become a fine nurse and quickly learned more medicine than most of my orderlies had mastered in years of cleaning up after battles.

"You will be very useful when you undo my hooks," Ann said. "I can't recall the last time I was so tired. You will need a place in the village to hold surgery hours after this. I did not like the look of Frau Rutherford's eye, and you will doubtless be accosted in the churchyard tomorrow."

Something about Frau Rutherford's black eye had caught my attention as well, but my mind was all cobwebs and moonbeams. When we reached Belle Terre, a sleepy groom took the horse, and Ann grabbed my medical bag from under the seat.

"I would have forgotten my bag," I said as Ann all but led me up the front steps. "I should have two. One kept in the stable, one at the house. You'd like Berkshire, Ann."

I was nearly babbling, so I shut my mouth. When we reached our bedroom, I managed to undo Ann's hooks and tend to my ablutions. When I sat, I had to remind myself that my boots should come off before I retired to the Rack of Husbandly Doom.

Ann pulled off my boots and generally got me undressed and into a dressing gown. I should have been mortified—or pleased?—that she'd see me without clothing again, but she was somehow in her nightgown, and I hadn't noticed her disrobing.

Battle fatigue, the soldiers called it. A state of weary, benevolent lassitude that merged dreams and reality. A pleasant and profound stupor that provided temporary distance from unsettling realities.

I woke sometime before moonset to find myself atop the covers on the vast canopied bed. I did not recall climbing onto the mattress. Somebody had draped a quilt over me, and birdsong fluted in through the open window.

A sweet summer dawn approached.

Six inches away, Ann slumbered on beneath the covers. She slept with the absolute stillness of the exhausted, on her side, as she'd always preferred to sleep in Spain. Her chest rose and fell in a slow, measured rhythm, and a surge of tenderness assailed me.

She'd stayed the course last night, kept her head, and seen me home. When I'd been nearly too fatigued to wash my own face, she'd looked after me. Nobody looked after me, save Ann. When she'd disappeared from camp, I'd realized how much her domestic presence had civilized me and my life.

She was a good woman, brave and stalwart. She deserved to be happy, and that boon was eluding us at St. Ivo's. I had just decided to take myself off for an early-morning ride—the gentleman's cure-all for any malady—when Ann opened her eyes and smiled at me.

~

I saw in Ann's eyes the moment when past mornings and present realities collided. She had cupped my cheek in her palm and even begun to move into my embrace when the welcoming light in her gaze shifted to bewilderment.

She retrieved her hand. "Hugh?"

"In the flesh, as it were." I wore nothing but pajama trousers and a predictable greeting from my cock to the new day.

"We... fell asleep," Ann said, extricating her braid from the covers. "You fell asleep. I was banking the fire, and I turned around, and a sizable Frenchman had collapsed on the bed. Even if I'd had the heart to waken you, I don't know as I could have. You were... *hors de combat*."

She rolled to her back. *Hors de combat* had been our term for the moments after intimacies when neither of us could move, speak, or think. We had enjoyed many such moments first thing in the day.

"Sorry," she muttered.

I told my masculine appendage to think of boiled spinach and other culinary abominations favored by the English. My masculine appendage thought only of Ann.

It's a fine morning for a hack through the woods. I rehearsed those words mentally, applying the merest touch of enthusiasm to them in the interests of not overplaying my role.

"Ann, may I hold you?" Where in seven married hells had *that* come from?

She turned her head on the pillow, her gaze cautious.

"Hold you," I said. "Only that. Last night has left me... You did not return to Belle Terre, and unruly crowds sit ill with you."

She scooted across the mattress and bundled against my side. "They didn't strike me as being quite so drunk this time, more fool I. I did not want to be a ninnyhammer, leaving you without your medical kit and without a way to get home. I knew you'd stay, and I knew... I was terrified, Hugh, but I was also furious."

I wrapped my arm around her shoulders, her warmth along my side both familiar and novel. Of necessity, bed had been one place where we'd talked. We'd had little enough privacy on campaign and little enough peace and quiet. The fringes of the day, upon waking or retiring, had been rare islands of quiet for us.

"Tell me about being furious."

"We both know how Wellington's glorious army behaved after breaking sieges," she said. "Ciudad Rodrigo was a horror. Badajoz was a three-day atrocity. But those soldiers had been through hell, seen thousands of their comrades die in a few scant hours, and that was war. It was wrong and vile, but it was war. What explanation, what possible explanation, could any of these villagers have for striking Mrs. Cooper? I saw her suffer that blow, and my anger eclipsed my fear."

"Did you see who hit her?"

"A man. His back was to me. I doubt he meant to strike her, but he meant to strike somebody. They all did."

"That is usually the prevailing sentiment in a brawl. Do we leave for Berkshire, Ann?" I wanted to. I aspired to practice medicine, to relieve the undeserved suffering of the sick and aged, of mothers in childbed, and children who deserved to reach their majorities.

She mashed her nose against my shoulder. Ann had a cold nose, something I'd forgotten. Her hands were also cool, which was lovely on a hot summer afternoon, but less agreeable on a winter morning.

"What has changed, Hugh? When I married you, you were a medical dogsbody. Any injury or illness merited your attention—a slight cough, a general's dyspepsia. You did not distinguish, and you never refused a patient. You wouldn't allow a patient to wait if you could avoid it. Now, you see a community that needs a healer of any stripe, and you are ready to pack your bags."

As I pondered Ann's question, I realized that she understood me in a way nobody else could. She'd seen me in battle, so to speak, seen me tear into my chosen career with the determination of a French bulldog and the ferocity of an English mastiff.

"I am no longer new to my profession," I said. "No longer in thrall to the practice of medicine. It is my calling, but a calling should not become an obsession. I thought if the English needed me enough and saw how necessary I was to their survival, then they might accept me." That wasn't quite right. "Maybe they might have respected me."

The room was gradually filling with the soft gray light of predawn. The lone warbler had been joined by a few others, a beautiful sound to accompany an unexpected conversation.

Another thought followed: Lady Violet had needed me. She'd been at low ebb when we'd become friends, a little lost, a lot lonely, *as had I*. I had viewed myself as her gallant and, more than that, as her... rescuer.

The word was distasteful. Violet had not needed rescuing. She had needed a friend and granted me the privileges of a lover and fiancé. How would I have fared with her as she'd continued to grow in independence and confidence? Would she have had any use for me and my medical ambitions then?

Ann patted my chest. "You should have been more concerned with whether the English deserved *your* respect, Hugh St. Sevier. The wounded always asked for you, and they would wait, bleeding and in pain, for you to see them when other surgeons could have seen them sooner."

"Earning me," I said, "the resentment of the other doctors. I often felt as if I fought a war within a war. A war for cleanliness, for basic supplies, for decent treatment of the injured. If they could walk, they were expected to march, and that... Why are we discussing this?"

"Because it is part of who we are?"

"Part of who we were. You never did answer my question. Shall we decamp for Berkshire?"

"No. Fiona is settling in, and you are forging a path back to your doctoring. I might well have a friend in Mrs. Purvis, and that is a start. Times are hard, and every village has its bad moments."

Last night had been more than a bad moment. The brawling might have quickly escalated into property damage nobody in St. Ivo's could afford and hard feelings that lasted for years. *Ann* had prevented that, with the simple expedient of rousing the vicar to fetch his pistol.

We remained entwined, and while arousal did not wane entirely, the moment was sweet. Ann had been an affectionate wife, once she'd realized that I would not interpret her every touch as an invitation to swive. Her casual pats and hugs, her hand on my arm or her fingers straightening my hair had become a source of fortification in a world that had frequently turned brutal.

Had I fortified her similarly? Apparently not enough. Every time I brought up leaving Belle Terre, I risked that Ann would agree to leave, but without me. We held property in Scotland, and Ann's family was there.

"We'll stay at Belle Terre for now," I said. "I have patients to see."

"We must find you a place to see them in the village, Hugh. Folk should not have to troop out to Belle Terre when they could instead consult you in the village on market days without making an extra trip."

I hadn't thought to open a market-day surgery, but that made sense. Ann generally made sense.

"I have to pee," she said, rolling away from me and leaving the bed. "Lord, summer nights are too short." She went behind the privacy screen and tended to nature's call. When we'd shared a tent, there had been no privacy screens. Was it progress that Ann would be this casual with me about her bodily functions?

"Ann, is there another reason you are willing to tolerate a longer stay in St. Ivo's?" I asked, sitting on the edge of the bed and feeling every one of my years. Ann was right again—summer nights were too short.

"We are here, Hugh," she said, retrieving a dressing gown from a peg on the bedpost. "We have paid our call on the vicar. We have been introduced in the churchyard. We have hired a housekeeper who cares for more than flirting with the local squires. Twice now, you have been called upon to deal with a medical emergency. In Berkshire, we'd have to start all over—again."

I took the dressing gown from her and helped her into it. "Starting all over might be preferable to what's afoot here in St. Ivo's."

She wrapped her arms around me, a good, snug Ann-hug, such as I'd taken for granted too many times in Spain.

"Lady Violet's family seat is a half day's hard ride from here," she said. "If she and the marquess buy the manor house at Ashgrove, they'll be a mere ten miles from St. Ivo's. Berkshire is the other side of London, Hugh, and that woman carries your child."

Well, yes. Violet's situation was never far from my thoughts, but she wasn't mine to think about, and the child would not be mine in any legal sense.

Which, of course, only increased my reasons to worry.

"Before that baby was conceived," I said, "I married you, and you gave birth to Fiona. The marquess has the burden and privilege of seeing to her ladyship. I have you and Fiona."

She gave me a squeeze. "We will be godparents to the baby, Hugh. Her ladyship mentioned this to me, by way of asking my permission. I gave it. A child cannot be loved by too many people, provided those people act responsibly." She eased away just when I would have tightened my embrace.

I needed Ann's courage, and her clear thinking. Needed her clear-eyed pragmatism and honor, but what—if anything—did she need from me?

"I had a thought as I fell asleep last night," she said, taking a seat at the vanity. "About Frau Rutherford."

Ann undid her braid, a mundane activity that nonetheless fascinated me. In the past weeks, I'd risen in the dressing closet, tended to my morning routine, and tapped on the door before passing through the bedroom. If Ann was still abed, she feigned sleep. Most days, she was already awake and gone from the room. I had never caught her at the vanity.

To see her in only a nightgown and robe, to see her hair unbound... What coursed through me was not desire, exactly, but yearning. Fierce, heartsore yearning.

She had said something... changed the subject. I whacked at my attention as I might have shaken the shoulder of a drunken soldier.

"What about Frau Rutherford?" I recalled a prodigious black eye on an otherwise tidy and quiet blond woman of about five-and-thirty years. She'd come to the vicarage with her husband, who'd had a gash on his arm... Ye gods, what a night.

"Frau Rutherford had an injury," Ann said, regarding me by means of the folding mirror. "An ugly black eye, all green and purple."

"Not much to be done of an injury like that. Ice, if it's available. Arnica, taking care not to get it in the eye itself. She said her vision was unimpaired."

Ann took up the brush and merely held it. "That was an aging bruise, Hugh. You taught me that. Bruises are red, then purplish, and only in the later stages, do they show up green, brown, and black. She did not get that injury last night."

None of our business. None of our business... And yet, I had treated any number of soldiers' wives with black eyes, bruising, and worse. If such abuse was not the business of a physician, whose business was it? Commanding officers, stalwart warriors all, dared not interfere. Chaplains, beacons of grace in the midst of savagery, ignored the bruised, limping, silent victims of marital discord.

"Shall I have a word with Vicar?"

"I can chat up Mrs. Cooper," she said. "The vicar's wife sees more than she lets on. Somebody ought to have a word with Nigel Bellamy, Hugh. The king's man should have been on hand last night, and he for damned sure can't allow any more hound races."

That somebody would not be me. "Are we attending divine services?" I asked as Ann began brushing her hair.

"We absolutely are, and we are taking Fiona."

My wife had made up her mind, and I knew better than to argue with her. When would she make up her mind about our marriage?

I retired to my dressing closet, donned the appropriate Sunday-morning finery, and accompanied Ann down to breakfast. My mood was incongruously cheerful, given the likely tedium of Sunday services with a sullen and worse-for-drink congregation.

Ann had hugged me. She had shared a bed with me. She had been casually private with me.

We were making progress. I was sure of it.

CHAPTER EIGHT

ANN

"Your husband tasked Hap Purvis with seeing the green set to rights," Marigold Fletcher said. "Hap rounded up anybody who was half sober to assist. Once the inn closed, Mrs. Anderson sent the staff from the inn to help too. You'd never know we had a riot here a mere twelve hours ago."

A sapling in the yard of the cobbler's shop had been broken off about two feet from the ground. The top of the little tree lay a few yards away, wilting in the midmorning sun. Oilcloth covered a window of the lending library, and dirt stained the steps of the inn where somebody had smashed a pot of Mrs. Anderson's red salvia. A stretch of the blue salvia growing beside the chandler's emporium had been trampled.

"There was a battle," I replied, "though I'm not sure what the combat was about. You have my sincere thanks for your assistance at the vicarage last night. Do we know how the brawl started?"

I was walking Miss Fletcher home from divine services while Hugh introduced Fiona to young Benedict Purvis outside the smithy.

My next objective was the dry-goods store, which once again stood open for business—or for browsing—contrary to every Sabbath law in England.

"How does any war start?" Miss Fletcher replied. "Somebody insulted somebody else. Somebody threw a punch. Somebody else defended a friend, or so they will claim. The hound races are a pretext to over-imbibe for many in the village. You and Monsieur St. Sevier will think very badly of us, but it's best you know the truth of St. Ivo's."

She spoke with the resignation of an infantry wife midway through campaign season.

"But what is the truth?" I asked as we reached the blue gate before her cottage. "Did you notice Frau Rutherford's black eye?"

"How could I not?"

"Did she tell you how she came by it?"

"Frau Rutherford keeps mostly to herself and her shop," Miss Fletcher said. "She has small children, and they tend to consume a woman's energies."

Miss Fletcher studied the green, which—despite Hap Purvis's efforts—still wore a bruised and trampled air. The child's discarded top had been placed under one of the oaks, like a wreath at the base of a headstone, and the shawl had been draped over a bench.

"What do you know of the Rutherfords generally?" I asked.

Miss Fletcher's gaze swung to me. "You are concerned for Trudy. My mother is, too, but one does not interfere between man and wife. The Rutherfords have been here only a couple of years—they hale from Leipzig. One doesn't ask too many questions."

The Battle of Leipzig had involved more than half a million soldiers from more than a dozen nations and had resulted in tens of thousands of casualties. Fighting in the city itself had been ferocious, as the defeated French had mounted a rearguard action to allow Napoleon's Grande Armée to scuttle off and lick its copious wounds.

The aftermath of the battle had been horror on an unfathomable scale. Nobody with an iota of consideration would inquire too closely of a family that came from Leipzig.

A change of subject was in order.

"Who is your landlord?" I asked as Miss Fletcher passed through the gate to her little yard. "I noticed your gutters could use some attention."

From where I stood outside the gate, I could also see that the windows on the upper floor were overdue for a glazing, a serious matter if left untended for much longer. Rust was beginning to show on the standing-seam tin roof, and the stone walkway wanted attention as well.

"Our landlord?" Miss Fletcher asked.

"The person responsible for making repairs on the cottage, the one to whom you pay rent." None of my business, really, but two women living on their own might be reluctant to approach a landlord to request repairs.

"The owner of the cottage is your husband, madame, but Mama and I do not pay rent. The aldermen were to have made some sort of arrangement with Belle Terre's steward—the cottage in exchange for relief from some tithes—to allow Mama and me to use it as a sort of dower property for the vicarage."

The excessive dignity of Miss Fletcher's posture suggested that nobody had said anything to Hugh about this arrangement. Belle Terre was paying its full share of tithes as far as I knew, and nobody was looking after the Fletchers' cottage.

Had Thaddeus Freeman known of this situation? As the former magistrate, he ought to have exerted himself to apprise Hugh of it—or Mr. Cooper should have, or Nigel Bellamy.

Men. Some men, anyhow. "And you've been here, what, five years without any maintenance? I will say something to my husband. High summer is the perfect time to see to a dwelling, so please do make a list."

"Madame... I doubt any agreement was ever made between the village and Monsieur St. Sevier regarding the cottage. Papa died, and

Mama and I had nowhere to go. The cottage was vacant, and when the aldermen gave us a key, we did the best we could with the place."

St. Ivo's had made squatters of the former vicar's family, another reason why the village's fine folk would like to see Hugh remain an absentee owner.

"I am certain no such arrangement exists," I said, "but that oversight is easily rectified. Monsieur will be looking for someplace in the village to consult with patients on market days. The village can help him solve that problem."

Miss Fletcher smiled at me, and the shift in her expression turned a pretty countenance dazzling. "You are fierce, madame, and resourceful. My mother likes you, and she likes very few people, though you mustn't tell anybody I said that about Vicar Fletcher's elderly missus. She's the reason half this village can read, the reason half the babies born here didn't die. If Elizabeth Bellamy knows how to keep her brother's books, that's because Mama taught her some basic accounting."

"You are proud of your mother," I said. "My mother was formidable, too, and my granny still is. We'll see to your gutters, Miss Fletcher, and again my thanks for your aid at the vicarage last night."

We curtseyed, and she hurried into the cottage. No smoke curled from the chimney, suggesting that once again, the Fletchers would have no Sunday feast.

Or perhaps they simply regarded the day as too hot to cook a roast. I waved to Hugh across the green—he had Benedict on his shoulders and Fiona by the hand—and made my way to the dry-goods store. Mrs. Fletcher was worried for Frau Rutherford, and given that Mrs. Fletcher hardly left her cottage of late, that worry had to predate my arrival in St. Ivo's.

A dry-goods store to me was any establishment that dealt in products other than hardware or foodstuffs. Johann Rutherford's shop expanded that definition in so far as he seemed to sell a little bit of everything. Fabrics were available in tidy bolts stacked along the back wall, safe from the sun. He also sold the haberdasher's assortment of sewing supplies—needles, threads, scissors, embroidery hoops, yarn, knitting needles, and so forth.

Another shelf near the back held a selection of books, most of which were clearly used.

Another shelf displayed weights and measures for cooking.

On a table toward the rear of the shop, he'd set out large green glass jars full of various blends of tobacco, and next to those was a selection of patent remedies. Bottled scents, smelling salts, cosmetics, hairbrushes and combs... Mr. Rutherford ran more of a general store than a dry-goods

shop.

The inventory was all artfully displayed and free of dust. The windows were spotless, and the plank floor swept, and yet, on a fine summer day, the shop had a slightly musty scent. Hap Purvis, looking spruce in his Sunday finest, was examining a selection of quizzing glasses, and Mrs. Anderson was sniffing scent bottles one by one.

Elsewhere in the building, a child cried with a sort of tired determination I associated with infants between their first and second birthdays.

"Madame." Frau Rutherford curtseyed behind the counter. "You come to browse?" She was a tall, sturdy woman with blond hair in a neat chignon. One of her eyes was a pretty blue, and the other was hard to look upon, so livid was the bruising.

"I do come to browse," I said. "You have a larger selection than I've seen in most dry-goods stores."

"My Johann says we must offer what is needed. In St. Ivo's, much is needed."

An understatement. "Monsieur would agree with you. You do a brisk business in patent remedies?"

She took out a cloth and began dusting the spotless counter.

"More in winter, when the old people ache. You will please pardon my Fredericka. Her teeth are exploding."

Trying to learn French, Spanish, and a smattering of German, I had made many similar blunders.

"Erupting," I said. "Erupting from the gums, as a volcano erupts. We also say she's teething."

Frau Rutherford repeated *teething* silently. "*Zahnen, auf Deutsch*. From *der Zahn*, for 'the tooth.' That child should have forty teeth by now, given how she complains."

I picked up a blue bottle with a fancy label. "Harbuckle's Heavenly Helper might ease her discomfort." I uncapped the cork and took a sniff. "Mostly brandy, I'd guess, with honey, spices, and a little laudanum."

Frau Rutherford put away her dusting cloth. "My Johann says the remedies are not for the children. Fredericka must learn that crying does not make the teeth stop hurting."

If Fredericka was teething, she was probably less than two and a half years old. "Must she also learn that nobody cares about her discomfort?"

Frau Rutherford took the Harbuckle's from me and replaced the cork. She set it among the other patent remedies and shifted each bottle about half an inch to the left.

"The mama does not argue with the papa, madame. Fredericka will soon fall asleep—she naps at this time—and rest will ease her pain."

I wandered down the row of shelves until I faced the books. Sermons, mostly, and a few Gothic novels. Nothing for children, no books of recipes, no travelogues, but then, the lending library might have those.

"Does your eye hurt?" I asked, taking down one of Mrs. Burney's tales.

"No, madame, thank you for asking. Are you looking for anything in particular?"

"I'm here on behalf of my daughter," I said. "In summer, the children can play outside by the hour, climbing trees, building dams in the streams, or picking berries. When the weather grows cold, they need indoor entertainments. A deck of cards, a sketch pad, some rousing adventure stories."

Frau Rutherford beamed at me. "*Genau*, madame! I tell this to my Johann. Children cannot always work and study. Who makes the toys for the children in St. Ivo's? I make dolls for my girls, and I could make more dolls for the shop. We have scraps of fabric and yarn. I can sew when the children are in bed in the evening. Johann says we must offer something for the boys if we are to offer dolls for the girls."

"Boys like toy swords," I said, thinking back to the little fellows who'd been underfoot in Spain. "Those should be easy enough to make. They like toy horses and little spyglasses. I daresay my Fiona would enjoy those items too. All children enjoy puppets."

"Marionettes!" Frau Rutherford said, giving the word a German flavor. "This is a fine idea, madame. I will speak of this with my Johann."

Did the poor woman have no thoughts of her own? Must everything be discussed with Johann? "Toy soldiers are also wildly popular with most children."

"No soldiers," Frau Rutherford said. "No swords. Johann says to make play out of war is evil. I agree with my Johann."

I ran my hands over balls of soft wool and chose four of a lovely sky blue. Mrs. Anderson appeared absorbed with her perfumes, and Hap Purvis had moved on to study the books. Elizabeth Bellamy had come in, and she was pretending to examine packets of needles.

"Does your Johann make war out of being your husband?" I asked quietly.

Frau Rutherford's friendly air faded into confusion. "Madame? My English is not... War out of being my husband?"

"The injury to your eye happened some days ago, Frau Rutherford, and I suspect you are very careful not to fall down steps or otherwise bash up your face. Something or someone struck you, hard, and that concerns me."

She put her hand up to her eye, pressing her fingers lightly over the bruise. "My Johann would never... He is not like that, madame. You are mistaken."

Said every woman ever to suffer violence at her husband's hands. "Your Johann was overheard yelling at you earlier this week," I said. "He went on at length, and Mrs. Cooper has a few words of German. She caught him calling you a stupid woman." *Dumme Frau* translated all too easily.

Frau Rutherford took the blue yarn from me. "I am a foolish woman, but the bruise to my eye was an accident. White goes well with this blue, or the cream is good too. I can get more of this color if you like, but you must order soon, or it won't be the same dye lot. The London mercers always say it's the same, but they are making lies."

Was Frau Rutherford being honest? She wrapped the yarn in brown paper and used a length of the yarn itself to tie up the package. Artful of her, also frugal.

She passed me the bundle and marked something down in a green ledger book. "You pay another time, yes? At Wednesday's market."

"Wednesday, then."

I had learned all I could from Frau Rutherford, namely that she was married to a domineering man who felt justified in calling her names and ordering that a small child suffer alone.

"If Mrs. Purvis and I were to start a knitting group," I said, "would you be free to join us?"

Elizabeth Bellamy frankly stared at me, though my question had been addressed to Frau Rutherford. Elizabeth brushed past me, jostled my arm, and loudly greeted Hap Purvis who was nose down in a novel.

"Thank you very much for the invitation," Mrs. Rutherford replied, "but I must mind my children. We have not all the governesses, madame, and Mrs. Purvis's boys are old enough to mind themselves."

"Then her boys can mind your toddlers. What evening would be most convenient for you?"

"Come, madame. We put your package into the gig, yes?" She took me by the arm and gently steered me toward the door, sparing Elizabeth a bright smile.

When we reached the lane in front of the shop, Frau Rutherford dropped my arm. "You must not think me unfriendly, madame. I like Mrs. Purvis, and I am a good knitter. Right now, though, Johann is unhappy with me."

She marched at my side as if we were pushing across Spain before winter arrived. "So unhappy he can't allow you from the house for an hour to knit and enjoy a cup of tea with the neighbors?"

"*Die verdampten Hunderennen,*" she muttered.

Hund was *hound,* and *rennen* was *to run*. She'd cursed the hound races. "I beg your pardon?"

"I make a small *Wette*... a bet. On the races. I win, but Johann is unhappy. To wager is to risk, and we have not enough coin as it is. Johann says one trusts in God, not in a lot of stinking hounds. I almost always win. I am careful never to bet more than I have—spare pennies, *ja*?—and I learn which hound is the best to run. I tell Johann I save some extra from the household money, but he watches the ledgers, and there is no extra. I tell him about the bet. He is very angry. I will not make another bet. I give Johann my word, and we kiss on it."

A German custom, or the Rutherfords' own little ritual of reconciliation? Frau Rutherford's bet wasn't anywhere on Freeman's list, but then, he'd said his list was incomplete. Johann Rutherford, by contrast, had been in the short column of winners.

"Did your husband strike you, Frau Rutherford?"

"*Nein*. Never. Johann's people are *Mennoniten*. A little like your Quakers. No war, no duels. No violence toward others. He yells. Only yells, and I was foolish. We will speak no more of this, madame, and you will come on Wednesday and pay for the yarn." She passed me the package and gave me the same toothy smile she'd offered Elizabeth Bellamy, a ghoulish display given that black eye.

Herr Rutherford sauntered out onto the porch of the store, smiling genially in our direction. I nodded in return, but I was puzzled by Frau Rutherford's recitation. She had prevaricated about her black eye—*accident* covered a multitude of possibilities—but she had reminded me that Freeman's list of winners and losers was not exhaustive.

Frau Rutherford had bet on the hounds and other women likely had too. Who had held their bets, and who among them had lost a substantial sum?

Fiona hollered at me to come see Benedict's papa's horses, and I set the package under the seat of the gig. Fiona was making a friend, and that had to be a good thing. I thought back to the start of my day, in a bed shared with my husband.

The interlude had been sweet, pleasant, and reminiscent of many mornings early in our marriage. We'd always been able to talk in bed, and sometimes *only* in bed. If proximity to me on a bed had been any sort of test of Hugh's self-restraint, he'd done a fine job of hiding his desire.

As for my own desire... My husband was an attractive, charming man and a profoundly skilled lover. I'd missed him terribly as a woman misses her mate. Nonetheless, our morning interlude had been simply affectionate, and perhaps that was a good thing too.

~

"The races must end," Hugh said before Elizabeth Bellamy had even poured the tea. "A dog is beaten, and we shrug, fine Christians that we are, but Frau Richardson's black eye might also have resulted from a disagreement over the hound races."

Nigel Bellamy made a face as if the milk had gone off. He'd received us in his formal parlor, which even on a summer day had a slightly shabby, neglected quality. The dried hydrangeas on the sideboard were disintegrating. The mirror behind them had a coating of dust.

The lady of the house, Nigel's mama, was off at the seashore for the summer, and perhaps the staff had grown lax in her absence.

"One cannot simply end a commercial venture," Nigel said, "because a husband and wife take to spatting, St. Sevier. Rutherford himself does a brisk business on race nights. I realize matters got out of hand on Saturday, but we'll go on from here, sadder and wiser."

"Mrs. Cooper is having dizzy spells," Hugh continued as if Bellamy had not spoken. "She is elderly. If she should fall, she might break a hip and never walk again. I lay this risk at the feet of the hound races. Geoff Springer's knee was dislocated, and he'll have to be careful for the rest of his days. Once the joint has been abused, it's never again as sound. He's young, Bellamy. Little more than a boy, and he will not be careful."

I knew my husband's temper. I'd seen it unleashed on generals, colonels, and the lowly fellows who drove wagons for the horse artillery. If annoyed, Hugh could wield profanity and impressive volume in several languages, but when he spoke in the clipped, quiet tones he was using now, he was truly enraged.

Elizabeth passed the tea around, though Hugh had declined to partake. I sipped my weak China black and wished that we'd thought to bring Thaddeus Freeman along on our call. Though Freeman made me uneasy, if Bellamy would not listen to Hugh, perhaps he'd listen to the decorated war hero and former magistrate.

"I cannot help that Geoff Springer is a hothead," Bellamy said, sipping his tea. "While I share your concern, St. Sevier, I don't see how, legally, I can stop the village from holding the races. The aldermen have passed their little ordinances, decreeing that the races will be held. Anderson pays them most of the entry fees to compensate for the use of the green, and that is money the town very much needs."

"Does St. Ivo's need that coin more than Mrs. Cooper needs to be able to walk?" Hugh replied in exquisitely civil tones. "Does St. Ivo's need the coin more than the Donohue family needs the head of its household? Donnie Vaughn should be tried for attempted murder of Arden Donohue, and I will cheerfully testify against him."

Bellamy took a cake from the plate his sister held out to him. "Your word will not convict him, St. Sevier. I give offense when I say that, but you would be painted by the barristers as bitter, given your own recent brush with the law. Moreover, your inherent revolutionary tendencies make you partial to the poorer families in the area."

I wanted to hate Bellamy, but he was merely being honest. According to some in England, concern for the less fortunate was not Christian, but rather, dangerously revolutionary. The lower orders—so this enlightened thinking went—should resign themselves to their hardships, and rely upon God to reward their sacrifices in the hereafter. Pandering to their discontent with soup kitchens or workplace reforms was unkind and likely to foment rebellion.

Anything distasteful to the squires and lords, or injurious to their wealth, had become likely to foment rebellion.

Decent wages.

Safe working conditions.

A chance to vote in even local elections.

Housing that didn't literally collapse in a high wind.

Safe drinking water.

All dangerously revolutionary. Unpatriotic, even.

"Hap Purvis, among others, saw the same incident," I said, "and Noah Purvis detests the hound races."

"I'll have a talk with Vaughn," Bellamy said. "Another talk."

"Talking will not repair the window of the lending library," Hugh retorted. "Somebody tossed a rock at that window, Bellamy. The lending library offends nobody, but some foolish boy or half-drunken yeoman thought he'd add to the general mayhem by destroying property he won't have to replace. Do the wise village fathers intend to spend all the entry fees fixing windows that should never have been damaged?"

A silence stretched, broken only by the sound of Elizabeth stirring her tea.

"We had a riot when news of Napoleon's first abdication came," she said. "Jeb Palmer tried to climb the steeple and broke his arm on the cobbles. The Mattinglys' horse spooked, and Cara Mattingly got tossed into the creek. That was back in Vicar Fletcher's day. He preached on temperance for the next month, and we were better behaved after that."

She smiled at her tea, as if recalling fond memories. She'd have been in the schoolroom that many years ago and had likely not experienced the mayhem firsthand.

"There, you see?" Bellamy said. "St. Ivo's has had its high spirits for the nonce, and we'll all be chastened and humbled going forward. I'll threaten Vaughn with charges for disturbing the peace again, and he'll keep his tail between his legs until the new year."

Hugh remained silent, though a muscle leaped in his jaw.

"You already lectured Vaughn," I said, "and disturbing the peace was the offense of record in that case too. If our neighbors suffer no consequences for their violence, then violence will remain an acceptable response to any disappointment. Take away the races for the rest of the year, and they might rethink their destructive impulses."

Bellamy scrubbed a hand over his face. "I agree with you, madame, but as you say, I've taken the measures that lie within my power—I've rattled the magistrate's sword—and I honestly do not see what else I can do without overstepping my authority. My predecessor lost his post for that transgression, if I might allude to the obvious, and I really think your case is better made to the aldermen."

Hugh speared Bellamy with a magnificent glower, but disdained to speak. The aldermen were Nigel's father—away at the seashore—Winthrop Dreyfuss, and his neighbor and friend, Donnie Vaughn.

"You can attend the next race meet," I said. "If the king's man is on hand, outright criminal behavior is less likely."

"I will attend Saturday's gathering," Bellamy said. "I've asked Freeman to as well. I grasp the nature of the problem. I simply lack the authority to resolve it. We have few enough diversions around here and few enough occasions to socialize. The races are a tradition, and we English are loath to meddle with tradition."

We English. A gauche reminder that neither Hugh nor I claimed the great privilege of Englishness. Thank the everlasting powers for small mercies.

"We had traditions in France as well," Hugh said, rising. "An expensive and ineffective monarchy, a rapacious ruling class, a rural population in thrall to an equally greedy church... We endured centuries of those traditions, and we did not modify them gradually when we had the chance. Millions have died in France and elsewhere as a result of our foolishness." He waved an elegant hand. "*Quel dommage.* At least we were not bereft of our traditions."

Elizabeth set down her tea cup with a *plink!* "I'll see our guests out, Nigel."

Nigel rose slowly. "You are angry, and justifiably so. Saturday night was a disgrace, and as a physician, you are outraged. I am sympathetic to your concerns. Elizabeth was there with some of her friends, and if anything had happened..."

"We were fine," Elizabeth said. "We bided with Mrs. Fletcher until matters calmed down. Other ladies passed the time with Mrs. Purvis. We weren't in any danger."

I wanted to rail at her: If Donnie Vaughn's torch had been tossed at a thatched roof, if rock-throwing had started up in earnest, if somebody had thought to interfere with one of Anderson's barmaids ... Elizabeth had been in danger. She was too sheltered and smug to have known it.

"We will take our leave of you," I said, "and thanks for the tea."

Elizabeth accompanied us to the front door, where we again went through the ritual of sorting hats, bonnets, gloves, and walking sticks.

"The races aren't all bad," Elizabeth said, handing Hugh his top hat. "I won a fair bit on Lionheart. You mustn't tell Nigel, but the wagering on the races is quite lively."

Hugh passed me my bonnet, along with a look any wife would have understood. *For the love of God, please get us out of here.*

"Then Lionheart's last victory wasn't a fluke?" I asked.

She entrusted my parasol to Hugh. "I know a good runner when I see one, madame. Old Hector's getting on, but Dreyfuss can't admit that. I often make a bit of spare change on the races, as do most of the ladies. We never bet much on any one match, but we do like our little wagers, and we enjoy discussing the various competitors. Nigel would disapprove, which is just too bad. My pin money is mine to do with as I please, isn't it?"

I had reason to know that the Bellamys were struggling financially, as most landowners were, at least compared to the effortless wealth they had enjoyed for generations. The Corn Laws kept the price of grain artificially high, but the great masses whose lives depended on bread would not put up with protectionist tariffs on foreign wheat forever.

Those masses, for the most part, did not vote, though, and Hugh's observation about refusing to allow a society to make gradual changes came back to me.

"We will see you Saturday," I said as Hugh tapped his hat onto his head. "And your brother as well.

Elizabeth bobbed a curtsey, we bid her farewell, and Hugh made no protest when I took up the reins.

"We are not moving to Berkshire," he said as I guided the horse down the drive. "We are moving to Scotland, as far from these blockheaded Englishmen as we can get. America looks promising too."

We weren't going anywhere. Hugh would never turn his back on his child—his other child—or on that child's mother.

"Nigel Bellamy behaved as expected," I said. "We did not honestly believe he'd stop the races."

"True, but the *vicar's wife* was assaulted, and all Bellamy could do was bleat on about English traditions." Monsieur muttered on in his native tongue, while I guided the horse onto the lane.

"I do wonder about one thing," I said.

Hugh propped a boot on the fender and turned his face to the sun. "Madame will enlighten her husband."

"Elizabeth said the ladies generally do well by the wagering. If the ladies are generally winning, then at least some of the men are generally losing. Why fiercely defend a tradition that results in so many of the fellows being lighter in the pocket?"

"*Parce que les hommes sont stupide,*" Hugh said, very Frenchly. "Because men will give up coin in exchange for the excitement of a wager and the pleasure of drunken brawling. Men are such fools that they will go to war simply because a king or general says it's time for some bloodshed, *mes amies*. A few martial airs and a handsome uniform, and off we march to our doom."

"I haven't heard you rant like this since we were on campaign."

"I feel as if I am at war, Ann. At war with foolishness and stubbornness. You are not wearing driving gloves."

He took the reins from me in a maneuver we'd perfected in the first week of marriage.

"We could move to Scotland," I said. "Lord Dunkeld's seat is not eight miles from our property in Perthshire."

"You tell me that your cousins regard that property as their home, and I am only willing to order my life so far to accommodate his lordship and Lady Violet. She is a good, dear woman whom I will always esteem, and she is to be the mother of my child. I respect Dunkeld as well, but I cannot..."

How had we got onto this topic—again? "Hugh?"

"She is my past. You are my wife and my future. Is it time we started sharing a bed, Ann?"

With a quiet, polite question, my husband had ambushed me. I wanted to leap from the gig and run headlong across the countryside, but I'd already fled my husband once before.

Look how that had ended.

"Soon, Hugh. I hope soon, but not just yet."

"Is there something you need from me, madame? Some assurance, some proof of my intentions?"

"You are not the problem."

We drove along in silence, the verdure of rural England all around us. I owed Hugh more than what I'd said, but he spoke again before I could come up with a way to approach the next step in our dealings.

"I will move my effects into the bedroom across the corridor from your apartment," he said. "If the servants gossip, they gossip. I cannot go on as we have begun, Ann, though I will not press you for what you cannot give freely. I, too, hope that *soon* comes quickly."

The pain that quiet declaration caused me had old echoes, all the way back to Spain. Hugh was patient, but not endlessly so, nor should he be.

"I understand," I said.

When we arrived at Belle Terre, he handed me down from the gig, escorted me up to the house, and then shut himself in the estate office, where, in our present circumstances, I dared not follow him.

CHAPTER NINE

HUGH

"I am not the problem." I muttered these words in French to Charlemagne, who responded with a flick of his hairy ear as he plodded along the lane to the village. "Is this a good thing, that I am not the problem, or a bad thing? If I were the problem, I could fix me. But if I am not the problem..."

That meant *Ann* was the problem, and yet, nothing about my wife struck me as problematic. She was quick-witted in ways I was not. She was a devoted mother, and the staff at Belle Terre respected her. She was honorable—too honorable, perhaps, but no, one could not be too honorable.

She was attractive to me. She always had been. The years had added gravity to her Celtic good looks, and I had learned to value women for more than their strong stomachs in the infirmary or friendly smiles elsewhere.

Not just yet, she had said.

Charlemagne shied at an invisible rabbit, as was his habit when my attention wandered from the important business of riding my horse down a lane we'd both traveled dozens of times. He enjoyed a brisk morning hack, but trundling about in the afternoon heat tried his equine nerves sorely.

Or so he would have me believe.

"What tries Ann's nerves?"

Crowds, bigotry, dishonesty, musty wardrobes, disloyal staff, drunken excesses, public lasciviousness, injustice. Ann had enjoyed our marital romping—as best I could tell—but she'd never been comfortable with the ribaldry that passed for soldierly good cheer.

Neither had I. I had seen that ribaldry become a loathsome evil when sieges broke, to the everlasting shame of the entire British Army.

A disquieting thought leaped out from the hedges of my musings. "Could Ann love another?"

Marrying me had been an alternative to what would have amounted to serial rape, a lowering recollection. Having been all but forced into marriage with me, wouldn't Ann—thinking herself again a widow upon my supposed death?—relish the chance to choose a man on her own terms?

"I will have to ask her."

Charlemagne snorted—at the dust of the road, of course. Summer was a dusty season.

When was a good time to ask one's wife if her affections were fixed elsewhere? And what mental infirmity had prompted me to announce that I would voluntarily surrender my cot in the dressing closet for the pleasures of solitary insomnia?

The answer to that question was obvious: Arrogant stupidity had prompted my decision. I had been desperate for Ann to instead invite me into the marital bed, and she had called my bluff.

As the arched bridge came into view, I offered up a prayer for Lady Violet and Lord Dunkeld. *May the good God spare them from stupidity.* The child, which I was coming to think of as *our* child in a general sense, needed parents and step-parents in charity with one another.

The village appeared to be enjoying a peaceful afternoon nap. Mrs. Fletcher was watering the salvia that grew so prettily beside the livery barn, a sole equine hanging his head over a half door to watch her. She refilled her can at the livery pump and moved on to the beds edging the green itself.

Other than her placid progress, the village was somnolent in the heat of the day. I left Charlemagne at the livery and took myself to Herr Rutherford's shop. According to Ann, Frau Rutherford claimed her black eye had been an accident, one supposedly unrelated to Herr Rutherford's ire at his wife's betting. However the injury had occurred, I wanted to see that the eye was healing.

When I arrived at the shop, I found the lady behind the counter, tending her ledgers.

"*Guten Tag*, monsieur." She had a pretty smile, but her gaze was wary. "May I help you find something?"

An infant of perhaps eighteen months fussed in a low cradle set by the window. She kicked at her blankets, but wasn't upset enough to climb from her cradle.

"Somebody doesn't care for the sun directly in her eyes," I said. "Or perhaps she's teething?"

"Fredericka has a difficult nature. *Sie ist unzufrieden.* And yes, her teeth are e-rupting. I learn this word from Madame St. Sevier."

My German was rusty, but I'd acquired the rudiments of necessity in Spain. Most of the German states had been England's allies at some point during the war, and many of my patients had hailed from German-speaking regions.

Frieden meant *peace*. Frau Rutherford had described her daughter as fussy, dissatisfied, unpeaceful. In my experience, very young children often mirrored their mother's state of mind. I smelled no evidence of a soiled nappy, and the little girl was in good weight, but she was audibly unhappy.

"How is the eye?" I asked, nudging the cradle out of direct sunlight with my boot.

The child grew quiet and focused on me.

"My eye is ugly, monsieur, but it does not hurt. If you are here to accuse my Johann of smacking me, then you must not."

When I had no idea where her Johann lurked, I would not broach that topic. "I am here to pay for my wife's yarn, if you'll let me know the amount due?"

The child resumed fussing in a tentative, tired fashion.

"*Ach so,* the yarn. Yes. We say *Garn auf Deutsch.* A pretty blue." She consulted her ledger and quoted me a modest sum.

I passed over the coins as Fredericka gave up fussing and closed her eyes with a small sigh. "You might try a little oil of clove on her gums," I said.

"Oil of clove?" Frau Richardson spoke the phrase carefully.

I rooted through my limited store of German. "*Nelkenöl.* Oil of clove. On the gums." I made a motion as if brushing my teeth with my finger. "Some mothers prefer whisky, but I have found the clove more effective."

"I did not know of this. We have some oil of clove with the remedies." Frau Richardson came around the counter and bustled down the aisle. "I will try this. Fredericka fusses because she is tired, and she is tired because her sore teeth give her no peace. I thought she might like the breeze by the window, but you are right. The sun is too warm."

"Or too bright. Your eye does appear to be healing. How is Herr Rutherford's arm? I'd be happy to look at it while I'm here."

Frau Richardson began sorting through tins and bottles arranged on a display table. "I change the dressing, and Johann fusses worse than Fredericka. They are alike, those two. Johann's wound heals."

"Do you know how he came by it?"

"He goes to the inn when the dog *Löwenherz* wins, and somebody pushes Johann against the steps. He falls and cuts himself on the thing for scratching mud from the boots. It is very dirty, so I make Johann go to you at the vicarage, and you clean the wound carefully."

"As long as the wound bled freely for a time, and you are keeping it clean, all should be well." I'd doused his arm thoroughly with cask-strength whisky, one of the best disinfectants known to medicine—if a bit painful upon application—then poulticed the gash with honey.

"Oil of cloves," Frau Rutherford said, uncorking a small blue bottle and sniffing the contents. "*Ja*?"

I sniffed too. "*Oui*. Rub a drop or two on her gums, and she might quiet down. I would not advise the patent remedies, though. They can be very strong." I picked up a bottle of Harbuckle's Heavenly Helper. "This one, for example, would send a grown man to sleep and leave him with a sore head."

"Old Mrs. Fletcher swears by the Harbuckle's. We stock it for her, though we sell an occasional bottle for sore joints or *Schlaflosigkeit*. Sleep-lackingness. I forget the English word."

"Insomnia. Harbuckle's will send a patient to sleep, but much like strong drink, it can cause other miseries."

"Madame sniffs and says it is brandy and laudanum. Johann forbids it for the children."

"Wise man. In a dire emergency, perhaps, but not for a child who's merely fussing. *Auf Wiedersehen*, Frau Rutherford."

She beamed at me for offering a farewell *auf Deutsch*. "I will tell Johann that you asked after him. *Adieu*, monsieur."

We parted with the mutual good cheer of foreigners on English soil. I was proud of my ability to retrieve a few words of German, though I was also puzzled. Why, when a mob had been threatening to riot, had Johann Rutherford abandoned his shop and nipped over to the inn, where the worst of the drunkards would have been found?

That question plagued me as I looked in on Mrs. Cooper, who was healing adequately, if feeling a bit worn out by the heat. Before she could ply me with tea—why did the English insist on drinking hot tea in oppressive weather?—I put a question to her.

"You and Mr. Cooper have been married for some time," I said as my hostess escorted me to the door. "Have you any advice for couples who face... difficulties?"

She turned a potted fern that sat on the sideboard. "Advice such as trust in the Lord and all shall be well? If you want that sort of advice, you must apply to Mr. Cooper."

"I want helpful guidance."

Mrs. Cooper gave me the sort of patient look she'd probably been aiming at her spouse for years.

"Ann and I became separated in Spain," I said, though I assumed our past was common knowledge. "We each believed the other to have been a casualty of war. We are only recently reunited, and there is... awkwardness." Estrangement between spouses who'd been sharing a bedroom, if not a bed.

Mrs. Cooper muttered something genteelly profane about *that dratted war.* "Your wife adores you, monsieur. When Madame St. Sevier came to tell Mr. Cooper to get out his pistol, she was most upset. 'Hugh cannot abide gratuitous violence,' and 'Hugh will try to patch them all up, but nonsense like this cannot be patched up, and they won't thank him for trying.' She was concerned *for you*, sir, beside herself with worry."

Ann had not been beside herself. A much younger Ann had watched a pack of louts dicing to see which one of them would be the first to rape her. Had I not known what the stakes of the game were, I would have said—based on her expression—that she'd been bored.

"She was not beside herself." Concerned, perhaps. Vexed, more likely.

"How well do you know your wife, monsieur?"

Interesting question. "Apparently not that well."

Mrs. Cooper handed me my hat. "Perhaps that is the difficulty? You expect a woman who has been through war to take a near stranger to her bed. You are not the young husband she agreed to marry. She is not the wife you knew on the Peninsula. Many couples marry on little acquaintance, but that is their choice, and they usually have family to help them get off on a good foot. Do I take it Madame St. Sevier followed the drum?"

"She did."

Mrs. Cooper patted my arm in a manner that suggested I was the one recovering from a blow to the head. "War is awful for men, but it's never-ending purgatory for women whether they are on campaign or *merely* praying for husbands, sons, and brothers. Perhaps Madame St. Sevier has known too much of hell and not enough of earthly joy? Befriend your wife, monsieur, and the rest might sort itself out. Importune her for her favors, and you could reopen a wound no lady wants to acknowledge. She loves you, of that I am certain."

On that bewildering little homily, Mrs. Cooper gently shooed me out the door and into the merciless afternoon sun.

Who was Mrs. Cooper to assure me that my wife loved me? The vicar's missus was recovering from a head injury, which made her mental faculties unreliable at best.

Mrs. Fletcher waved to me from the flower bed opposite the smithy, and I waved back.

As I crossed the green, I returned to my musings. I would ask Ann if she pined for another. Perhaps a laird's son had caught her eye —or perhaps the laird himself. The Scots had charm, they were hard workers—Ann set great store by a willingness to work hard—and they would appreciate Ann's pragmatism and her beauty.

She might well be madly in love with a kilted laddie, while I spent my nights waiting for her to summon me from my cot.

I paused on the steps of the lending library and decided that before my decree regarding separate bedrooms could be implemented, I would rescind my decision. If Ann and I were to struggle on, we'd do so as husband and wife.

Farther down the green, Herr Rutherford swept his spotless steps. The rhythmic *ping* of a hammer on hot metal sounded from Purvis's forge, and a tabby cat lolled about on the drystone wall surrounding the graveyard.

A peaceful village, to appearances.

The interior of the lending library was cool and shadowed, sitting as it did in the shade of enormous maples. The space was a simple rectangle, with windows on three walls and plank flooring. The broken window had been boarded over from the outside, adding to the gloom. Bookshelves ringed the room at waist height, and a pair of reading chairs were arranged before a cold, well-swept hearth.

Miss Fletcher sat behind a battered desk, glasses perched on her nose, a book in her hand. Her brows were knit, and she did not look up when I walked in.

"Just put the books on the return shelf," she muttered. "I hope you enjoyed them."

"That must be a fascinating tale," I replied, mindful that I was alone with an unmarried young lady. Doctors occasionally found themselves in such circumstances of necessity, but I was hardly paying my call in a medical capacity.

"Monsieur!" She popped to her feet and curtseyed. "I do apologize. I'm struggling through *The Doctor in Love* in the original French, and I must admit, the humor is slow to dawn when I'm trying to recall an irregular participle."

The play had other translated names. Some referred to it as *Dr. Cupid* or *The Love Doctor*, but I'd also seen Molière's little comedy flying under the banner of *Love Is the Best Physician.* The doctors cast in the farce were a lot of posing, argumentative buffoons, though the play had a happy ending for the young lovers.

"May I assist with any vocabulary in particular?" I asked.

She closed her book without marking the page. "I should be assisting you. Are you searching for any particular sort of book?"

No, I was not. My objective was to warn the young lady about the addictive properties of Harbuckle's Heavenly Helper.

"My pride has sent me in search of a particular sort of book. One hopes for your discretion."

"Of course I can be discreet. We haven't many medical books, though, if that's what you seek."

"I am looking for a manual about how to care for hounds. English country gentlemen are supposed to be experts on canines of many stripes—harriers and lurchers and spaniels and so forth. I have no interest in blood sport, but with a male patient, what does one discuss to put the fellow's mind at ease? A man may be too poor to own a horse, and yet, he will have a loyal hound. The Faraday sisters know more about canines than I do. This is embarrassing."

She peered at me as if I were a small boy who'd spun some tale involving highwaymen and a school assignment gone missing.

"You want to know what could poison a dog, don't you? I have wondered that very thing myself. I weed all the beds of salvia that Mama so conscientiously plants and waters about the green, and weeding gives one an abundance of time to think."

She and Ann would get on famously. "I hope we have had our last hound race in St. Ivo's, Miss Fletcher, and our last riot."

She returned Molière to a shelf behind the desk. "The races won't stop, monsieur. If we get a rainy night on Saturday, the next meet will be postponed, but the beasts need exercise, and until the hard frosts start, the men need their entertainments."

"What has frost to do with anything?"

"Once the ground freezes, and damage to cropland is less likely, the fox hunting begins."

"There, you see? I am such an ignoramus about country life, and Belle Terre's library is no help. If I seek improving tomes, I may bury myself in them by the hour, but practical information is not to be had."

None of this was bringing me around to the topic of Harbuckle's hell brew, nor did I appear to be convincing Miss Fletcher of my sincerity.

"Mama and I love animals," she said, "and Mama says poisoning a hound would be an act of desperation. She was most of the reason why the hare-coursing stopped. Those poor little beasts, chased without hope of escape. Hardly sporting. Papa agreed, and he talked the aldermen around. So we have the races now, and I doubt the aldermen will give them up."

The aldermen were a trio of self-satisfied Squire Lumpkins,

though their authority over the village was apparently real. Dreyfuss struck me as the most sensible of the three, and he was ever convinced of his own wisdom.

"Do you know what will poison a hound, Miss Fletcher?"

"Grapes. I know not why, but Mama swears it is so. Beer, wine, ale, and spirits are bad for them. They get drunk as we do and on much smaller quantities. Milk can give them diarrhea."

Who in his right mind would give a dog milk? But then, dogs were dogs. A country-dwelling canine in the vicinity of a dairy might find a pail of fresh milk on his own and ingest it without human prompting.

"I would not have thought milk bad for anybody," I said, "though I'm aware that some older people avoid it. Perhaps poison was not the right word. Do you know how to sedate a dog?"

A large gray slate had been hung against the library's front wall, and upon this slate was a rendering of the cursive alphabet. Miss Fletcher used a rag to rub the letters away.

"I have been racking my brain on that very topic," she said, "but midwifery and tending small wounds doesn't provide much education regarding sedatives, much less the sedation of hounds. Mr. Purvis might know because he does some animal doctoring. Mr. Faraday is probably our best source on canine husbandry. He is our master of foxhounds, and he does dote on his pack. Thetis likely knows as much about hounds as her father does, and Elizabeth Bellamy has her father's love of dogs."

Miss Fletcher dusted her hands and crossed the room, brushing past me. "This discussion reminds me of a pair of volumes old Mr. Bellamy donated. Not Nigel, but rather, his grandfather. The old fellow went to his reward about five years..."

She tiptoed her fingers along a row of bound books, going title by title. "That's odd."

"We're having a sudden flood of interest in hound management?"

She went to the desk, boots thumping on the hard plank floor. "I can understand why one title might be loaned out. Some squire is thinking of keeping a pack or breeding his bitch, but both at the same time..."

She leafed through a ledger book, apparently as curious as I to know who had borrowed those books.

"I stopped in the dry-goods store before I came here," I said.

"That place is amazing." She flipped another page and ran a finger down a column. "They have something of everything. Mama and I agree that Rutherford would do better in a larger town, or even London, but we'd be lost without him. Acquiring goods through the mail is expensive and time-consuming, and then one never quite gets what was promised."

"I noticed that they stock a number of patent remedies. Frau Richardson says that your mother is partial to one in particular."

"Mama's joints do pain her." Miss Fletcher flipped the ledger forward a few pages. "If she's in too much pain, she cannot sleep, and then the lack of sleep makes everything worse. She sometimes naps through the worst heat of the day, and it can take a dose of Harbuckle's to send her off. I would hate to think of winter without that remedy on hand, monsieur."

"Be careful with it. The ingredients are powerful, and they can cause a state similar to inebriation. Your mother uses a cane, suggesting she's already unsteady on her feet. Old bones break too easily and don't heal well."

"I am always careful where Mama's health is concerned. She spent too many years haring over hill and dale from this sickroom to that lying-in, and she deserves a few years of ease."

Miss Fletcher turned the ledger around for me to read. "Thaddeus Freeman has had both books. He took them out two weeks ago. He's allowed to keep them for a month. I have looked over the entries for the past three months, and he's the only person to borrow those titles. They are quite venerable."

"Too venerable to be of use?" I asked.

Miss Fletcher returned to the gray slate and began writing out simple French words. *Bonjour, adieu, s'il vous plaît, merci.*

"I have been on the library volunteer staff for ages," she said, "and I am in great demand as a reader too. The elders in particular like for me to read to them, and I know our collection well. I cannot recall Mr. Freeman ever borrowing another book on so bucolic a topic, and he is not a man to treasure a book for its historical value."

And he had borrowed these two *before* Lionheart's victory. "Mr. Freeman enjoys an expansively curious mind," I said. "Like me, he might be trying to address a gap in his squirely skills. Why the French words, Miss Fletcher?"

She added a few more phrases. *Je suis d'accord*—I agree. *Bon voyage. Bienvenue.*

"Because there is more to life than St. Ivo's blasted hound races, monsieur, and more to learning than samplers stitched from Proverbs for the girls and proper handwriting for the boys. The better families send their sons to Mr. Cooper for some Greek and Latin, but the poorer children have only my feeble efforts."

She put down her chalk and remained facing the slate. "I'm sorry. I ought not to complain. I like teaching the children, and it's only for a few months each year." She dusted her hands again and faced me. "I've been meaning to raise a topic with you, but haven't found the right occasion."

To my horror, Miss Fletcher appeared near tears. Fortunately, Ann had given me the benefit of her discussion regarding the cottage repairs.

"I have been negligent," I said. "I do apologize. As the owner of your cottage, I have not kept up with the maintenance. I am most sorry for that oversight, but I did not realize that dwelling was part of Belle Terre's holdings. The land steward recently retired, and he doubtless meant to bring the matter to my attention, but it must have slipped his mind. Do you have a list for me?"

She blinked. "A list?"

"Of repairs. Repairs are the exclusive responsibility and right of the landlord. I grasp that much English law, at least."

I watched integrity war with practicality in Miss Fletcher's pretty blue eyes. Integrity carried the day on a tired sigh. "Monsieur, we pay no rent. We are little better than squatters."

"The situation has been explained to me. Belle Terre's tithes are reduced to compensate for the use of the cottage. All is in order in that regard. You owe no rent, but I have been remiss about the repairs."

My announcement should have occasioned relief, a smile, some manifestation of good cheer. Miss Fletcher balled her hands into fists and stared hard at the slate. *Good day, goodbye, please, thank you.* She might well have been counting to ten in French.

"I was not privy to the negotiations," she said. "The aldermen and your steward worked something out, or claimed they did, but I doubt any documents were signed. You are within your rights to turn us out."

If I behaved with that degree of barbarism, Ann would desert me all over again, and this time, she would stay gone.

"You and your mother care for the cottage and keep the drunkards and vagabonds from making free with it. You will set my mind at rest if you stay."

That much was true. The notion that two women should somehow make their way in the world without income or property, friends or neighbors... Nobody with any honor wanted that on his conscience, even less so a gentleman of means.

"Mama and I have only each other," Miss Fletcher said, "and she considers this village home. We have good memories here." That recitation bore little warmth, though it was, again, probably true. How honest we were, Miss Fletcher and I.

"Then you and your mother must make a complete list of needed repairs, and I will see to them before cold weather arrives."

Miss Fletcher returned to her desk and put the ledger away. "Mama will be relieved. Thank you, monsieur."

Her thanks bore an air of martyrdom, or... shame? Shame seemed more likely. I put on my best jovial physician's smile and bowed my farewell to her.

Charlemagne was happy to return home, despite the later afternoon heat, though I kept him to a walk. I wanted time to ponder what I had learned on my jaunt to the village.

The cause of Frau Richardson's black eye remained a mystery.

Mrs. Cooper believed Ann loved me. Another puzzle.

I must ask Ann if she had left a dear friend of the kilted variety in Scotland.

Freeman had taken a sudden interest in the care and raising of hounds.

Miss Fletcher believed in education for the village children.

I was back at Belle Terre and handing Charlemagne off to a groom before it occurred to me what detail among the orts and leavings of my excursion bothered me the most: Any man who sought to borrow a book from the lending library would find himself alone with Miss Fletcher, however briefly.

And that state of affairs apparently troubled nobody, though Miss Fletcher was unequivocally the daughter of a gentleman.

~

Ann had supper served on the terrace. We kept country hours, not only out of consideration for the staff, but also because this afforded us time with our daughter. Fiona joined us for our outdoor meal, a very great privilege in the eyes of the nursery staff.

For Ann and me, Fiona's presence had become an assurance that no difficult topics would be raised. I was thus prevented for the duration of the meal from countermanding my decision to sleep across the corridor from my wife.

"Will you take me to France one day, Papa?" Fiona asked as I sliced off a bite of cheese for her from the selection on the tray. "Mama says France has *montagnes gigantesques et beaucoup de beaux châteaux*."

Ann reached for her wineglass, hesitated, then drank.

"Your mother is correct," I replied, serving Ann a portion of her preferred Stilton. I chose the cheddar we made at Belle Terre. "France is very beautiful, as are her mountains and castles, but lately, France is also very poor."

Fiona's gaze bounced between her parents. "We are not *pauvres*, are we?"

Had Fiona experienced poverty in Scotland? I had so few details about my daughter's early years. I knew only that Ann had been lucky to find her way to a Scottish regiment, after a period of imprisonment at the hands of Spanish irregulars and the French military. As Napoleon's defeat by the massed European armies had become inevitable, informal prisoner exchanges had occurred, despite official policies to the contrary.

Nobody had wanted to put food in the mouths of the enemy, or slow military movements by coddling captives.

"We are not poor," I said, "and your mother and I will always look after you, but one is discreet about financial matters, Fiona. We discuss them only with family." A silly point on my part, because Belle Terre itself shouted of wealth and privilege.

Fiona held her piece of cheese up to the westering sun like some sort of gustatory sextant. "You did not take care of us in Scotland, Papa. Cousin Donald said you were as worthless in death—"

Ann muttered in Gaelic about discussing the topic later. I had taken to closeting myself in the estate office with a Gaelic primer, and one of our grooms was an Ayrshire lad. I tried out my faltering Erse on him, and he corrected my pronunciation with ruthless good cheer.

In Spain, better than half the enlisted men had been Irish or Scottish. Commands had been given in both English and Gaelic, lest a battle be lost in translation. I had also studied medicine in Edinburgh, where I'd picked up a fair amount of both Lallans and the Highland tongue. My Gaelic was coming back to me, though I allowed Ann the fiction that she and Fiona retained a private means of communication.

"I am sorry I was not with you in Scotland," I said, "and I am very glad that you have come to England to be with me now."

"I like England." Fiona shifted her cheese to sight on the mares' paddock. "Benedict Purvis says summer doesn't end here until *An Dàmhair*."

"October," Ann said. "Child, do you plan to wave that cheese around all evening, or shall you eat it?"

"Both." Fiona grinned and flourished the cheese like a scepter, then popped it into her mouth. "I love cheese."

"I love you," Ann replied, "but a meal is more pleasant when shared with a supper companion who isn't speaking with her mouth full."

Fiona made a face, though she did finish chewing without offering further comment.

Ann and I exchanged a parental smile, and the moment took on a piercing sweetness. The soft light of the summer evening, the humor any parent needed to keep close at hand, the good meal enjoyed with my wife and child at our own table...

I had been the worst kind of idiot to insist on a separate bedroom.

"May I be excused?" Fiona asked when she'd finished another slice of cheese.

"You may," I said. "I will be up to read you a story later."

She would have scampered off, but Ann caught her eye.

Fiona flung a curtsey at us. "Good evening, Mama, Papa. Thank you for a very fine meal."

"Well done," Ann said. "I will tell Miss Prather that your manners are most impressive."

I watched Fiona walk back into the house, then topped up Ann's wine. "She is so young to be learning all the proper touches. I hate to think of her growing up so quickly."

"Good manners are an asset," Ann replied. "You want her to learn her wines. I want her to learn... so much."

I had taken to allowing Fiona a sip of my wine at our noon meal, one sip only. "My father and my uncles taught me and my brothers about wine one sip at a time. Wine remains one topic all Frenchmen, regardless of creed or political leanings, can agree upon: Ours is the best."

"We Scots agree about whisky too. Ours might not be the best, but it's ours. My granny started every day with a wee nip, and so did I, until I left for Spain."

Off in the woods, the birds had begun their evening chorus. Such a beautiful sound, and yet, it reminded me of the times I'd wandered a former battlefield looking for survivors as the birds sang the sun and many a fallen soldier to their rest. Women had wandered those battlefields as well, and all too often, their searching had ended in sorrow.

"Why did you follow the drum?" We had never discussed this. Ann had interrogated me at length about why a Frenchman would patch up Wellington's soldiers—I'd patched up Napoleon's injured as well—but I had not bothered to ask my young bride about her own motivations.

"I was in love," Ann said, her tone ironic. "I was enthralled with the notion of getting out of Perthshire and away from my family. Life on a farm is brutally hard work and endless worry, even on a prosperous farm. Life on campaign would be hard too—I knew that—but I would be free, *a married lady*, privy to all the mysteries of adult womanhood. More fool I."

"You did not love your husband?" I could picture him, a tall, grinning, bonnie laddie, with all the exuberance and blockheadedness of very young manhood.

"I was determined to get out of Scotland. He was determined to get under my skirts and willing to marry me to achieve his objective." She gazed off at the vast green canopy of our home wood. "I was more than happy to let him under my skirts, too, once we'd said our vows. Young people are idiots. He should not have died so soon. I should not have married him. Regrets are pointless, but that doesn't stop them from taking up residence in the heart."

I mentally kicked myself again for having quit my cot in the dressing closet. "I do not regret marrying you," I said. "I would very likely have worked myself to death but for your influence."

She swiveled her gaze to me, eyes glinting with either remembered ire or unshed tears.

"And the damned English officers would have left you for the scavengers. Somebody had to take you in hand. Those officers were more protective of the regimental cobbler and blacksmith than they were of you."

She had been protective of me. I had not understood at first why Ann had been so enraged at me for collecting the wounded from a battlefield or keeping endless hours in the infirmary. My initial thought had been that widowhood had put her at risk for a dire fate once, and she wasn't about to let a second husband slip through her fingers, lest she face that fate all over again.

In time, I'd come to see that the meals she'd brought to me, the lectures she'd delivered to my orderlies, the camp stool that she'd carried to the infirmary herself, had been purely for my benefit.

"I never thanked you for marrying me," I said. "I am thanking you now, Ann. The crows lost a feast when you spoke your vows with me." I kissed her hand, and she found it imperative to study the stable yard at the bottom of the hill.

"You were too good a man, and too skilled a physician, to be allowed to die of stupidity. I've been thinking about that list of bettors Freeman gave us."

At that moment, I did not give a shovelful of horse manure for Freeman's damned list. "Our past makes you uncomfortable."

She slipped her hand free. "Our past is complicated. I'm not sorry I married you, Hugh. But we deserved a better start."

I gathered up all my courage and prepared to announce that I would not be leaving the dressing closet after all.

What came out of my idiot mouth? "Ann, when you and Fiona were living in Scotland, was there somebody else?"

She looked honestly confused. "What kind of somebody else?"

"A man, a possible husband. A lover, a fellow who needed to be taken in hand and had the sense to enjoy that privilege?"

Her expression suggested that I had concatenated languages, as Fiona often did. "Another man? I didn't want another man. I wasn't much of a wife, but I could be a devoted mother, so that's what I did. Fiona would not have understood what another man was *for*, and my cousins... There was no other man, Hugh, but I have asked myself if expecting you to disentangle yourself from Lady Violet wasn't grossly unfair of me. I could have sent you a letter, but the post is unreliable, and I... I wanted to *see* you. For myself. I wanted Fiona to at least know what her father looked like."

Now I was the one left trying to parse half-comprehended fragments of meaning. "A part of my heart was given to you in Spain, Ann. Not in the usual way, over poetry and flowers, but over hot meals, shared blankets, and strong coffee. Violet could never have that part, no matter how much I cared for her or she for me. I do not pine for her." I *no longer* pined for her, a result of both the passage of time and the challenge of trying to rebuild a life with Ann and Fiona.

"You don't miss her?" Ann asked.

I considered the question. "I find I do not, not in the sense you mean. She would have pounced upon your comment about the bettors list, for example, and this very significant conversation you and I are having instead would again be put off."

"About that list..."

To blazes with the perishing list. "All men, I know, and mostly men who lost money."

"Purvis didn't lose, and Rutherford didn't lose."

Both names provoked a mild, reluctant curiosity. I had declared my love for my wife—more or less—and she was maundering on about St. Ivo's wagering fools.

"Purvis claims to hate the hound races," I said, "and Rutherford is purported to be no fan of betting."

Ann finished her wine and stood before I could hold her chair.

"Rutherford is no fan of *his wife* placing bets, according to Frau Rutherford, and Purvis is canny. He'd place a small bet to appease appearances, while muttering into his beer at home about the folly of it all."

"I'll have another look at that list later," I said, rising and offering Ann my arm, "though it occurs to me that the whole problem will soon be moot. Colder weather will see a return of the hounds to the hunt field, and then nobody will care that the races were rumored to have been fixed."

"Perhaps, but I have the sense something larger is afoot here, Hugh. A few of our neighbors conspired to send you to the assizes. Others have broken the law for coin. Something is yet amiss in St. Ivo's."

Ann and Lady Violet had this much in common—a tendency to see the truth, however inconvenient. St. Ivo's appeared to be a pretty, unremarkable English village, but such villages did not have riots over hound races. Rather than admit that, I remained silent.

"Let's make a pass through the stable," Ann said. "Charlemagne will appreciate a carrot."

I took her hand, to which she did not object, and we made our way slowly down the hill.

"I spoke without thinking," I said, "when I informed you that I'd be sleeping across the corridor. I spoke out of frustration and pique."

"Our situation would frustrate a saint, Hugh, and you are not quite a saint, though I have seen you work miracles. If you wanted to remove to Berkshire to oversee the fruit harvest, I'd understand."

Having exiled myself to a guest room, I wasn't about to compound my folly by leaving for Berkshire, and bedamned to wifely understanding.

"I am sorry for my outburst, Ann, and if it's all the same to you, I will maintain my present quarters."

She was silent as we approached the stable yard. The lads were occupied with putting the older horses out for a night at grass and bringing in the young stock that had grazed through the heat of the day. Charlemagne was yet in his stall, because I often went for an evening hack.

"I've set Purvis to finding you a mare," I said, "though I assume you aren't averse to a handsome gelding if I come across one of those first?"

"Geldings do not come in season," Ann said. "The convention of putting women on mares, when mares are periodically rendered distracted and out of sorts by the demands of nature, makes little sense to me. Find me a sane, sound equine of any stripe, and I will be grateful."

I was grateful for my sane, sound wife. For her devotion to Fiona, for her patience with me. "Then you don't mind having me sleep in the dressing closet?"

She fished a pair of carrots from the box outside the saddle room and fed one to Charlemagne. "I mind, Hugh. You cannot get proper rest on a cot that's too short for you. I think of you there, night after night, when I know what a lack of sleep does to the nerves. You used to carp on that very theme."

Charlemagne consumed his carrot and made sheep's eyes at my wife. She stroked his nose, and I was jealous of my horse.

"I want you to be comfortable," Ann went on, and my hopes rose like doves on the wing. "You need your rest, particularly if you are to resume doctoring the ailing and infirm. A healthy body resists disease more effectively than one that is run down, or so you claimed, and regular sleep is the bedrock of all good health."

"So it is." This was the power of a humble and sincere apology. A man willing to set aside his pride and admit an error in judgment was not only freed from his cot, he was permitted the very great comfort of slumber in the marital bed. From there, possibilities multiplied in my imagination like stable cats.

Late-night chats as Ann and I aided each other to disrobe.

Reading to Ann by the fire before bed.

A glancing touch beneath the covers...

"I should never have let you spend all those nights in the dressing closet," Ann said, "and today I had your things moved into the blue guest room. I'm sure you will sleep much better there, and I won't feel as guilty thinking of you tossing and turning on a hard cot."

Charlemagne craned his neck and pulled back his lips in that undignified equine maneuver that looked like an equine having a good laugh.

"I am blessed with a most considerate wife," I said. "If we might return to the house, I will spend some time in the estate office reviewing accounts."

Ann fed Charlemagne the second carrot and then accompanied me up the hill. We did not hold hands. We did not walk arm in arm. I felt like a very great fool, in part because I had no idea what my wife was thinkinng.

Was she relieved to have me out of her dressing closet? She'd said no other man had caught her eye, and I believed her.

I did repair to the estate office, and to the comfort of some good French brandy. I stared at the list of bettors, though my mind refused to focus on St. Ivo's riots and races. By morning, I was thoroughly out of sorts, because I had added one more insight to my store of eternal verities.

A man—a husband—could toss and turn in a fluffy, lonely four-poster just as miserably as he ever did on a wretched little cot.

CHAPTER TEN

ANN

Hugh had not offered to join me in the marital bed, but rather, to resume spending his nights in the dressing closet. Was he trying to balance my failure as a wife with his pride before a house full of gossiping servants? Hoping that familiarity would breed attraction?

I was wildly attracted to my husband. I had been in a reluctant way even in Spain, even while married to another. I had not liked that Hugh was a physician and that he dealt by choice with the human body in its most inglorious frailty, but I had liked *him*.

His determination, his intelligence, his *honor*. Women in a military camp quickly learned who was an officer and who was a gentleman. The two did not overlap as neatly as we had been led to hope, a fact to which I could testify in disgusting detail. Hugh, no matter how exhausted, frustrated, or angry, had occupied the most rarefied end of the gentlemanly spectrum.

He'd married me not out of pity, but rather, out of duty, which was in a way worse. A pitiful object could provoke compassion. A duty... duty and love struck me as mutually exclusive, though a soldier was taught that they were one and the same.

I puzzled on my marriage as thunder rumbled in the distance and Fiona stumbled through her work at the pianoforte. I pretended to embroider the hem of one of her pinafores, but the foul weather meant poor light for close work.

Hugh was in the estate office, which had become his husbandly retreat. I was loathe to intrude on him there, even more so after our conversation earlier in the week regarding sleeping arrangement, regrets, and losing bets.

Fiona brought her piece to a close on a bungled cadence. "Today is Saturday," she said, hopping off the bench and joining me on the sofa. "Will we go to the hound races?"

I hated those hound races. They symbolized for me the rot lurking beneath St. Ivo's rustic veneer. Frau Rutherford's mysterious black eye, Mr. Purvis betting on the races he purported to abhor, Mrs. Cooper's head injury inflicted by a person unknown. Donnie Vaughn, village alderman and bully-at-large. To use Hugh's terminology, the village appeared to be in the grip of a wasting disease.

"If the rain keeps up, the races will be postponed," I said. "Would you like to try a few stitches?"

She joined me on the sofa, took my hoop, and studied the section I was working on. "*Un papillon bleu.* Do they have blue butterflies in France?"

"I imagine so. France is little more than twenty miles over the water where the two countries are closest. On a clear day, you can see from one shore to the other across the Strait of Dover."

Fiona took up the needle and added carefully to the butterfly's wing. She had her father's fine dexterity, his steady hands. How I loved the touch of Hugh's hands, had gloried in his capacity for tender caresses...

"When will Papa take us to France?" she asked.

"We haven't been at Belle Terre that long, Fiona. Why this interest in France?"

Her tongue peeked out of the side of her mouth. "Papa was born in France. He has a French accent, and he speaks French the best. Then he went to England, and Scotland, and Spain, and France, and back to England, and again to Scotland. You saw him in Scotland and said, 'That is Papa! He is alive!' And so we came to England."

Hugh read to Fiona at bedtime. He was too shrewd to view that exercise simply as a means of sending his daughter off to peaceful slumbers.

"You have been subjecting your father to interrogations."

"What is interrogations?" Her stitches were as good as mine.

"*Questionner*." I mentally rooted about for the closest Gaelic term. "*A cheasnachadh*."

More stitches followed. "Papa travels much."

Ah. "He does, but you won't lose him to France or Spain, Fiona. He might have to travel to Berkshire, or elsewhere on business, but he will always be your papa."

"He was my papa when we lived in Scotland, and I never saw him. He never read me stories. He never took me up on Charlemagne. I don't want him to be that sort of papa again. I want him to be my Belle Terre sort of papa."

Had the child plunged a dagger into my heart… "Parents must travel sometimes, especially fathers. Your papa has business in London, a house there. A house in Berkshire. He cannot take us with him everywhere, Fiona, but he will come back to you."

She speared me with one of those looks a child aimed at an adult who had let the truth inadvertently slip into view. "He comes back to *us*, Mama. I want French butterflies on my pinafore. I will ask Papa what color the butterflies are in France."

She shoved the hoop at me and popped off the sofa. "I hear a carriage! Is Papa going somewhere? Is somebody having a baby? Maybe Benedict has come to play!"

Benedict would not arrive in a carriage. The rainy weather would induce Thaddeus Freeman or Nigel Bellamy to take a carriage, though I wasn't in the mood to entertain either man.

Hugh appeared in the doorway. "Are we expecting guests?"

"We are not, but somebody might be making a morning call."

Mrs. Trebish was perfectly capable of answering the door, but she would have to be summoned from belowstairs, and Fiona had already pounded down the corridor. As Hugh and I entered the foyer, I could see that the coach coming up the drive was a fine vehicle indeed.

A foursome of matched grays pulled a heavy, well-sprung conveyance. The wheels were painted blue. The coachman wore silver and blue livery. Behind the coach, a sleek chestnut mare trotted daintily through the muck.

"She couldn't leave us alone," I muttered, straightening Hugh's hair with my fingers.

"That coach does not belong to Lady Violet," he said, holding still for me.

"The coach likely belongs to Dunkeld, and that mare is doubtless his pretext for calling. Had he come alone, he would have waited for decent weather and brought the mare over on a lead line. That rolling barge is for the benefit of her ladyship, Hugh, and you are not sleeping in a guest room if she is to spend the night."

A procession of emotions flitted through serious brown eyes. Puzzlement, astonishment, and then—of all things—humor.

"It shall be as my wife wishes," he said, tucking a lock of hair behind my ear. "Fiona, away with you. This is not Benedict, but rather, Lord Dunkeld and Lady Violet. They will doubtless insist on visiting the nursery, and you had best make us proud."

"His lordship talks like Mama!" Fiona observed, scampering up the curved main stairway. "I like him."

I liked Dunkeld, too, mostly. He'd lifted a considerable weight from my conscience when he'd offered for Lady Violet. I hoped they were here to inform us of their nuptials, but apparently not. As Hugh shepherded us through a round of overly cheerful greetings, Lady Violet was still addressed as Lady Violet rather than Lady Dunkeld.

She was, to the eye of a careful observer, carrying a child.

Because her dress was of the old-fashioned empire design, the pregnancy was not immediately obvious, though I noted Hugh making one of his characteristic visual inventories, and his gaze lingered on her ladyship's face.

She was in anticipation of motherhood, and she and the marquess were as yet unmarried. Some difficulty apparently required sorting out, and a small, complicated part of me was pleased that they'd come to us at Belle Terre with their problems.

"How are the denizens of St. Ivo's treating you?" Lady Violet asked as I passed around the requisite cups of tea. We were in my private parlor, because I'd had the fires lit, and because... Violet and Sebastian, Marquess of Dunkeld, were family after a fashion.

The men exchanged a look, and Hugh left it to me to answer her ladyship's inquiry.

"Carefully, not quite cordially. The former vicar's daughter is friendly, though she's also relieved not to have to fill her aging mama's shoes as midwife now that Hugh is on hand. Vicar and Mrs. Cooper are welcoming, in their way, and Freeman has dropped by once or twice. Hugh has been asked to serve in a medical capacity on several occasions when no other resources were available."

"So we must wonder," Dunkeld murmured, studying his tea, "are the rest of them leaving you in peace out of shame because St. Sevier was treated so shabbily earlier in the year, or are they lying in wait?"

The marquess was a handsome man, in a dark-haired, craggy Scottish fashion. I liked him, and not only because his burr was the sound of home. He had the particular humor unique to the Scot, both subtle and hilarious, and he trotted it out at the most unexpected times. Then too, he was honorable, and I would always esteem a man of integrity.

"Or is the village doing a little of both?" Lady Violet mused, helping herself to a second cup of tea. "Some resent you. Some want to welcome you, but don't know how."

"Is Fiona managing?" Dunkeld asked.

The question was shrewd, because the subject upon which I would expound most enthusiastically was my daughter—our daughter.

"She is recovering," Hugh said, surprising me. "The father she barely knew was taken away without warning, and she is alert for any further mischief. She distrusts Freeman, but she has taken a liking to some of the children in the village. With children, one needs patience, *non*?"

The ensuing silence suggested that with spouses, prospective spouses, and former prospective spouses, one needed patience as well.

"Tell me about the mare," I said. I knew Dunkeld to be quite the equestrian, and if Hugh had any confidant at Belle Terre, it was Charlemagne. His lordship obligingly waxed eloquent about bloodlines, conformation, and temperament while I wondered what my husband was feeling at the sight of his former and now *enceinte* lover.

What was I feeling, for that matter?

Some apprehension, simply because Lady Violet and her Sebastian were unexpected callers, but I myself had insisted that we construct a history of cordial relations with them.

I was also uneasy for more private reasons. Hugh and I had not made much progress toward normal marital relations, and that was my fault. Would Lady Violet, with her nose for puzzles, ferret out the marital details and lecture me for failing to fulfill all the wifely offices?

I almost wished she would, but then, she had yet to become the Marchioness of Dunkeld, and therein doubtless lay a tale as well.

"You must stay the night," Hugh said. "I know Violet to be an intrepid traveler, but the roads are miserable at present. I request that her ladyship exercise caution for the sake of my nerves."

Another silence ensued, and I realized that Hugh and Violet had not addressed each other directly in fifteen minutes of polite conversation.

"How are you feeling?" I asked her ladyship. "And you might as well be honest, or Hugh will conduct a medical interview over the soup course at supper."

Dunkeld rose and began a circuit of my parlor. He pretended to study the pressed forget-me-nots framed over the sideboard, then the cutwork Fiona had recently completed. The effort was simple, but it was hers, and I treasured it.

"You might as well tell them," Dunkeld said, back to the assemblage, "or I will."

My mind flew back to the many women who'd consulted my mother and grandmother regarding the progress of a pregnancy. Lady Violet was still carrying, but perhaps the child had ceased moving?

Hence, her unwillingness to marry the marquess.

"Shall I leave?" I put the question to her ladyship, but I was also giving Hugh the opportunity to send me away.

Lady Violet turned a magnificent glower upon me. "Please do not abandon me to the fussing and fretting of two grown men. One is bad enough."

"Perhaps there's nothing serious to fuss about?" I suggested.

"Precisely." Her ladyship sent a fulminating look at Dunkeld's rigid back. "I am unwilling to entrap his lordship into holy matrimony until the arrival of a healthy child is all but a given. This has vexed him exceedingly, but then, he is easily vexed of late."

Dunkeld took out a flask and half turned to salute in Violet's direction. "*A Dhia, thoir dhomh neart*."

Hugh could apparently translate that—*God, give me strength*—because his lips quirked.

"Violet," Hugh said, "stop prevaricating. Has the child ceased moving?"

"The little fiend goes on regular maneuvers," she replied, her tart words belied by a violent blush. Her ladyship then sent me—*me?*—a beseeching look.

"She bleeds," Sebastian said. "A few drops, streaks… Don't ask me how I know this—I was not snooping—but I know."

Hugh studied Violet with a lips-pursed, brow-furrowed expression that I recognized. He was mentally diagnosing, sorting symptoms, causes, and treatments with an efficiency that had saved many a life.

"When did this start?" he asked.

Violet, for the first time, met his gaze. "From the beginning," she said. "At first, I thought, 'Well, maybe I'm not carrying.' But it was never more than a whisper. It's still no more than a whisper, but Dunkeld will fly into the boughs over nothing, and I am still very much with child."

"Is there a pattern?" Hugh asked. "Every few days, every few weeks, always in the morning, never upon waking?"

Dunkeld had ambled to the window, where he stood, flask in hand, watching the rain.

"I don't notice anything upon waking. Usually, only at the end of the day, and I will go for weeks without any symptoms."

"Any cramps?" I asked, because I suspected Hugh might avoid that inquiry.

"Never. I am as healthy as that mare Sebastian is so proud of."

A particular tension seized the marquess's shoulders. I would not have been surprised to hear the sound of teeth grinding.

"No," Hugh said, rising to face her ladyship, "you are not. Some traces of blood early in a pregnancy are common, particularly after vigorous activity or at the time when the courses would normally have arrived. You are no longer early in your pregnancy, my lady."

"Don't you dare scold me, Hugh St. Sevier." Violet was on her feet, skirts swishing. "You have no idea, none of you, what it's like to carry a child and fear a third… disappointment. I want this baby. I want this baby desperately, and I feel fine, but then *he*,"—she jerked her chin in Dunkeld's direction—"went rooting through the laundry."

Dunkeld faced her, his flask in a white-knuckled grip. "I've told you and told you, I was searching for a receipt in my breeches pocket, Violet—"

"And he has been worse than the Regent with a gouty toe ever since. I am *fine*."

She was not fine. She was worried half out of her mind, in a situation beyond her control, and in a body beyond her control.

"I had spotting with Fiona." I poured myself a second cup of tea, though I was not particularly thirsty. "Started about halfway through. I was in France by then. My diet was less than ideal, and I went from marching for miles one day to sitting upon my backside for hours the next. The worst days seemed to be when I had the great good fortune to enjoy the loan of a mule. War and childbearing are an awkward combination."

Hugh considered me as if I'd sprouted fairy wings. "I did not know this."

"I wished I'd died once we put out to sea. If Fiona is a good sailor, I will be very much surprised."

"You had spotting?" Lady Violet had lowered her voice on that last word. "Truly?"

"Streaking, never more than a few drops of anything approaching red. My family includes several midwives, so I did what I could to address the situation."

Dunkeld raised a dark eyebrow at me. "And that would be?"

Hugh appeared unwilling to hold forth as the medical expert in the room, so I answered his lordship's question.

"Rest," I said. "If not lying abed, then at least putting my feet up. I became much more careful about any herbal teas or seasoned dishes I was offered. No cat's-claw, pennyroyal, sage, thyme... My mother had a list, and she suspected some women have specific sensitivities."

"Oh, now you've done it," Violet said, plopping back down in a wing chair. "Now he will forbid me to walk and insist I follow a lowering diet."

"No lowering diets," Hugh said, very firmly. "Plenty of fresh greens and red meat, organ meat if you can."

Violet shuddered.

"And she's to rest?" Dunkeld asked.

Her ladyship was back on her feet and sailing across the parlor. "Do not refer to me in the third person when I am present. I grow weary of reminding you, Dunkeld."

His lordship offered return fire, his burr thickening as he bounded over *ye wee besom* and *drive a puir mon daft* and galloped on to round the flag at *the de'il knows why*. In the midst of this verbal affray, Hugh caught my eye.

His eyes were dancing, and I could see a certain absurd humor in the situation too. I also realized that I cared for her ladyship and the growling marquess, as did Hugh—as should we both.

"Rest," Hugh said, "is not complete inactivity. If her ladyship were to put her feet up for an hour in the morning and afternoon and avoid lifting anything heavier than a full teapot, she would be taking reasonable measures to ensure the pregnancy ends well."

"And red meat and fresh greens," Dunkeld added. "Not endless trays of bread and cheese."

"I like bread and cheese," Violet retorted, "and St. Sevier has not forbidden them to me."

The combatants turned to Hugh for a decree. "Ann will make you a list of the items her mother found suspect. Other than those—and I caution you particularly against pennyroyal tea—your diet should be one of moderation and variety."

"That means I can have my bread and cheese."

"In moderation," Dunkeld snapped. "Moderation is not half a loaf before noon, Violet."

The bickering resumed, and Hugh took the place beside me on the sofa. "They have the stamina, *non*?" he muttered.

"They are frightened witless, Hugh."

"As am I. I will never again be quite as convincing with my all-will-be-well speeches to the expectant papas. Did you really have spotting with Fiona?"

"Right up until the week she came into the world. You will be more convincing with the papas for being more sympathetic. Should we send the pugilists to neutral corners?"

Lady Violet was seized by a yawn, and Dunkeld possessed himself of her hand. Their voices dropped into a conspiratorial range, Dunkeld's head bent near to her ladyship's.

"He loves her," Hugh said, his voice puzzled. "Truly loves her."

And I love you. I did not dare say those words aloud, but they were true. When had they come true—come true again? Sometime between when Hugh had delivered Mrs. Grant of little Sixtus and when he'd stolen a sip of my tea two minutes past.

"She will be safe with him, Hugh."

"But will she have sense enough to be happy?" The comment was interesting, for being just the slightest bit judgmental regarding her ladyship. "Shall we have my things moved from the blue guest room?"

"I asked Mrs. Trebish to see to that when I sent for the tea tray."

"*Bon*, and his lordship will want the green bedroom. Her ladyship might be well advised to nap now." The rest of my tea disappeared, along with a piece of shortbread.

"And I am to make that suggestion?"

"Violet sees an ally in you, not another pontificating male. She was raised with a surfeit of pontificating males, then she married one. I suspect part of my appeal was simply that I did not often attempt masculine proclamations with her. We will—"

A tap on the door heralded Matthews, the first footman, looking somewhat nervous. "Beg pardon, madame, monsieur. Mr. Nigel Bellamy has come to call. I put him in the library because the fires were lit in there. He said his business were somewhat pressin'."

"He's the magistrate now?" Dunkeld asked.

Hugh nodded. I wanted badly to reach for my husband's hand—or send him off to Berkshire, with Bellamy none the wiser.

"Whatever pressing business he has," Violet said, "he can air it before his lordship and myself as well as before his host and hostess."

I could see Hugh equivocating, male pride, or something, warring with common sense. In the grand hierarchy of British society, the marquess was nobody to trifle with and neither was Lady Violet.

"Let's not keep him waiting," I said. "Matthews, another tray please. The weather is beastly, and Mr. Bellamy will appreciate a hot cup of tea."

Lady Violet took my arm and accompanied me to the library. I gathered she enjoyed the dismay on Bellamy's face when she made her entrance, with Hugh and the marquess arriving in our wake.

Bellamy bowed stiffly at the appropriate times, then announced that his errand was not social.

"So you've come to arrest somebody?" I asked. "Or perhaps we're back to illegally detaining the innocent in this shire? Do tell, Mr. Bellamy, because nothing less than hanging felonies appear to bestir you from your abode."

Bellamy stared at a spot past my left shoulder, and a cold skein of dread snaked through my middle. I would not survive watching my husband led away by the king's thugs again—and neither would Bellamy survive any such attempt.

"As it happens," Bellamy said, "I'm here to ask you a few questions, madame. Have you recently purchased yarn from the dry-goods shop?"

"I have. I made my selection on Sunday—a pretty blue—and my husband paid for it later in the week, as seems to be the local custom."

Bellamy flicked a glance at everybody else in the room. "I would like to see your workbasket and your reticule."

Hugh, the marquess, and Lady Violet all seemed to grow two inches in height at that demand, but we were dealing with rural England's version of a petty despot. Placating him and sending him on his way was the wiser course, as I well knew.

I crossed the room and retrieved my workbasket from its place by the sofa. "You'll find the yarn on top."

He had begun rocking up and back on his heels, like a stall-bound horse weaved before the door. "And your reticule?"

"I'll fetch it." What on earth could he be about?

"I cannot allow that, madame. I'll fetch it, if you don't mind."

"No," Lady Violet said, "you shall not. Madame need not suffer the indignity of you rooting through her personal effects when I am on hand to retrieve the requisite item. And lest you think I am colluding with madame in some larcenous conspiracy, his lordship and I arrived less than an hour ago and have been nowhere but the public rooms."

Her tone could not have been more disdainful.

"Take his lordship with you," Bellamy said. "I'm told it is a beaded reticule, a pattern of roses."

"You'll find it in my wardrobe," I said, "hanging on the left side, where it has been all week. I seldom need it between one Sunday and the next."

Lady Violet and Dunkeld quit the room, and I felt Hugh's fingers wrap around mine.

"We importune you," he said, "to stop a local event that has grown so violent as to encompass attempted murder, and you do nothing but offer to scold a man who cares nothing for your lectures. Now you are here to accuse my wife of some petty crime based on nothing more than gossip. When his lordship and Lady Violet return, you will explain yourself, and you will do so most thoroughly."

Hugh's exquisitely polite tones told me he was furious. I was gratified to know that he was protective of me. Mostly, though, I was terrified, and thus I clung to my husband's hand while Bellamy rooted through my workbasket like a terrier on the scent of a rat.

~

As Bellamy dumped the contents of my reticule onto the low table before the sofa, I caught a sympathetic glance from Lady Violet. Hugh and I occupied the sofa. She and the marquess had taken the wing chairs opposite, while Bellamy roamed at large.

To my very great relief, my reticule held only the usual items. Pocket comb, coin purse, a plain handkerchief, and one embroidered with the St. Sevier family crest. Also a pencil and small sketch pad with some of Fiona's childish drawings, four plain hairpins, and two spare green hair ribbons for those occasions when Fiona lost one.

"No knives," Dunkeld said. "No treasonous dispatches. Not even a volume of bawdy poetry. Madame leads a boring life, apparently."

Bellamy blinked at the detritus of my life. "Have you an everyday reticule?"

"Because I do so little socializing and go on even fewer mercantile outings, I need only the one, mostly for Sunday. I leave it in my wardrobe from week to week, though the maids, footmen, and housekeeper would all have access to it if they sought to pry."

Lady Violet gathered up my things and returned them to the reticule. "You owe Madame St. Sevier an explanation, Mr. Bellamy."

"Or an apology," Dunkeld added. "I myself would be very curious to see a search warrant."

Bellamy appeared to realize only then that he stood like a dull scholar before the speech-day jury, while the rest of us sat.

"To be honest," he said, "I had hoped it would not come to search warrants or arrests."

The tea tray arrived, and Hugh asked Matthews to bring one of the chairs at the reading table over for Mr. Bellamy. I would not have been that gracious.

When the footman had withdrawn, Bellamy took his seat and declined a cup of tea.

"Items have gone missing from the dry-goods store," Bellamy said. "Rutherford was insistent that I follow up. He is fanatic about his inventory and brought his complaint to me. My sister Elizabeth happened to overhear him and noted that you had been in the shop shortly before Rutherford noticed his goods were not where they should be."

To my consternation, Dunkeld had taken it upon himself to pour out for Lady Violet. He added a dash and dollop to her cup and passed it over with aggressive solitude. Lady Violet set the cup down and poured out for him in turn.

"Your sister is a witness in this affair," Hugh said, "and yet, you do not recuse yourself from the role of magistrate. Has it occurred to you, Bellamy, that if Elizabeth was in the shop at the same time my wife was, then Elizabeth must be regarded as a suspect as well?"

Bellamy, pale to begin with, looked positively cadaverous at Hugh's question. "I grasp your logic, monsieur, and I had hoped the whole business was merely a misunderstanding. Madame put an item or two in her bag simply because one runs out of hands, then she forgot to add them to her tally. If so, then a few pence would address the oversight."

Dunkeld put a piece of shortbread on her ladyship's saucer. "If the local magistrate were enforcing the law, nobody's shop would be open on Sunday, and allegations of customers walking out without paying for goods would not occur."

"A fair point," Lady Violet said, sitting forward. "Why on earth was the dry-goods store open on the Sabbath, Mr. Bellamy? Why would your sister be shopping on the Lord's day? I find this very puzzling."

Bellamy's cheeks acquired a pinkish hue. "I'm not about to send anybody to jail simply for... for allowing people to browse when they have to be at the village for divine services anyway."

"You don't want to see anybody go to jail, ever," Hugh said. "You would not arrest Donnie Vaughn for brandishing a torch at a man who could not defend himself. I suggest that sending *guilty* people to jail is part of the job, Bellamy."

Too late, I recalled that Bellamy had been a captive during the war—as I had. "Are you satisfied that I am not the thief, Mr. Bellamy?"

He looked anything but satisfied. "Lord Dunkeld, do you give me your word that her ladyship removed nothing from this reticule prior to presenting it to me?"

Dunkeld turned his best lairdly glower on Bellamy. "I give you that assurance."

Lady Violet sipped her tea with all the dignity of the queen mother.

"Then I will absent myself." Bellamy rose and bowed in my direction. "With apologies for having had to pay this call."

"I'll see you out," I said. "St. Sevier, if you would pour me a cup of tea?" I sent Hugh my best do-as-I-say smile, and he picked up the teapot.

Bellamy and I made a rapid progress to the front door.

"I do apologize, madame. It's just that Rutherford sees thieves lurking behind every bush, and Elizabeth would not keep silent, and all of this over a length of satin binding. I don't even know what satin binding is. Elizabeth says she saw you admiring some blue satin binding to go with the yarn you purchased."

I had browsed the sewing notions generally and did not recall paying any attention to the available bindings. I would not have purchased binding until my project was complete and precise measurements were in hand.

"You've searched your sister's effects?" I asked, holding his coat for him.

He nodded. "Elizabeth is shrewd. If she stole this stuff, she'd have it well hidden before she accused you. She's my sister, and I love her, but as the oldest girl in the family, she learned to be devious when necessary."

I passed him his hat. "Did you come here to exonerate me?"

"I hoped to, and I have, to the extent that searching for missing goods nearly a week after they disappeared means anything. I know that you of all women deserve to be left in peace, but the whole village is on edge these days, and this was the best I could do."

"I will explain your motivation to my husband and to our guests, but I believe you have a point."

He tapped his hat onto his head and pulled on his gloves. "You do? If so, yours is the minority opinion on the matter. I do not want to be magistrate, you know, but Freeman bungled the job, and Faraday took his turn before Freeman, and I..."

"You wanted to do your bit." I disliked Nigel Bellamy, but I felt some sympathy for him.

He peered out at the bleak day and sent me an equally bleak look. "You had a rough time of it in Spain. A very rough time of it, from what I heard. When does one begin to feel normal again, madame? When does one start to live again?"

He could not know how rough, nor was I about to enlighten him. "You have started. This willingness to wade into the petty nonsense of the shire, to remonstrate with your sister, to take in a blameless hound... That is the beginning. Life beckons, and knowing full well we are not being invited to a feast, we yet take a step in life's direction and find a few crusts or a ripe apple along the way. Time helps, but you must be patient and compassionate with yourself."

"You are kind," he said, taking up a gleaming mahogany walking stick. "Thank you for that. If we do hold another bedamned hound race, I will be plainly in evidence for the duration of the event, and I mean to have a word with Rutherford about all this Sunday browsing. If folk drink to excess Saturday night, they can buy their patent remedies in advance or suffer the consequences."

He bowed smartly and took his leave, letting a gust of cold air into the foyer. I returned to the parlor, knowing exactly what I would find.

Lady Violet held the spool of blue satin binding. "I had it in my pocket," she said. "We guessed that was the last place Bellamy would dare look. I made Sebastian remove it from your reticule so that he could attest to my innocence."

I took my place beside Hugh. "Bellamy said he came here to exonerate me, but he has also all but told me that I have an enemy in Elizabeth."

"*We* do," Hugh said. "Why?"

"Maybe she was warning me," I said. "Binding is used to edge fabric. On shawls and blankets so the stitching doesn't unravel and to give the piece a pretty finish."

"You mean that binding is bought to be displayed," Dunkeld said slowly, "and you would never dare display an item you'd stolen."

"Elizabeth knows that," I replied, "or whoever sent me this warning knows that. Frau Rutherford might have put that binding in my purse. Hap Purvis was in the shop at the time, as was Mrs. Anderson, and… I forget who else. I also carry this reticule with me to the village on services, and half the shire mills around in the churchyard before and after services. All that aside, Bellamy certainly wasn't interested in asking me about other possible suspects."

Lady Violet was on her third piece of shortbread. "Then Bellamy isn't fit for the job, but warning you about what? St. Sevier, is the shire up in arms against you again already?"

She sounded nigh delighted at the prospect. I wanted to dash my tea in her ladyship's face, but I instead allowed my husband to take up the narrative.

CHAPTER ELEVEN

HUGH

Frenchmen were supposed to be sophisticated in matters of *amour*, though sitting next to my wife and beholding my former lover as she bickered with her prospective spouse, I felt none of the savoir faire my heritage should have bestowed upon me.

I had dreaded seeing Violet again. Our situation was too *désordonnée*, too messy. And yet, the ladies were managing quite well. Dunkeld, for his part, had been sufficiently concerned for Violet to bring her to me, the only physician in whom she was likely to confide her symptoms.

And for my part? Ann and I faced an increasingly complicated situation at St. Ivo's, one that had escalated to potential criminal charges—aimed *at my wife*. Violet Belmaine was adept at deciphering riddles, and our riddle was in urgent need of a solution.

When the king's man had come for me earlier in the summer, Ann had been left to cope with the situation as best she could. Only because of her willingness to recruit allies was I eventually exonerated. I now had a taste of the rage and bewilderment she must have experienced.

And the fear.

"St. Ivo's is in thrall to hound races," I said, by way of explanation to our guests. "These occasions are an opportunity for wagering, drinking, and informal pugilism. The stated purpose is to condition the dogs for rigorous work in the hunt field, but ten minutes of galloping about the green twice a month isn't likely to achieve that effect."

"So the races are a village fair without benefit of church influence?" Lady Violet asked.

"Something like that," I replied. "The shops all stay open, the inn does a brisk business in libation, and even the blacksmith is expected to be available at his forge—when he's not refereeing boxing matches. An underdog owned by one of the poorest families has twice prevailed, and now rumors abound that the races were fixed. One could argue that the rumors are supported by evidence."

"One could," Ann muttered, "also pass the whole matter off as the nasty grumblings of those who can't take losing a few shillings in stride."

Dunkeld scrubbed a hand over his face. "No force on earth beats the gossip of an English village for speed, power, and inaccuracy, but what has any of this to do with you?"

Ann was watching me, so I weighed my reply carefully. "In one sense, nothing, except that as a medical man, I know soporifics and stimulants better than anybody in the shire."

Dunkeld cursed fluently in Gaelic, while Lady Violet frowned at the teapot. "You are dealing with cowards, then," she said, "because rather than confront you with their suspicions, they instead accuse Ann of shoplifting goods she could buy with her pin money a thousand times over. Not very bright of them."

"But effective," Ann said. "I will not patronize the shops on my own again."

My wife, who had been through hell in Spain and God knew

what thereafter, was afraid. "We will decamp for Berkshire," I said, "and leave these wretches to sort themselves out."

I meant that decision to comfort Ann and to put our guests' minds at ease. St. Ivo's had nothing of substance to do with Ann and me. I owned a monstrosity of an overgrown wood here, an oversized house full of expensive art nobody appreciated, and acreage largely farmed by others.

Ann shook her head. "Mrs. Grant would have died a miserable, lingering death but for you, Hugh St. Sevier. Her child would have perished with her. The Purvis lad would still have a dislocated arm, and nobody would have been on hand after the riot to patch up the wounded. I ran in Spain. I will not run now."

She had *run* in Spain? That wasn't quite the same thing as giving up on a marriage, was it? I wasn't about to pursue that inquiry before witnesses, but Ann had doubtless disclosed more than she'd meant to.

"You're inciting riots now, St. Sevier?" Dunkeld asked. "I hadn't taken you for the rioting sort."

"Hugh did not start the riot," Ann said, going on to explain the utter mayhem the match race had engendered.

"The sensible thing to do is to halt the races," Violet observed. "Autumn is all but upon us, and the whole business strikes me as doing significant harm and not much good."

Her ladyship was as practical as ever—when it came to other people's business. "The benefits of the hound trials are subtle, but widespread. The shops benefit. The publican benefits enormously as both a purveyor of ale and a sort of race steward. The village benefits from leasing out the green. Those who wager successfully benefit, and in some cases significantly."

"Who loses?" Dunkeld asked.

"Those who bet on the wrong dog," I said, "and they are eager to try their luck on the next race meet, so nobody favors closing down the races."

"Are the matches rigged?" Violet asked.

Ann spoke while I rummaged around for an equivocal diagnosis.

"We don't know. One of the losers showed some symptoms of having been drugged, but his fine, upstanding owner had also beaten him, so the symptoms proved nothing. The blacksmith claims to detest the races, but he was among the winning bettors. The dry-goods merchant remonstrated with his wife for placing a wager, but he was also among the winners. He sells patent remedies, and one of those could easily have been used to drug a dog."

Something about the way Ann was not looking at me now piqued my curiosity. "Ann?"

She studied the reticule that sat beside the teapot. "Marigold Fletcher knows something of herbs. She was inspecting the hounds last Saturday when you and I arrived, and she is discontent at St. Ivo's."

"Is discontent a motive?" Violet asked.

"It's not revenge, passion, or greed," Dunkeld said. "Aren't those the usual justifications propelling the villains in the Gothic novels?"

"Those villains are men," Violet snapped. "A paucity of imagination follows almost necessarily from their gender."

At that moment, I was glad Ann was my wife. Violet was dear, determined, and blazingly intelligent, but she was, to use Ann's word, discontent. Impending motherhood might well be to blame—meaning I was to blame too—but this restless, tart quality had also been part of Violet the widow and Violet the intended.

I trusted that Violet the mother would not suffer the same acerbity, but Violet the marchioness was unlikely to spare her spouse.

"Her ladyship has a point," Ann said slowly. "Ava Purvis claims to detest the hound races, because they demand another late night from her husband for the convenience of the squires. Elizabeth Bellamy won a small sum betting on the underdog, of which she was inordinately proud. Mrs. Fletcher—Marigold's mother—took a very dim view of Donnie Vaughn beating his unsuccessful contender. Johann Rutherford upbraided his wife severely for betting on the races—though she won—and then turned around and placed his own bet. The ladies are involved in this too."

"The wealthy squires are involved," I added wearily. "The village aldermen, the vicar and his wife, and the poorest families barely hanging on. The whole village has an interest in these races, for better or for worse."

"You describe a pot about to boil over," Dunkeld said, "with neighbor set against neighbor, mother against daughter, and so forth. The hound races strike me as a symptom of some worse malaise. St. Sevier, you are the physician. What's your diagnosis?"

"Fiona would say the whole village is in want of a nap and a snack." Why had that observation popped into my head?

"Fiona will be dying to greet you," Ann said. "She saw the coach, and that means she saw the mare, and that means..."

"A girl after my own heart." Dunkeld got to his feet and offered Violet his hand. "My lady, shall we pay our respects to the nursery?"

"We'll see ourselves up," Violet said, getting to her feet with a touch less grace than usual. "And if it's not ceding the field utterly, I myself could do with a nap." She smiled at me a bit guiltily.

I stood and assisted Ann from the sofa.

"I've put his lordship in the green bedroom," Ann said. "Your ladyship is in the blue. I'll look in on Fiona with you, once I've put my workbasket to rights."

The marquess escorted Violet from the room, and Ann leaned against me. "Violet wanted privacy to harangue the marquess."

"Or the marquess is planning on haranguing her. The Scots are infamously brave. Maybe Violet wanted privacy to apologize for some ungracious remarks." I assayed an arm around Ann's waist and brought her into a loose embrace. "Her ladyship is, as you say, unnerved by impending motherhood."

"As well she should be. Are you tempted to cosset her?"

"I'd get the worst of that effort, I'm sure. If there's cosseting to be done, I will leave it to you and Dunkeld. Violet likes to scrap, and I do not like to scrap. We would have had to deal with that fundamental difference, or it would have eventually corroded our entire marriage."

Ann looped her arms around my waist and tucked ever so slightly closer. "You both like to solve problems, Hugh, but you have different approaches. Why am I glad to see our guests?"

"Because they are reinforcements and because we worry for them. I suppose that makes them friends." The word settled more easily into my mind—and heart—than I'd anticipated.

"Bellamy terrified me," Ann said. "Violet is right—women are involved in whatever is amiss here."

How pleasant, to converse with my wife not face-to-face—I couldn't see Ann's eyes because she'd laid her cheek against my chest—but heart-to-heart. We'd often stolen such moments in Spain, respites from the world and all its ills.

"Not only women," I said. "The biggest winners were poor men."

"Underdogs," Ann murmured. "And like underdogs, whoever supports these races—or rigs them or sabotages them—will be tenacious and wily. Do you really want to move to Berkshire, Hugh?"

Yes, I really did. An early start in the morning would have suited me well. "Freeman was an overzealous magistrate, while Bellamy is nearly passive. Matters here could easily deteriorate, and we have few allies."

"Or the whole mess will be forgotten as soon as we get a hard frost."

I thought of Bellamy rooting through Ann's personal belongings and making no attempt to develop a list of other suspects.

"I know this, *mon coeur*. If Bellamy, his sister, or Johann Rutherford—if *anybody*—thinks to threaten you or Fiona, I will defend you. They can burn our home wood, demolish Belle Terre, and salt the wells, and I will shrug at their foolishness, but another threat to my wife, and with all the savagery for which the French are regularly vilified, I will keep you and Fiona safe."

She hugged me, though I had no idea where that speech had come from. My heart, perhaps.

"It won't come to that." Ann gave me a little squeeze that was so fundamentally *Ann* I nearly kissed her, but she stepped away too quickly.

She moved toward the door, so I called after her. "Were you running from me in Spain?"

Her back was to me as she shook her head. "Never that, Hugh, but now is not the time to revisit the past. We have guests."

I thought she'd beat retreat on that observation, but she instead faced me. "You called me your heart, just now."

"I did." Was I to be berated for being affectionate when private with my wife? The words *you hugged me first* begged to be spoken.

"I always liked that about you—the casual French endearments. I still do." She took up her reticule, kissed my cheek, and left.

As I restored order to Ann's workbasket, I tried to make sense of that last exchange. Not long ago, I had referred to Violet as *mon coeur*. She had ceased to be my heart, which was as it should be. Clearly, I was no longer the center of her aspirations either.

But years before I had met Violet, Ann had been my heart, my darling, my dearest. I closed the lid of the tidied-up workbasket and decided that matters with Ann had taken a few steps forward. She had sought my embrace, we were back to sharing a bedroom in some fashion, and she had not run from me in Spain.

So from whom or what had she fled? And when would she share that tale with me?

~

"Your mind is not on the game, Dunkeld." I sank yet another ball into a corner pocket of the billiard table. His lordship had been distracted at supper, and when Ann had offered to light Violet up to her bedroom, Dunkeld had surrendered all pretensions to making conversation.

He'd declined port in favor of whatever Highland brew he carried in his flask, while I had pretended to enjoy a civilized brandy.

"If your intended was half gone with child," he growled, "refusing to marry you, and being stubborn about something as simple as napping at midday, would you be focused on a silly game?"

I set my cue stick in the rack and took Dunkeld's from him rather than trounce him for a third time.

"Her ladyship was my intended first, it's my child she's carrying, and she herself asked to take a nap this afternoon. She doesn't want you entrapped by a pregnancy that ends too soon."

"*She* doesn't want to be entrapped into marriage with me." This admission was ripped from the vast and chilly depths of Dunkeld's manly dignity. His lordship had been in close communion with his flask throughout our games, and I suspected the water of life was in part responsible for his admission.

Violet's fretful Scottish swain was overdue for a tincture of truth.

"Her mother died when she was but a girl," I said. "Violet had no sisters, no kindly step-mama, to take a hand in her upbringing. Before she was out of the schoolroom, her best friend—her first love, if I am to be mortifyingly honest—went off to war without any explanation she could grasp. Two previous pregnancies ended in loss. Her execrably immature disgrace of a husband died after only a few years of marriage. Her family left her to mourn virtually in exile when they should have rallied in her support.

"Then her ladyship," I went on, "from some well of misplaced optimism, found the courage to allow me to court her, and I, too, disappeared as if the fairies snatched me away. Did you expect she would fall swooning at your feet when you proposed to her?"

Dunkeld gave me a thunderous scowl, though behind the Scottish pride, I detected a hint of genuine curiosity.

"When I proposed to her, I expected her to be... relieved." Dunkeld went to the sideboard and began sniffing the stoppers in my decanters one by one. "*I* was relieved. That woman has been driving me daft since I was a boy."

Good for you, Lady Violet. "Have you made any attempt," I said, "any attempt at all, to woo her?" I thought back to long walks with her ladyship in the park, endless hours shared in traveling coaches, pleasant evenings squiring Violet about in Society.

My wooing had been so subtle and gradual, that the decision to court Violet had sneaked up on me as much as my affections had stolen over Violet's awareness. She had told me in hindsight that had my approach been any more direct, she would have sent me packing.

"Wooing?" Dunkeld let a stopper fashioned to resemble an eagle clink back into the bottle. "Is that when a fellow drags a lady the length and breadth of the realm, involves her in everything from missing brides to disappearing bridegrooms, nearly sees her drowned, and gets her with child? If so, then I must disapprove, St. Sevier, seeing as my bride is in a delicate condition and all."

"One does not brawl with the only physician in the shire, my lord. Besides, Violet and Ann would banish us both to the carriage house if we resorted to fisticuffs, and you are not in fact angry with me. You are worried for the woman you love, and you don't know what to do about it."

Dunkeld made a circuit of the table, retrieving balls from pockets. "Now you diagnose affairs of the heart, about which you know nothing. You've been at the brandy all evening, St. Sevier. Best watch that. You're a married man now."

"And you are fuddled." Which, oddly enough, endeared the marquess to me. "What I can tell you, as the man whose marriage proposal Violet accepted before yours, is that she needed and deserved wooing, and I failed to realize that for far too long. I thought she was being coy, trying to pique my masculine pride into overt displays of pursuit. I have no interest in such games."

"You are an idiot. Violet could not be coy to save her soul. She's shy and not as worldly as she seems, but never coy."

Her ladyship would not like to know Dunkeld and I discussed her, but she and Ann had discussed me, and I genuinely—desperately—wanted Violet and Dunkeld to be happy together.

"Your lordship is very confident of your opinions about Lady Violet, and you are right. She has no talent for manipulation. I am not English, not of her world, and I was mistaken in my surmises. She sorted me out, and I learned to trust her. When left to make up her own mind, when encouraged to speak her mind, Violet deals very well. When harassed and lectured and taunted, especially by men, she retreats."

"Not for long," Dunkeld muttered, tossing the white cue ball from hand to hand. "I suppose you've been wooing your wife, then?"

The Scots excelled at the art of the ambush. "I am sleeping in the dressing closet."

I expected Dunkeld to have a laugh at my expense. He instead placed the cue ball on the table and racked the rest of the set. "Better than the carriage house. Is there hope?"

I thought of Ann, leaning against me, her arms around my waist. "Yes."

"You are wooing your wife, then? Stealing her tea? Letting her ride your horse? Rubbing her feet?"

Heavenly angels. What whisky did to a proud man's self-possession. "Rubbing her feet?"

Dunkeld found it necessary to choose carefully among a half-dozen identical cue sticks. Again. He rolled them on the billiard table, sighted down each one, and tried balancing them on his palm—as if I'd allow faulty equipment in my game room.

"Dunkeld, I will now speak to you as a physician and as a physician only. Given that Violet is having symptoms which can presage a miscarriage, intimate relations are ill-advised. Exercise restraint, for the love of God, and expect to exercise more restraint—*months* of restraint—after the child arrives."

He set his cue stick back in the rack. "One hasn't any choice in that regard. You will please forget I said that."

"At least you aren't sleeping in the damned dressing closet on a cot made for a child."

He smacked me on the biceps. "Poor fellow. Perhaps Gaelic charm is overrated, but your lady has been through much. Your lack of appeal might not be the entire problem."

I did not rub my arm. "What are you going on about?"

He began fussing with the fire, poking at the coals, adding a square of peat, then poking some more. "Ann St. Sevier was mentioned as missing in the official reports, then as among the captives. Contrary to orders, I generally read whatever dispatches I carried, in case they had to be destroyed and the message conveyed verbally. The Bonapartist locals who got their hands on her up were not known for their hospitality. Then she was handed over to the French, who were—meaning no insult—also not known for treating female captives well."

I sank onto the sofa, grateful that Dunkeld had delivered that blow while pretending to study the fire.

"I was told..." I tried again. "The official word was that no one survived the attack on the band of deserters she was attached to. 'No survivors' meant 'no captivity.' I took a backhanded comfort from that. Ann hasn't provided many details about what actually happened."

Dunkeld set the poker back on the hearth stand. "You might be on that cot for a long time, St. Sevier."

His lordship had delicately alluded to the intimate violation women were prey to in wartime—and in peacetime. "If Ann needs me to sleep on the cot into my dotage, then on the cot I shall sleep."

The marquess resumed watching the fire, as if tossing peat and poking coals were a high art, and the results might want some refining.

"You love her."

"She is my wife." Why was it so hard to say the words? In the next instant, I heard myself reciting the litany of losses Violet had suffered. Next to them marched my own list—parents, brothers, home, homeland, cousins, aunties and uncles, and Violet.

And before Violet, I had lost Ann. Violet and I had had more in common than either of us had perceived at the time. I had considered her wounded by grief.

Physician, diagnose thyself.

"You love your wife," Dunkeld said. "That's... good. Violet said you did, and she seemed pleased about it. Relieved." He took to studying me. "Does Ann love you?"

"Does Violet love you?" She did. I knew she did, had since childhood, but her romantic feelings for Dunkeld had never been allowed to flourish, and his for her had got him a one-way passage to Spain's battlefields.

"She esteems me," Dunkeld enunciated carefully. "I hate that word. 'Esteem.' I esteem my damned horse when he clears a stile in good rhythm. I do not want… I am maundering. What do you suppose is really going on with these hound races?"

"Note the adroit change of subject. I have no idea what is afoot with the hounds. I barely know a collie from a spaniel."

"We should get them puppies." The marquess, probably forty-seventh in line for the throne, stretched out on the hearth rug as if he were an old hound himself. "The ladies. Get one for Fiona too. Hairy, stinky, slobbering hounds, and the womenfolk will delight in them, when a perfectly healthy Scottish marquess fails to impress."

I threw a pillow at that perfectly healthy—besotted—marquess, careful that it hit his lordship rather than sail into the fire. "Dunkeld, it's time you went to bed."

"Quite agree." He wedged the pillow under his head and turned on his side to face the fire. "Enjoy your cot."

I did not immediately leave, because my cot had no appeal, and Dunkeld, in his tipsy, blunt way, had put his finger on a number of troubling issues. First, I needed to let Ann know that whatever had happened to her in Spain, whatever had inspired her to leave the safety of camp, her past was behind us. I wanted to know what she wanted to tell me, but I also wanted to move into the future with her as husband and wife, whatever that meant for her.

Second, just as I had not properly examined my own history and wasn't well enough acquainted with Ann's, I needed to take a closer look at the history of the hound trials. A competent physician diagnosed a patient only after taking a thorough history. He was trained to consider everything from diet, to personal habits, to environment, to recreation, to employment.

Who *habitually* won money? Who lost? Whose dogs competed

successfully? Who entered time and again with no chance of winning? All that information could be relevant.

I could boast of no credentials as a husband, and I was the veriest tyro as a father, but I hoped that as a diagnosing physician at least, my skills were trustworthy.

I draped a blanket over the sleeping marquess and banked the fire, then took myself up to the bedroom I might never share with my wife. Ann was asleep in the big bed, the light of my candle turning her features to alabaster.

Good night, mon coeur.

I made my way silently to the dressing closet, peeled from my clothing, washed, and stretched out on the cot. But for that conversation with Dunkeld, I might have climbed in beside my wife, trusting that I did not trespass and yearning for her to take an affectionate notice of me.

Dunkeld's reminder had sobered me and left me hoping that, just as I was a competent physician, perhaps my skill as a friend might recommend me to my spouse.

~

At breakfast, Dunkeld posited the theory that the mare deserved the day to recover her energies. Violet—doubtless in retaliation for Dunkeld's attempts to confine her to quarters—declared a desire to spend her morning strolling the home wood.

Because stubbornness alone would inspire her ladyship to march around in Belle Terre's wilderness until Yuletide, Dunkeld predictably stated an intention to escort her. We were none of us, apparently, in the mood to attend divine services.

"I'll give you the keys to the cheese cave," Ann said. "You can admire our cheddars. Fiona says ours are the best in the world."

"They are quite good," I said, finishing my eggs. "I thought we might send one along to the Fletchers."

Ann topped up my tea. "On what pretext? We already sent over enough soupbones to feed a regiment, and the dog was in Bellamy's keeping the next day."

"The Fletchers are the former vicar's wife and daughter?" Violet asked.

Ann left it to me to reply. "The same. They dwell in a cottage owned by Belle Terre for which they pay no rent. The aldermen colluded with my former steward to establish the ladies there unbeknownst to me. Supposedly, Belle Terre's tithes were reduced in compensation for use of the cottage."

"Except they weren't," Violet said, helping herself to another slice of buttered toast. "You dwell in a den of thieves. Mrs. Fletcher was the midwife in her earlier years?"

"She was," Ann said, "and she's something of an herbalist. Her daughter does what she can at a lying-in, but I suspect being a midwife without ever having given birth is difficult. Not because the science eludes her, but because she will lack credibility with her patients. She knew enough to summon Hugh, for which I commend her."

Dunkeld paused in the middle of ingesting a mountain of eggs. "Tell Mrs. Fletcher you are thinking of seasoning your cheese—flavoring it with caraway, dill, and whatnot—so it will fetch a higher price at market. The French cannot leave a good cheese to stand on its own, as is known to all. Send her a cheese so you can ask her opinion regarding the ideal herbs for your scheme."

The marquess's insight should not have surprised me. Outside of matters relating to the love of his life, he was a shrewd man and commercially astute.

"That is a fine idea," Ann said, "both as it relates to the Fletchers and as it relates to the cheese. We have more than we can possibly consume, and it would fetch a decent sum in London."

I thought of the Donohues and Grants, of a family too poor to buy a bottle of cod liver oil, and children who might never walk without pain because of that poverty.

"Any subterfuge that puts more food in the Fletchers' larder is acceptable to me. My lady, enjoy your stroll in the woods. Madame, if I might have a word?" I rose, bowing to the company, and Ann joined me in the corridor.

"Where are you off to?" she asked, fluffing at my cravat. I had come to prefer the coachman's knot, both because the style was loose and because it showed off lacy edges, in the style of an old-fashioned jabot. Ann arranged the edges of my neckcloth just so, and I was assailed by a need to hold her.

Not paw her, not press my attentions upon her, but to simply hold her as the day began.

"I am off to the library. I bethought myself that we need more than one list of bettors, wins, and losses if we are to find any patterns in the wagering. I want to send Freeman a note..."

Ann had taken my hand and was leading me not in the direction of the library, but rather, toward my study.

"I put them in here," she said, opening the study door. "The staff is unlikely to come in here without your permission, and I didn't want anybody snooping."

"Put what in here?" Ann rarely ventured into my study, just as I usually gave her parlor a wide berth.

"The wagering records," she said. "I had the same thought as you and sent off a note to Freeman before our guests arrived yesterday. One race, or one set of races, won't show us any larger patterns. Freeman could get the records from Anderson without raising any eyebrows, so I begged that favor from him."

"You did not beg."

She opened the drawer on the right side of my desk. "Of course not, but if Freeman feels indebted to you, then I'm not above giving him a chance to work off his guilt." She withdrew a sheaf of papers and set them on the blotter. "This is the whole summer thus far, and Freeman collected Elizabeth Bellamy's betting history from her personally. I haven't had time to study the lists, but while Lady Violet is leading Dunkeld a dance in the woods, I thought we might get started."

"Light exercise is good for her," I said, taking a seat on the opposite side of the desk. "And Dunkeld needs to refine his dancing. Might I have my spectacles? They are in the other drawer."

Ann handed them over and took the seat behind the desk. "Shall we list winners and losers?"

"And sums won or lost. Which beast won and who owned that winner might also be of interest. I suspect we are not looking for the large windfall or catastrophic loss, but rather, a subtle trend marked by occasional reverses."

Ann passed me half the tallies. "Elizabeth Bellamy said she usually won. Not a lot, but consistently. That stuck with me for the pride in her voice. She keeps the Bellamy books, and I suspect she could do a better job of running the property than either her father or her brother. Instead, she's their unpaid house steward."

I considered my wife, who had anticipated my suggestion that we more closely examine the wagering. The wife who had weathered Bellamy's insulting visit the day before and who was a gracious hostess to my former intended. I thought, too, of Dunkeld falling asleep on the floor before the hearth and admonishing me to woo my wife.

"Do you know, madame, how highly I regard you?"

She pretended to organize the papers before her. "I harbor a corresponding respect for you."

I waited, hoping there was more. Locking the door and *showing* Ann there was more came to mind, but no. It was for Ann to lock—or unlock—the doors.

"I feel safer when you aren't across the corridor," she said, taking up a pencil and drawing a sheet of foolscap from the tray to her right. "Even in sleep… I sleep better, I needn't fear my dreams."

While I had slept very little. "Then I will relinquish any plans to sleep across the corridor. Might I have a pencil and paper too?"

We fell to our respective tasks, and in my case, progress was slow. Ann had not asked me to share her bed. Maybe she had asked me for patience? I had a great deal of patience, or I had when the challenge had been Violet's moods and crotchets. I had patience with Fiona and with those who needed my medical skills.

With Ann, my stores were apparently limited.

"The big winners tend to vary," Ann said an hour later. "A particular hound does well for a few races, then goes off his game, or is displaced by a new champion. Nobody dominates the field for long."

I looked at my own lists, seeing the same pattern. "It's as if a hound is set up to be the favorite, then knocked from his pedestal. If that's the trend, then why would Donnie Vaughn be such a sore loser?"

Ann stood and stretched, her hands braced on her lower back. A memory rose, vivid and sweet, of her stretching in the same manner when wearing only her chemise after a night of glorious lovemaking. She'd looked at me over her shoulder as I'd sprawled on our bed, and her gaze had held such approval and affection...

Where had that Ann gone? Would I ever deserve such a look again?

"Lionheart is young," she said. "I doubt he competed in earlier years, meaning he might be Dervid Grant's first winner."

"Did Grant lose in the weeks prior to his victory?"

Ann brought her papers around to my side of the desk, took the chair beside mine, and sorted through the sheaf. "He won and lost pennies. Elizabeth Bellamy spoke the truth when she claimed she usually won. Not always, and not vast sums, but when the champions fell, she was usually betting on the underdog who defeated them."

"Is she supporting the unappreciated canines of St. Ivo's because she's their kindred spirit?" I mused. "Or is she rigging the races?"

Ann set her lists on the desk. "We can find evidence of rigging, Hugh, a pattern of winners and losers that defies any other explanation, but that won't tell us who is behind the scheme, or how they are carrying it off."

"The lists might tell us whom we should watch if we want to gather more evidence, or whom we should confront. You are determined that we bide at Belle Terre, because I am needed here, and that means that we must get to the bottom of the situation with the hound trials."

Ann took my spectacles from my nose and replaced them in the drawer. "I am plagued by the feeling that St. Ivo's suffers more than a case of crooked races, but I know my perspective is colored by the village's unfortunate treatment of you."

"Darling wife, you were all but accused of shoplifting by a magistrate who did nothing to investigate the allegations properly. Your jaundiced view of this village is based on facts."

She resumed her seat at my side. "They lie," she said quietly. "The aldermen lied about arranging lodging for the Fletcher women. Noah Purvis claims to detest the races, and then he wins money off them far more often than he loses.

"Rutherford is no better," she went on. "His shop does a brisk business on the Sabbath, and everybody pretends otherwise. He, too, claims to abhor wagering, but he's another consistent small-stakes winner. The whole village brawls on the very green, and the so-called magistrate will arrest no one, and yet, I am accused of petty theft over a length of ribbon. Frau Rutherford waited on me almost the whole time I was at her shop. Why the dishonesty and hypocrisy? Why are they so angry, and what are they afraid of?"

Her question held old and weary bewilderment.

"I know what I am afraid of," I said, rising and drawing Ann to her feet. "I am afraid of losing you again and of losing Fiona before I even truly know her. I realized something last night."

Ann offered a slight smile. "The wisdom of the billiard table?"

"Something like that." The wisdom of the besotted marquess? "I have lost much, and with Violet, it was as if a part of me knew she wasn't mine to keep. I did not know how or when she and I would be parted, but..."

"But you had lost France, your brothers, and me. You lose the occasional patient in peacetime, and you lost many while at war. I'm sorry."

"No more apologies, please. I am attempting to be manly."

She leaned against me once more, her arms around my waist. "I'm still sorry, Hugh. I did not mean to deal you a blow when I left in Spain, or another blow when I returned from the dead."

I wrapped my arms around her and rested my cheek against her hair. "I am glad you returned from the dead, Ann. Never doubt that." More words begged to be spoken. *What happened in Spain? I hated sleeping across the corridor. I love you.*

I was gathering my courage to offer any one of those overtures when somebody rapped on the door.

"St. Sevier, are you in there?" Violet called briskly.

Ann squeezed me, stepped back, and opened the door. "We have been reviewing the betting history of St. Ivo's hound races. Some patterns are emerging."

Violet strode into the room, Dunkeld in her wake. "The very thing," she said, "that I told Sebastian we ought to be doing. Are you making lists? The situation wants lists and theories. St. Sevier, Have I taught you nothing?"

"You taught me much," I said, not caring who read what innuendo into those words. "Let's adjourn to the library, and Ann and I can show you what we've found so far."

Ann gathered up our lists, and the ladies preceded the gentlemen out the door.

"Did you enjoy your constitutional in the home wood?" I asked his lordship before we'd quit the office.

"You should be beaten thoroughly for the state of those acres, St. Sevier. You have an armada worth of lumber in deadfall alone, to say nothing of your standing timber. The squirrels will grow obese on your nuts, and I nearly guddled a two-foot trout in your stream while Violet watched."

"The woods are beautiful, and you wanted to coax her ladyship into wading with you."

Dunkeld made for the door. "You really ought to take those woods in hand. You could make a fortune if you did. We take forestry seriously in Scotland, and I could give you some pointers."

"I am a physician, not a woodsman," I said, "and you take forestry so seriously that you have a leaf in your hair." I plucked said leaf from his lordship's dark locks and handed it to him. "Her ladyship must be very distracted to allow you to parade about in such disarray."

Dunkeld smiled piratically. "The woods are beautiful. You are correct about that much. Let's join the ladies, shall we? If we leave them unsupervised for long, they will plot uprisings on top of rebellions, while we poor sods are left to bumble about barefoot in the undergrowth."

"I do not bumble, Dunkeld. See that you don't either."

He allowed me to have the last word—for once. Perhaps sporting about with leaves in his hair agreed with his lordship.

CHAPTER TWELVE

ANN

Lord Dunkeld had dragged Hugh off for another hike through the woods, the stated objective being a discussion of all the ways Hugh might make money off a lot of overgrown trees. The result was to leave me alone with Lady Violet in the library, the remains of our luncheon sitting on trays.

"What do the winners have in common?" Lady Violet muttered, tapping the blunt end of her pencil against her lips. "I can feel a pattern here, but I cannot see it." She sat back, tossing the pencil onto the sheaf of papers before her. "Without the fellows, it is somewhat quieter, isn't it?"

I was opposite her at the reading table. Without the fellows, it was somewhat more awkward. I glanced at the clock.

"I will swear you went up to take a nap if you will promise to at least put your feet up while you work at your correspondence or read your novels."

Violet aimed a glower at me. "I put my feet up the whole time the men were on hand. I feel better with this pregnancy than I did with either of the other two."

I tidied my own stack of papers into a neat pile. "And yet, you are more worried?"

She angled herself, probably so that she could rest her feet on the chair at the head of the table. "Why, when God saw fit to punish Adam, was Adam merely banished from the garden? But Eve was not only banished with the spouse she'd angered, but also made to bring forth her young—every one of them, for all eternity—in pain and suffering? Why was Eve condemned to death a portion of the time when those young come along? Not an impartial Deity."

She closed her eyes and leaned her head back before going on. "Eve was just being sociable with the serpent, as any polite lady is supposed to be. Adam probably took the bigger bite of the apple."

"But," I replied, holding up a finger, "it was all *the woman's* idea. They still trot out that excuse when it suits them. Do you believe God will punish you for something by taking this child from you?" This child *too*?

Lady Violet opened one eye. "Hugh says you're very brave. You are also perceptive. I hope he appreciates that about you."

A question lay in those words. "And if he doesn't?"

"I will have a word with him."

I should have been offended. Who was Lady Violet Belmaine to lecture *my husband* on his duty to me? I was instead... touched. She worried, I suspected, not only for Hugh, but for me, and probably for Fiona too.

"Hugh has been the soul of kindness. We are making progress, but it feels like climbing some of the mountains back in Scotland. The last bit is the steepest part, and the fall from the highest precipice is the most treacherous."

"Oh, but the views from the summit," Violet murmured, closing her eyes and settling into the chair. "St. Sevier blamed himself for your abandonment of the marriage. Said you detested his medical calling, and he neglected you."

Hugh blamed himself? "The man is daft."

"Or was he smitten?" Offered in an innocent, sleepy murmur that fooled me not one bit.

"He was persecuted, and I hated that."

Violet circled her hand. I was to recite for her ladyship's edification—or for my own peace of mind.

"Hugh was so stubborn, and so passionate, and the English doctors hated him for that. He knew more medicine, and applied it with more skill, than all the rest of the surgeons put together. They were forever trying to catch him in an error or accuse him of stealing from the medical stores. When all else failed, they muttered in the mess tent about Frenchmen with divided loyalties, or doctors who spent too much time in discussion with wounded French prisoners."

"St. Sevier made the Englishmen look bad," Violet said. "This is not an aspect of his wartime service that he discusses."

Not with her ladyship, apparently. Probably not with anybody. "The wounded asked for him by name, would wait hours for him to treat them despite other surgeons being available. The generals and officers consulted Hugh when they could catch him in a private moment. They begged him to treat their diseases of vice, to attend their wives in childbed, and he never refused a patient."

"And his willingness to treat all and sundry probably earned him more resentment. Let's leave our lists for a moment, shall we? Those reading chairs look ever so much more comfortable."

I could refuse, but talking about the past was something I rarely did, and Lady Violet was—strangely enough—a sympathetic ear. We moved to the grouping by the hearth. I shoved a hassock before a wing chair, and her ladyship settled in with a pillow at her back and her feet on the hassock.

"You were saying that St. Sevier had a rough go of it in Spain, rougher than it need have been. Why did he persist?"

"Because he had a calling." Or a wife he was happy to avoid? "I could see that. He saved lives. He wasn't above consulting the local herbwomen and midwives, nor would he hesitate to harangue a general when a latrine had been dug in the wrong place. Where we did the washing, the cooking, the tending of the wounded... Hugh inserted himself into all of those decisions, and the senior officers listened to him, albeit grudgingly."

I took the second reading chair, and as soon as I sat, I felt my eyes grow heavy.

"St. Sevier can be forceful," Violet said, rearranging her pillow. "One doesn't notice that because he's so polite, and gallant, and what-not, but the average terrier is lackadaisical by comparison. I do believe he saved my life."

"He does not say much about his dealings with you." Other than to admit that he had been lonelier than he'd realized when he had taken up with Violet.

"The story isn't complicated. I was making a bad job of leaving mourning behind. The marriage had been unsatisfactory on both sides, though not without redeeming features—I'm supposed to say that because I'm a widow, et cetera and so forth. When the time came to put off my weeds..."

"You hesitated?"

"I went utterly to pieces. I had no energy, but I could not sleep. I was lonely, but wanted only solitude. I had no appetite, but ate at all hours. I was sick to my soul of my house, but had nowhere else to go. I was... dissolving. Hugh not only stopped that process, he made me see that I could refashion myself in any direction I chose. I will always esteem him for that."

She would always *love* him, for which I could not blame her. "Hugh would likely say the same about you."

"I won't be asking him. I have my hands quite full with Dunkeld, thank you very much."

That admission was gracious, a reassurance I would never have asked for. "Why haven't you married his lordship?"

Violet glanced around the library, her expression sheepish. "Dunkeld offered for me out of duty and friendship. I have agreed to marry him, but the timing of the ceremony will be at my discretion. He is a peer, through no fault of his own. He cannot be saddled with a wife incapable of giving him children—living, healthy children."

Of all the things that might have come out of Violet Belmaine's mouth, I could not have anticipated such... such utter tripe.

"You will have to do better than that, my lady. Dunkeld would cheerfully toss the title and all his castles into the North Sea if that would make you happy."

"It wouldn't. Sebastian's pride was crushed when my father refused to allow him to court me. My best friend at the time thought I was the one refusing him, and some little part of him still wants..."

"Revenge?" I well understood that notion.

"Restitution? Reparation? Sebastian was wronged by my father's scorn. Marrying me will right that wrong."

I could have fallen asleep in that comfortable chair, except that the conversation was too interesting.

"You are not the spoils of war, my lady, to be awarded to the victor. Have you any more excuses to parade before me? You haven't yet attempted to convince me that Dunkeld loves another. I would laugh outright, of course, but one must humor an expectant mother."

"You are awful."

Hugh didn't think so. His words came back to me. *Do you know, madame, how highly I regard you?* And the even more breathtaking, *I am afraid of losing you again and of losing Fiona...*

"We are cowards," I said softly. "We fear to be cast out of yet one more garden before we even grasp what harm we're responsible for this time, but life in paradise is not real, my lady. Marry the marquess. He will never betray you, never abandon you, never falter in his regard for you."

Her ladyship was wide awake and looking at me, her gaze curious. "Nor would Hugh treat you so cavalierly."

I might have told her then exactly why Hugh might toss me from our garden, but a tap on the door heralded the arrival of Matthews, come to collect the luncheon trays.

"There's a lively discussion going on down at the edge of the woods," he said.

"In French?" I asked.

"Several languages, from the sounds of it. His lordship and Monsieur St. Sevier are airing their vocabulary. Mrs. T said to tell you. Nobody's placing any bets."

"Meaning," Lady Violet muttered, swinging her feet to the floor, "that violence is not in the immediate offing. Four brothers does inure one to certain vicissitudes. What are they arguing about?"

"One of the stable lads came up for his midday meal. Hails from Ayrshire, so he can understand the Erse. He said it's an argu—a discussion about the home wood."

"The enchanted forest," Lady Violet said, pushing to the edge of her seat. "Dunkeld is smitten with those damned trees. He's keen to build ships, and that takes a perishing lot of wood. Pine will do for the planking—and pine he has aplenty in Perthshire—but the keel and frame are best built of hardwoods."

When did her ladyship discuss shipbuilding with the marquess? "We will leave the gentlemen to their discussion," I said. "If they come to blows, Matthews, you will let us know. Though attempting to pummel the shire's only physician would be foolish of his lordship, and he does not strike me as a foolish man."

"Aye, madame. Mrs. T also said to tell you she'd like to move half day from Thursday to Wednesday this week."

Mrs. T ought not to have put Matthews up to making that request, but she was one to dodge a confrontation, an impulse I also understood.

"Why?" I asked as Matthews gathered up the last of the trays. "Wednesday is market day, and I can't see Mrs. Trebish forgoing her weekly trip to market."

"Oh, we'll all be over at the village this Wednesday. The races what got rained out are to be held Wednesday after market. Should be a jolly time, if nobody gets to scrappin'. Mrs. T has a shrewd eye for a fast hound. We all tend to follow her lead."

I was tempted to refuse Mrs. T's request. The last thing the village needed was another riot.

"I do believe we'll be staying through Thursday," Lady Violet said, "if you and monsieur can stand us that long."

"You must stay as long as you please." That came out inhospitably, so I mustered some honesty. "I enjoy having your company."

Matthews paused by the door. "Shall I send Mrs. T along, madame?"

Violet and her marquess were on hand to attend Wednesday's races with us, and more Belle Terre staff in the village meant more eyes and ears that were somewhat loyal to Hugh and me.

"No need for that," I said. "The change in half day is agreeable to me, provided Mrs. T can manage around the outing to the village."

"Thank you, madame. I'll let her know." He jaunted off, clearly happy to be the bearer of good news.

"We will attend those races," Violet said. "Don't think to dissuade me."

"If we are to attend the races, you had best put your feet back up."

"I'd stick out my tongue at you were I not a lady." She returned to her previous posture, feet up on the hassock.

I stuck out my tongue at her, and we were both still in good spirits when the men rejoined us. What's more, we had come to some interesting conclusions about who might be rigging the races.

"You will tolerate my doting, please," Hugh said as he handed me down from the coach. "The green is more crowded than ever, and I do not see Nigel Bellamy when he ought to be sitting beneath the oaks looking magisterial."

"Elizabeth is in discussion with Noah Purvis," I replied, linking arms with my husband. "Or she's practicing her flirting on him. That suggests Nigel is likely at the inn. He seems to avoid strong sun."

Hugh peered over at me as the coach rolled away toward the livery. "I had not noticed that, but he does seem to avoid bright light, doesn't he? The curtains are drawn in his parlor even when he's entertaining guests."

"Perhaps he's melancholic or perhaps his eyes are sensitive to light. The hounds must still be penned in the livery." Caging animals generally disagreed with me, but the stalls of the livery at least meant the dogs weren't tied, and they were out of the heat and away from the throng on the green.

The crowd was restless, as the last of the market vendors tried to earn some extra coin by lingering at their booths. Herr Rutherford stood on the steps of his shop, beaming both at Ava Purvis, who appeared to be plying him with some kind of question, and at the milling villagers.

Anderson had moved tables and benches to the side yard of the inn, and a cluster of men loitered near the taps. The ladies were at the tables under the oaks, some knitting and all keeping a weather eye on the green.

By agreement, Lady Violet and the marquess would watch the races from the vicarage porch, though Vicar and Mrs. Cooper were on the steps of the lending library, in earnest discussion with Miss Marigold Fletcher.

"Where is Freeman?" Hugh muttered, taking my hand. "He should be here as well."

"Why?"

"Because he knows more than he's telling us, and we do not trust him."

I adopted the slight smile of a woman who was humoring her husband's social ambitions. "*Why* don't we trust him, other than the obvious?"

"Why did he take out those books from the library?" Hugh tipped his hat to Mrs. Donohue, who had one child by the hand and an infant on her hip. "Why could he provide the whole summer's betting records virtually overnight unless he was being careful not to allow any one dog to dominate the field for long?"

"Freeman might want to see the races fold up," I replied, "but he had no means to rig them. He doesn't make up the heats, doesn't house the dogs before the races start, doesn't seem to know very much about canines generally."

Hugh drew me to a bench outside the lending library. "And his horse likes him."

"What has that to do with anything?"

"Would a man who has earned—and encouraged—the devotion of one animal turn around and drug others? As you say, would Freeman even know how? Did he learn to poison hounds while devising and breaking codes for Wellington?"

Lady Violet and I had considered at length the questions of means, motive, and opportunity. Noah Purvis and Johann Rutherford had access to soporifics, as did Marigold Fletcher, if we considered her herb garden. For that matter, Anderson, with endless stores of spirits and ale, could also have affected the outcome of the races by the simple expedient of offering one dog a bowl of water and another a bowl of ale.

Noah Purvis professed to detest the races, even while he consistently won small sums wagering on them. Rutherford claimed to decry the wagering while he, too, consistently won modest sums. Anderson's coffers were enriched by the races regardless of who won, and Marigold Fletcher's name had not appeared on the lists of bettors.

Elizabeth Bellamy laughed at something Noah Purvis said and touched his meaty arm. I was reminded of Mr. Purvis's claim to have seven sisters.

"You are frowning," Hugh said, bending near as if sharing a husbandly confidence.

"Elizabeth Bellamy. Something she's said, done... She's not wearing blue satin binding is she?"

Hugh and I ambled closer just as Elizabeth parted from Mr. Purvis with a jaunty little curtsey.

"Purvis," Hugh said. "*Bonjour*! How fares the intrepid explorer of trees, haylofts, and pirate caves?"

Mr. Purvis bowed to me and extended a hand to Hugh. "The lad's fine, though I think you've inspired him to perfect his yelling. Has a natural talent for it. Gets that from his darling mother. We have pleasant weather for our races, at least. I hate to see the hounds galloping flat out in the worst of the heat."

The weather was lovely, though the quality of the late afternoon sunlight confirmed that these might be our last hot days.

The weather was also a safe, superficial topic. I had expected better from Noah Purvis. "What is your Ava haranguing Mr. Rutherford about?" I asked.

Noah's gaze went to where his wife yet remained on the steps of the dry-goods shop. "She probably wants some bit of thread or yarn that Rutherford doesn't stock. Always at the mending or tatting or knitting. Have you placed your bets?"

Wagering on a race that might well have been rigged struck me as a poor use of my pin money. Before I could offer that observation, Hugh spoke up.

"How, exactly, does one place a wager?" he asked.

"Anderson keeps the book, or Mrs. Anderson does when himself is presiding over the taps. He chalks the odds on the board, and you tell him who your winner is. He's keen on Lady Charlotte this time around, or Mrs. Anderson is. He takes the money, makes a note in his book, and then you order a drink and a meat pie, and he takes more of your money. Of course, he might well have reaped a fair bit of your coin at luncheon and as you wet your whistle throughout the day."

"You don't care for Mr. Anderson?" I asked.

Purvis glanced around. "The man is simply trying to stay in business. The coaching doesn't bring in that much custom anymore, and he has a family to feed. If you'll excuse me, I'm for a pint myself before I finish at the forge for the day."

I watched him stride off in the direction of the inn, his head and shoulders visible above the crowd. "Why do I sense sadness in Noah Purvis?"

"Maybe the apparent rapport between Mrs. Purvis and Herr Rutherford detracts from our blacksmith's good cheer," Hugh said. "Or perhaps Purvis harbors a tendresse for Miss Elizabeth."

Ava Purvis and Johann Rutherford? I shuddered at the thought and recalled Frau Rutherford's earnest recitation, every other sentence peppered with *my Johann*, and the final flourish, *we kiss on it*.

"Noah would not stray. He might appreciate from a respectful distance, and he probably does flirt without thinking about it, but he's loyal to his missus."

Hugh kissed my cheek. "As am I."

Before I could respond to that startling declaration, Anderson set up a racket with his soup ladle and iron triangle. Rutherford bowed over Ava Purvis's hand and crossed the green to the inn. Ava's next gesture was to shade her eyes and scan the crowd until her gaze apparently lit on Noah, heading across the grass.

She hurried from the dry-goods store around the green to the smithy.

"Mrs. Fletcher is dedicated to her salvia, isn't she?" Hugh said.

The lady used her watering can to good advantage all along the walkway before her cottage.

"Salvia can be used to take down inflammation," I replied. "And it's pretty." Mrs. Fletcher moved to her window boxes, generously drenching more flowers. "I thought she napped in the late afternoon."

"Maybe market days are too noisy for napping."

"Or the prospect of another riot makes sleep impossible. They're bringing out the hounds."

The various owners were leading leashed dogs from the livery to the row of lambing pens set up in the center of the green. Most of the beastsds were prancing and propping, while Old Hector appeared unimpressed with the crowd.

"Lionheart is among the competitors," I said. "And he looks to be in fine fettle."

Lionheart was leaping about, straining at the leash, and generally comporting himself as if he were mad for the starting line.

Or simply mad? *Maddened?*

"I like the look of that brindle beast bringing up the rear," Hugh said. "Good deep chest, powerful quarters, has a ready-to-do-business look in his eye."

The hound in question seemed to view the hubbub on the green with bored detachment. "*Her* eye, and you a physician."

"But not a veterinarian."

The competitors for the first heat were consigned to their respective pens. The owners remained in a little clutch nearby, doubtless on the lookout for anybody seeking to drug the dogs.

"Let's have a look in the livery, Husband. I want to get away from this crowd."

Hugh obliged by escorting me around the green. "You want to look at where the dogs were held, as do I."

The livery was deserted, the help presumably across the way placing last-minute bets. A few of the horses stabled on the green side of the aisle hung their heads over half doors to watch the crowd. Most of the equines were napping or lipping at piles of hay.

"The empty stalls are labeled," Hugh said. "Old Hector here, Lionheart across. Doncaster Lad and... Sharpshooter housed together. Lady Charlotte had her own stall. That must be my brindle."

I studied the stalls, not sure what I expected to find. Each had a water bowl, though Lionheart had apparently stepped in his. The remaining inch of water was muddy, and Lady Charlotte's water wasn't exactly pristine either.

The stable smelled strongly of horses, hay, and manure. I lifted Lionheart's bowl and sniffed.

"Hugh?"

"Hmm?" He left off scratching the nose of Squire Freeman's gray.

"Smell this." I passed him the bowl.

He cautiously passed it near his nose. "Bitter. It's faint, but..." He exhaled, then sniffed again. "Familiar, though I can't place it. Let's inspect the others."

Lady Charlotte's water also had a peculiar scent, though it wasn't precisely foul so much as it appeared her ladyship had availed herself of it liberally. The scent of the water was slightly off, though. Not in the same way Lionheart's was, but noticeably, to me anyway.

Hugh was not convinced of my findings regarding Lady Charlotte, though we agreed that Old Hector and the others had plain water in their dishes.

"What do the two of you think you're doing here?" Thaddeus Freeman was climbing down a ladder that led to the hayloft. He made an awkward job of it, given that he had only one good hand. His horse whuffled at the sight of him.

"Finding evidence of race tampering," Hugh said. "And you?"

"I've watched these hounds for the past two hours, and nobody has tampered with anything."

"You've watched," I retorted, "but you haven't *investigated*. Smell this." I fetched Lionheart's bowl for him.

"Dirty," Freeman said, shrugging. "Or maybe dosed with some ale. Many a squire has likely shared his pint with his canine companion, and if so the ale was diluted."

The color was right for ale, but the scent was wrong.

"Who watered these hounds?" Hugh asked.

"In the past two hours, nobody that I know of. Why? For all you know, Lionheart's owner gave him watered ale before he went over to the inn for his own drink."

I wanted to dump the *watered ale* over Freeman's head. "The smell bears littlee resemblance to ale. Somebody brought whatever I'm smelling and poured it into Lionheart's bowl. Lady Charlotte's water has also been adulterated but with something different. Take a whiff." I passed him Lady Charlotte's bowl.

Freeman wrinkled his nose. "Not ale. Could the dogs have simply stepped in their bowls?"

"As overwound as Lionheart is, he very well might have," Hugh replied, while I nosed her ladyship's bowl again and then Lionheart's. My memory went to those difficult months of pregnancy, when the scent of...

"Coffee," I said, shoving Lionheart's bowl at Freeman, and taking Lady Charlotte's from him. "Somebody laced Lionheart's water with coffee. As long as he's been confined, as hot as this stable gets at midafternoon, he'd be bound to drink it, despite the off flavor. If these hounds have been slurping away at their bowls for the past two hours, then Lionheart might well rocket about the green."

I closed my eyes and took another whiff of Lady Charlotte's bowl. Not coffee. Something faintly medicinal, herbal... I had caught the scent before somewhere, but could not place it.

Freeman was glowering at Lionheart's bowl. "Now that you name it... yes. Coffee. Monsieur, what do you know of the effects of coffee on dogs?"

I could see my husband thinking the words, *Je ne suis pas vétérinaire.* He took Lionheart's bowl from Freeman and set it across the barn aisle on a high shelf.

"Coffee can kill a dog," he said. "I saw it happen in Spain. Poor thing had seizures, became comatose, and could not be roused. I believe the creature ate coffee grounds. Lionheart's serving was significantly diluted. I would have been unable to place the scent in these surrounds."

"Nor could I," Freeman said. "Nobody went into the stalls while I watched, I can tell you that. If they tampered with the bowls of water, it was ages ago."

Hugh collected Lady Charlotte's bowl and set it on the far end of the high shelf. "The last thing Lionheart should do now is exert himself. His heart rate is likely accelerated to begin with, and—"

A sharp report suggested the race had just begun.

"We don't know who did this," Freeman said, "and I'd advise against making accusations when you have no suspect."

"We have suspects," I said, taking Hugh's hand, "and we have motives. All we need is a little more proof, though it might be too late for Dervid Grant's dog."

Hugh and I left the stable, Freeman with us, just as the pack of hounds came barreling around our end of the green. Lionheart, still regarded as an underdog, was well out front, while Lady Charlotte—the favorite—was several lengths to the rear.

~

The hounds crossed the finish line in the same order as they'd run the last half of the race, with Lionheart leading the charge and the favorite lolloping along at the back of the pack. Dervid Grant fastened a leash on the underdog who'd become the reigning champion. Lionheart, whether flush with victory or overwrought with the effects of coffee, could not keep still.

Lady Charlotte, by contrast, sat in a panting heap at her owner's feet, and the crowd that had been roaring before went ominously quiet.

"I cry foul," Winthrop Dreyfuss said as Old Hector, also panting but still upright, leaned against Dreyfuss's leg. "I can accept that Old Hec might not be in such fine shape this year, but I bred Lady Charlotte and raised her from a pup. I sold her to Cashmorton because he needed a first-rate bitch, and Charlotte was the best I had. Your mongrel ought never to have beat her, much less by lengths."

"I never went near Lady Charlotte, Dreyfuss," Dervid Grant retorted while contending with a beast leaping madly about at the end of the leash. "Lionheart is on his game is all. He's ready for another heat, while she's..."

Her ladyship chose then to sink to the grass, put her chin on her paws, and close her eyes.

"She's been drugged!" Dreyfuss snapped. "Any damned fool can see she's been drugged."

"She's worn out," Grant countered. "Your kind keep your beasts penned five days out of seven, and you let them out only when you need to hack your hunters. You don't allow your hounds to be *dogs*, and they haven't the bottom my lad has."

"I saw you, Grant." Donnie Vaughn elbowed through the crowd. "You were picking hawthorn on my land. Hawthorn can be used on dogs."

I slipped my hand into Hugh's, and because he chose then to step forward, he took me with him. "Grant was on my land," Hugh said, "and he was harvesting that hawthorn with my permission."

"Why?" Dreyfuss asked, giving Hugh the sort of sniffy perusal usually wielded by dowagers and chaperones upon tipsy younger sons. "Grant is in good health, and we have a *physician* he can consult if he's not."

No, they did not *have* a physician. They were lucky that Hugh was willing to bother with their ills and injuries. I was prepared to correct Mr. Dreyfuss's misconceptions until Hugh gave my fingers a slight pressure.

"Mrs. Grant is recently delivered of a child," Hugh said. "Her wardrobe became very close-fitting as her pregnancy progressed, and she developed some skin lesions as a result. I would not prescribe hawthorn for internal use when a woman is with child or lying-in, but for topical sores, it can serve."

That was all news to me, and Dervid Grant was looking a little bewildered too. Lionheart had taken to pacing in a circle around his owner, and Grant had to pass the leash from hand to hand as the dog orbited at a trot.

"Hawthorn is medicine for dogs," Vaughn insisted. "Ask Mrs. Fletcher. She's always reading the pamphlets, and she wouldn't lie. Grant cheated. The race was rigged. He stole from honest folk, and he needs to pay."

Frau Rutherford, a child in her arms, slipped away from the

crowd. Elizabeth Bellamy was easing in the direction of the livery, where she'd doubtless stowed her gig. I wanted to drag Hugh home to Belle Terre.

Across the green, Mrs. Anderson was harrying her staff to get the barrels of ale back into the inn, and on the vicarage porch, Dunkeld had his arm around Lady Violet's shoulders.

The whole village was bracing for another riot, or worse, and all I could tell them was that Donnie Vaughn was right—the races had been rigged. But not by Dervid Grant.

"Mr. Freeman," I said, "you were on guard duty in the livery, were you not?"

Dreyfuss, Vaughn, and the fellow named Cashmorton looked at me as if Lady Charlotte had joined the conversation.

Freeman sidled into the circle of men and dogs. "I did. From midafternoon on, I waited in the hayloft of the livery, with a clear view of the stalls that housed the first heat of competitors. Nobody went into or out of those stalls, except for the owners. Patrons and employees of the livery were on the premises, but they did not go into the stalls. Only the owners went into them, and only the stalls that housed their respective dogs."

"Then Lady Charlotte was given a slow-acting poison," Dreyfuss said. "Old Hec probably was too."

The crowd around us now was mostly men, though Marigold Fletcher was also among them, standing between Noah Purvis and Johann Rutherford. Noah would keep her safe, but why was she still here, and why was her expression nigh terrified?

Elizabeth Bellamy's gig rattled past and was soon over the arched bridge. She'd chosen a prudent time to be least in sight.

A shiver passed over me, despite the mild evening air. Least in sight—*or invisible*. Elizabeth's gig departed at a smart trot as a thought coalesced in my awareness.

"Hugh," I whispered, "Elizabeth wasn't on the betting rolls, and yet, she claimed to be a modest, consistent winner. Freeman provided us her betting history."

"Side bets?" he murmured as the gig disappeared from view.

"Frau Rutherford was also not on the rolls, and she, too, said she won small sums fairly consistently."

Noah Purvis and Johann Rutherford had been the modest, consistent winners. Ava Purvis had been consulting with Rutherford, and Elizabeth Bellamy with Noah Purvis… who had seven sisters and adored his wife.

"The ladies are placing bets through intermediaries," I said. "Purvis and Rutherford do abhor the races, but they have been inveigled into participating in the wagering, so their guns are spiked."

"Clever," Hugh said quietly as Lionheart finally sat, tail thumping nineteen to the dozen. "The real winners are obscured, and the critics are silenced, but how does that relate to drugging dogs?"

The two were connected, I knew they were. I also knew that the mood of the crowd had grown uglier, and one of Vaughn's cronies had slipped off to enter the livery. He emerged a moment later with a length of rope coiled in his hand.

At the same time, Lady Violet kissed Dunkeld and turned loose of him. The marquess quit the vicarage porch at a steady march, and the crowd parted for him.

"Grant is to blame," Vaughn said. "He's made a killing on the wagers these past two weeks, and he stands to win again today. That's thievery, rigging a race just because a man's too lazy to support his family."

"If anyone is lazy," Grant retorted, "it's you, Vaughn. You're a sot, and you beat a good dog because you wanted the winnings that were rightly mine."

I heard the sound of a knife sliding from a metal sheath.

"Go to Ava Purvis," Hugh said, dropping my hand. "Go quickly. These men mean murder."

Dunkeld shoved through the inner circle and took the place at Hugh's other side. "Getting ugly fast," he muttered. "A fine village you have here, St. Sevier."

Lady Violet remained on the vicarage porch, but she wasn't looking at me. She was looking at Marigold Fletcher. Miss Fletcher stood on the edge of the circle, her shawl clutched tightly about her, as if she were powerless to look away from an unfolding tragedy.

"This isn't about winnings," Vaughn nearly yelled. "This is about harboring a lying, cheating thief in our midst. Grant wants coin, and he won't work for it. He's too busy swiv—"

"Hold your tongue." I had spoken with the same authority I used on squabbling housemaids and feuding footmen, though my heart was beating like an artillery barrage. I wasn't about to sit idly by while this putrid excuse for a man maligned a decent couple.

"You have no proof," I went on, "and you have much to answer for. If anybody had a motive to rig these races, you did. Through your own criminal behavior, you lost possession of a hound who might have won you a tidy sum. You cannot resist the lure of drink, and your many acres are neglected. Your neighbors know this, and yet, because you're an alderman, they allow you to browbeat a fellow who works hard to provide for his family."

Hugh and Dunkeld stood at my back, while Freeman had taken the place beside Grant. Nigel Bellamy had bestirred himself to quit the inn and also placed himself near Grant.

"Somebody drugged these dogs," Dreyfuss said, though his tone was as puzzled as it was pugnacious. "Look at 'em."

Lady Charlotte was catching forty winks at her owner's feet, and Lionheart was yet incapable of sitting still.

"Are you insinuating that Mr. Freeman drugged the dogs?" I asked. "He has admitted to lurking in their vicinity for hours, and he detests these races."

Dunkeld's dark brows rose, while Hugh looked subtly amused. Freeman nodded to me, and I wished I could stick out my tongue at him. Let the great war hero know a few moments as the object of suspicion, however fleeting.

"I'm not saying that," Dreyfuss muttered. "Freeman's a good

fellow. Known him man and boy. Served with distinction and has the injury to prove it."

Many a scoundrel had bought a set of regimental colors. I kept that sad lesson to myself.

"We have no suspects with both opportunity and means," I said. "No witnesses to any wrongdoing—again. We have only race results that some of us disagree with."

"We have evidence," Dreyfuss retorted. "The hounds are off. This lot has seen Lady Charlotte run with the pack. She's a prime animal, and she's acting like a pensioner. Lionheart is young, but he's not stupid. He's acting stupid."

So was I, trying to reason with a lot of half-soused men, but I sensed that they might listen to me, while a harangue from Hugh or Dunkeld would simply get their backs up. What was needed was for Grant, Dreyfuss, and the others to *listen* to one another.

"Mr. Grant." I turned to Lionheart's owner. "What say you?"

Dervid Grant looked at his dog, who was panting heavily and still thumping his tail like a puppy promised a treat.

"Lionheart isn't himself, that much is true."

"Who objects to disbanding the races?" I asked. "They've already caused one riot. On that same evening, my husband saw Donnie Vaughn and his associates menace Arden Donohue with a lit torch. Mr. Vaughn has suffered no consequences for what should have resulted in charges for attempted murder. The lending library was vandalized. Mrs. Cooper assaulted. Now I see that good fellow,"—I gestured to the man lurking in the shadows with his rope—"has perhaps taken a notion to hang a blameless hound, or worse. All for a few shillings of *beer money*? Is St. Ivo's to become lawless for the sake of what was meant to be entertainment?"

Donnie Vaughn spat, but of course waited for somebody else to refute my oratory.

"She has a point." Noah Purvis's bass voice rumbled across the crowd. "We lose sums we can't afford, and we have sore heads and sore feelings the next morning. Because of the races, you lot expect me to work until all hours even on a Saturday. I'm done with that, or my Ava will know why. Then you want the dry-goods shop open on Sunday so you can dose yourselves with patent remedies. Call me a Dissenter if you must, but that's not what the Sabbath is for."

Rutherford, shoulders back, chin up, spoke next. "If I do not open my store on Sunday, Mr. Vaughn comes to the back door before services. I can give him a bottle of the Harbuckle's, and he will pay later, but he does not pay. Miss Bellamy wants her headache powder, and Mrs. Pringle needs some willow bark tea. You people wake the baby. We have no peace on our Sabbath. I think, 'Why not let them come in the front door?' And in the front door you come. Trudy says, 'Please, no more,' and I listen to my Trudy. We don't wager on the races, and we make no Sunday exceptions for drunkards."

Hugh turned an eloquently severe gaze on the assemblage. "Is it moved, seconded, and passed that the hound races have been disbanded? All in favor, say aye."

A weak chorus of ayes followed.

"All opposed?" he asked with exquisite indifference.

A cricket's little song filled the silence.

"No more hound races," Hugh said. "What shall be done with the bets for this night's race?"

"Grant would have been the biggest winner," Anderson said, wiping his hands on a dingy apron. "I'm willing to forgo my five percent."

How magnanimous of him.

"Keep the damned money," Dervid Grant snapped. "I want an apology, Donnie Vaughn. You accused me of every lousy, lazy fault a man can have. I know you can't get a decent crop out of tired land. I know the lure of the bottle is hard to resist, and I know you like to talk big. What I will recall, though, is that nobody stopped you when you aimed your bile at me. Nobody but the Frenchie doctor minded when you damned near burned Donohue's clothes from his back. For myself, I don't care, but for my babies... For my missus... For my few friends... For this damned *dog*..."

He stroked a hand over Lionheart's head. "You will apologize," he said quietly. "You will. The hounds might well have been drugged, but I don't know anything about that. All I know is that a fine and *loyal* beast seemed to be hitting his stride, and a little luck was coming my way when I desperately needed it. This damned village had to ruin even that. If I had the means, I'd collect my family and leave. But I don't, and I probably never will, so I won't say the rest of what I think."

Even the cricket went silent, leaving only the sound of panting canines to fill the evening air.

Vaughn puffed out his chest and stuck out his chin, but with the low cunning by which his kind endured, he must have read the shift in the crowd's mood, because he held his peace.

Noah Purvis seemed to gain three inches of height, and his son Hap had materialized from the crowd. Vicar and Mrs. Cooper were in the circle now, too, as was old Mrs. Fletcher.

St. Ivo's was backing the underdog.

"Apologize," Mrs. Cooper said. "You were out of turn, Mr. Vaughn, and spoke without thinking."

Vaughn mumbled something.

"We didna hear ye," Noah said.

Vaughn, appropriately enough, fixed his gaze on Lionheart. "Mrs. Cooper is right. I spoke without thinking. I do apologize. No hard feelings."

I know not what well of decency or courage Dervid Grant drew upon, but he stuck his right hand out toward Vaughn.

Vaughn, looking somewhat bewildered, shook, then shuffled off toward the inn.

"Drinks on me," Dunkeld yelled, "but no brawlin' lads and ladies."

And because the marquess was paying, half the village followed in Vaughn's wake.

I sagged against my husband, my knees abruptly weak and my breath short. We had solved the problem of the races generally, and perhaps we had planted a seed of communal spirit at St. Ivo's, but we had also all but proved that the races had been rigged. A mystery remained as to who had perpetrated that mischief and why.

As I watched Marigold tuck up her mama's shawl and accompany Mrs. Fletcher back to their cottage, I realized that more clues regarding those last puzzles had been put into my keeping. I felt no compunction to share my insights with anybody. The problem had been solved. The mystery was no longer in need of unraveling. I was content with a partial victory.

I should have known better than to expect that my husband would settle for half measures.

CHAPTER THIRTEEN

HUGH

Ann was keeping secrets.

I recognized the look from just before she'd left me in Spain—distracted, bemused, and trying desperately not to appear as if her focus lay elsewhere. I could well imagine why she'd want to leave St. Ivo's after this day's work, but I would be damned if she'd abandon me again.

"Madame, you took risks," I said as we gained on the retreating forms of Marigold and Mrs. Fletcher. "You confronted a half-drunk crowd of men who were intent on violence."

The scene had brought back memories of my betrothal to Ann, if one could call her acceptance of my offer a *betrothal*. A crowd of men in an ugly mood had been contemplating even uglier acts as they'd tossed their dice and leered at a recently widowed Ann.

"You were with me," she said. "You took the same risks, and yet, I'm not castigating you on the village green, Hugh St. Sevier."

I heard a snort behind me—Violet. Where had she come from? And if Violet was trailing us, Dunkeld was also likely within earshot.

About which, I did not care. "I was so proud of you, Ann St. Sevier, I almost told Dunkeld to scamper back to his porch and let you deal with matters." I took her hand and leaned closer as we walked along. "You know who's rigged the races, don't you?"

"I heard that," Violet said.

Ann smiled. "We have a nanny."

We had a friend or two. "You, madame, have information about this whole mess you have yet to share."

The Fletchers passed through their gate. Mrs. Fletcher stopped only to pick up her watering can, and then the ladies disappeared into the house.

"Freeman is the logical suspect," Ann said, "but as you note, his horse speaks for him, as does his general character. I hate admitting that."

"While I," said Thaddeus Freeman, coming up on Ann's right, "am glad to hear it. Didn't mean to eavesdrop, but one develops the habit of listening."

"Or lurking behind oak trees," I retorted, drawing Ann to a halt. "Do we consider the matter of the hound races resolved?"

Freeman gazed across a green now devoid of all but a few stragglers. "I hate loose ends."

Dunkeld and Lady Violet joined us, and Noah Purvis ambled over from the direction of the smithy.

"Nice work, madame," he said. "I still wish we knew who'd drugged those hounds. Rotten thing to do."

Freeman scowled. "Are you accusing me, Purvis?"

"Nah," Purvis said. "You are like a hen with one chick when it comes to that idiot horse of yours. You might slap a glove across a fellow's face, but you wouldna skulk about to tamper with his dog."

Who would? And what did it say about Freeman—decorated war hero and former magistrate—that his horse was his character witness?

The door to the Fletchers' cottage opened, and Mrs. Fletcher herself emerged, carrying what had to be a full watering can, based on the way she set it on her front porch.

"Evening, all," she called, waving. Her shawl flapped in the evening air, which was still far from cool, and a hint of a notion of an idea fluttered through my imagination.

"Good evening, Mrs. Fletcher," I said. "Would you mind if we joined you?"

She gathered up her shawl. "I'm afraid we haven't enough chairs, monsieur, though I am sorry to decline such pleasant company."

"We can assemble in the garden, and all I'm asking for is a quick chat."

Ann had slipped her arm through mine, while Dunkeld, Violet, and Freeman were looking askance at me. Purvis looked merely curious.

"I've been boasting about your garden," Ann said. "Lady Violet is quite the gardener, and Dunkeld has an interest in botany as well."

Devotion to a product of fermented barley hardly qualified as a botanical interest.

Mrs. Fletcher's gaze went to the door of her cottage, and that one glance—resigned and resolute—told me much.

"Very well, around back with the lot of you. I'll just fetch Marigold, though I don't know as we have even a tea service for so many."

"No need for tea," Violet said with aggressive good cheer. "And I've had quite enough lemonade to last me until Christmas."

Purvis and Freeman brought up the rear, and we were soon standing about on Mrs. Fletcher's back terrace, all of us pretending to admire her potted herbs and strung beans. I had considered confronting my suspect without an audience, but in present company, the Fletchers would be among friends, did they but know it.

"We cannot offer you all a seat," Marigold said when she joined us, "but I do want to express my appreciation for what just transpired on the green. The races were getting out of hand. The horse races aren't as bad, for some reason, but this business with the dogs... it was never were a good idea."

Lady Violet had taken one of the two available chairs, and Mrs. Fletcher the other. That left Ann and Marigold standing and meant the other fellows remained on their feet as well. I didn't want us looming over Mrs. Fletcher, so I gestured for Ann to take a seat on the low wall edging the terrace. Dunkeld sat upon the stones at her ladyship's feet, and Purvis perched his immense bulk on the back stoop.

Freeman led Marigold to a potting bench and took the place beside her.

"Whose idea were the hound races?" I asked when the company had found seats.

"I'm not sure," Marigold replied. "The enclosed hare-coursing on the very green was too much, and Papa persuaded the aldermen to give it up. The hares haven't a fighting chance in that situation. I begged Papa to leave St. Ivo's if they were so determined on that cruelty."

"The owners were unwilling to muzzle their hounds," Mrs. Fletcher murmured. "We came up with the races as a compromise."

"We," I said, "meaning you?"

She looked at her hands, which I subjected to a physician's discreet perusal. No clear evidence of rheumatism, despite those hands having done a great deal of hard work.

"Thomas was willing to champion the idea," she said, "but yes, the suggestion was mine."

"The lending library was your suggestion, too, wasn't it?" I asked. "The collection is impressive."

Mrs. Fletcher looked away, in the direction of her glorious beans.

"That collection," Marigold said, "was far less impressive before Papa died. He willed his books to the lending library. Mama had intended for the village itself to build up the collection, but Papa's books are still the bulk of the titles."

Ann was watching me, as were Violet and Dunkeld. Purvis was studying the terrace's flagstones as if they held the secrets of eternal life, and Freeman was sitting quite close to Marigold.

"We could have used those books," Mrs. Fletcher said. "Could have sold half of them when Thomas died and donated the other half. The aldermen would not let me sort the collection. They just kindly sent a few stout lads to haul the lot wholesale to the lending library, to *save me the trouble.* Some of the most valuable titles—the ecclesiastical rarities—never made it to the lending library."

"The aldermen thanked us," Marigold said. "We saved them the effort of procuring books, and the whole village has benefited. Some apparently more than others."

"You saved them the effort of finding a midwife, too, didn't you?" Ann gently posed that question.

"Mama would never refuse aid to a woman in childbed," Marigold said, "and we still do what we can when there's illness or injury."

"For which," I added, "you are not compensated."

Mrs. Fletcher's gaze went to her daughter. "They know," she said. "They've puzzled it out somehow. I thought I was careful, but then, I thought St. Ivo's was a lovely little village."

"Mama, nobody knows anything. *I* don't know anything. Perhaps you are tired? The day has been taxing to all of us, and an early bedtime—"

Mrs. Fletcher held up a hand. "Marigold, I love you dearly, but I need not involve you in my schemes. This village doesn't consider you their responsibility, but they owed me, and I exacted payment as I saw fit."

Her soft words held a ferocious load of fury, and I knew not how to proceed. I had incidental observations and hunches to go on, no proof.

"They cheated you out of a roof over your heads," Ann said, "and devised the plan that put you in this cottage, didn't they?"

"Donnie Vaughn is a great one for saving money," Mrs. Fletcher said. "Thomas's contract only required that adequate provision be made for his widow in the event of his death. 'Adequate provision' was to steal the use of this cottage from Monsieur St. Sevier and hope he'd never notice."

"How do you eat?" Ann asked.

"They don't," I said. "Not as they should. I noticed that Miss Fletcher's clothing was sewn for a more robust frame, but I did not see the significance of that detail. No Sunday roasts, no tea tray for company. If Mrs. Fletcher lacks energy, it's because she's hungry, not because her advanced years have turned her frail."

"I have energy enough," Mrs. Fletcher said. "I am so sick of eggs and potatoes... I could expire of it, though I am far from frail on my good days. All the basil and tarragon in the world can't make eggs and potatoes other than eggs and potatoes. Ungrateful of me. Grant and Donohue leave the occasional fish or fowl on our back step. Otherwise, we would starve. Those men risk being hanged as poachers to do us a bit of kindness, and yet, it's Vaughn and Dreyfuss strutting about in the churchyard on Sunday."

"And without your good offices, the poorest children would die aborning," Ann said.

"And your good offices," Marigold murmured. "The Purvises try to keep us in butter, and Herr Rutherford pays me to sweep and dust the shop so Trudy has a few less chores to attend to, but we haven't much coin."

"We have *no* coin," Mrs. Fletcher retorted. "Marigold refuses to beg, and I refuse to starve. Does that make me a criminal?"

Freeman, the former magistrate, remained silent, though Ann spoke up.

"You drugged the hounds, ma'am. Monsieur says coffee can kill a dog, and I'm sure Dervid Grant would rather have Lionheart trotting at his side than any amount of winnings stashed beneath the mattress."

How did Ann know that? She was speaking from certainty, not hunches and guesswork.

"I'm careful," Mrs. Fletcher said, "and I do have an eye for a healthy hound. I watch for who has natural speed, and I let that beast gain a reputation as the favorite, then I tilt the odds just the least little bit and let it be known in certain quarters that the favorite is due to falter. I'm not always right, but my system has worked well enough to keep us from the poorhouse and see a few deserving others gain some coin."

"And that," Noah Purvis said, "is why Elizabeth Bellamy sashays up to me in a quiet moment and asks me to place a wee bet for her. I do it, but I feel as guilty as if I'd kissed the girl beneath the maypole."

"Herr Rutherford does it too," Ann said. "Which is why your Ava is occasionally deep in conversation with him and then tells you she was ordering thread or ribbon that never shows up."

The arrangement with accommodating gentlemen also explained why Elizabeth had warned Ann off with a passing allegation of shoplifting.

Purvis's dark brows drew down, then his expression shifted to a fond smile. "Avie and I struggle, with all those mouths to feed, and our lot has bottomless appetites too. They get that from their mother. My Ava is clever, and she knows I dislike the races. I'm not too keen on Elizabeth Bellamy either—a nervous filly, that one—but I feel sorry for the lass."

Freeman asked his first question. "Why? She's comely, she has family, she's in good health."

I could feel the ladies collectively wanting to cosh the squire for his brilliance.

"Elizabeth Bellamy," said Mrs. Fletcher, "is the only reason her family still owns any property. I taught her how to keep the books, and she took control of the family ledgers before she was out of the schoolroom. Her father is an idiot, her mother a hypochondriac. One brother is a fribble and the other hasn't bothered to learn how to manage land. Elizabeth has saved that family, and you can quibble with her means, but not her results."

"And for her efforts," Ann said, "she is probably begrudged a pittance in pin money which Nigel instructs her not to fritter away on peppermint sweets."

"Elizabeth is the Bellamys' unpaid clerk, secretary, house steward, and man of business," Marigold said, "and I am not paid to teach in the dame school. I—who had a more thorough education than any man in this village save Vicar himself—am *permitted* to teach there, to give me something to do, you see. Spinsters should rejoice at any chance to redeem themselves from lives of meaningless isolation."

"Now, Marigold," Mrs. Fletcher said, though she sounded more proud than reproving.

"Trudy Rutherford doesn't even have pin money," Marigold went on. "Not in the sense of having her own money to spend. She is in that shop at all hours, the children underfoot, the customers pestering her at every moment, while Dear Johann stands about on the steps all day, smiling at nothing. Then he takes a notion to look over the books and decides that Trudy isn't to spend so much on hair ribbons for their daughters. His great solution is to put the girls' hair into one braid rather than two, because he has never tried to sleep on a single lumpy braid."

"He's fussing over *hair ribbons*?" Ann said.

"The fussing isn't the worst of it," Mrs. Fletcher retorted. "The true insult is when he comes up with one dunderheaded idea and thinks himself a genius, while ignoring the fact that his shop would fail without his wife's hard work and common sense. The poor woman is so tired she stumbled into the smokehouse door and got that dreadful black eye."

And Trudy had come to Mrs. Fletcher for aid rather than allow me to treat the wound, probably in part because Mrs. Fletcher did not charge for her services.

"Without Ava to keep the books," Noah said, "my forge would fail. She's telling me to get spectacles, and she's right. You spend years looking into the flames in a darkened smithy, and your eyes eventually pay the price. I could no longer see to keep the ledgers even if I knew how. But as for pin money... I make the coin, and it disappears. Ava never complains outright, but... there's a strain, and the lads just keep growing and growing."

Noah was silent for a moment, staring hard at the flagstones, then he aimed a look at Mrs. Fletcher. "You told Ava when to bet and how, didn't you?"

Marigold looked as if she wanted to put a hand over her mother's mouth, but Freeman had at some point taken hold of that hand.

"I might have hinted," Mrs. Fletcher said. "I told Marigold how to bet, and she spread the word in certain quarters, once she realized how good I was at picking winners. Most weeks, I said nothing, but several times in the course of a summer, I'd make an informal prediction."

Freeman looked as if he was puzzling out a cipher. "You rigged the races and shared the winnings with those like yourself who have not been compensated for their labors? The other ladies, the servants, the poorest families."

Mrs. Fletcher adjusted her shawl and said nothing.

"Dervid Grant works himself to flinders," Marigold said. "Arden Donohue's skills with a fishing line got us through the winter. We owe those men, and Lionheart is a fine specimen. I asked Mama if she thought there was any chance Lionheart might win a race, but I never... Mama?"

I did not want Mrs. Fletcher admitting to criminal activity, and yet, she had to know she'd given herself away as the mastermind drugging the dogs.

"The watering you do," I said. "The cottage, the livery, the smithy... This end of the green blooms with blue salvia, and you take care of it."

"Salvia's not much work, once you plant it. A little weeding—Marigold sees to that, and the Purvis boys help. The livery provides the fertilizer."

Some of which doubtless ended up in this lovely back garden. "But this late in summer, the flowers need water, and water weighs about eight pounds per gallon."

Freeman must have caught my drift, because he picked up a watering can near the bench he shared with Marigold.

"A can that holds five gallons," I went on, "weighs about two and a half stone, and you are supposedly a frail old woman afflicted with rheumatism."

"She never fills the watering can to the brim," Marigold said. "Half empty, the can wouldn't weigh that much."

"She fills it nearly full," Noah said, "and totes it around as easily as some women carry a parasol. I know how a sore back or injured hand lays me low from time to time, and when I'm afflicted, I cannot pick up a hammer without feeling it."

"The stick isn't for show," Mrs. Fletcher said, brandishing her cane. "When I overdo, my back acts up too. The Harbuckle's helps then, as does bedrest."

But hauling water up and down the lane, tending to the salvia, and discreetly pouring a flask of coffee over a stall's half door into a water bowl had not overly taxed Mrs. Fletcher's energies. The shawl obscured much, as did the knack of being invisible. The shawl had also obscured...

The Harbuckle's. Lady Charlotte had been dosed with Harbuckle's Heavenly Helper, but how to prove that?

I was saved that trouble by my own dear wife.

"Harbuckle's," Ann said, "helps rig a race, too, doesn't it? A full-size hound probably weighs a little less than half what you do, so the dosing and timing weren't difficult."

Mrs. Fletcher seemed to shrink in on herself, and she again took refuge in silence.

"You need not admit anything," Ann said. "I smelled the elixir in Lady Charlotte's water bowl, and Frau Rutherford said she stocks it only for you. The game is up, and I commend you for running it well and generously, but the issue remains that you and Marigold need to eat, and you refuse to beg. More to the point," Ann said, looking at me, "those should not be your only alternatives."

~

Ann expected me to find a solution to the Fletchers' situation, but keeping them fed and housed was only half an answer. The larger issue was a community in bad economic spirits. The malaise had to do with money, power, and accountability for both, and I—a product of revolutionary France—was the least likely person to come up with an effective treatment for an English village.

But Ann, along with the rest of the assemblage, apparently expected me to, and for Ann, I would try.

"I can make Donohue and Grant my gamekeepers," I said, "and procure the requisite certificates such that they will ensure nobody is in want of a partridge or hare for the stewpot."

"Donnie Vaughn won't like that," Marigold said—with some relish.

"Donnie Vaughn," Freeman muttered, "should have been arrested for disturbing the king's peace, inciting a riot, and attempting murder."

"He's an alderman," Mrs. Fletcher retorted. "Nigel is new to the magistrate's post, and Vicar is old and looking to retire. Besides, the second alderman is Nigel's dear papa, and a more spineless bag of wind you never did meet."

And the third alderman was Dreyfuss, Vaughn's nearest neighbor and friend.

"How does one become an alderman?" Ann asked. "And how is an alderman unseated?"

"Has to do with the council," Purvis replied. "I'm supposed to be a member of the village council, but it doesn't do much other than meet for a drink once a year. We seem to elect the same aldermen over and over."

To my French soul, this village-rule-by-free-drinks arrangement was repugnant in the extreme, though I knew it to be a regular feature of rural English life. A man standing for the hustings was expected to spend great sums *entertaining* the voters in his district, such that many a fellow was inebriated by the time he cast his ballot, which he did publicly.

"The council," said Freeman, "is anybody who qualifies to vote in general elections, meaning the squires with land producing a decent income, and the merchants who qualify under St. Ivo's scot-and-lot rules."

"The *male* merchants," Mrs. Fletcher muttered. "Maybelle Pringle has been managing her millinery since Moses came down from the mount, and she pays the borough levies, but she is not on the council."

"I've thought about selling our herbs," Marigold said, "but a vicar's daughter is a lady. A woman who peddles tisanes is..."

"Not begging," Mrs. Fletcher said. "Or starving." A long look passed between mother and daughter. An herbwoman's skill might well save lives and ease suffering—and earn her a living—but she would never be considered a lady.

What was the benefit of being a lady if the primary privilege associated with genteel birth was desperation? "The council chooses the aldermen?" I asked.

"Aye," Purvis replied, "as best I recall, from among its own numbers. Those numbers have dwindled in recent years as families move to Town or sell up and emigrate. Dreyfuss, Vaughn, and old Mr. Bellamy run without opposition."

"Then it's time for some new blood," I observed. "You, Noah Purvis, would make a fine alderman. Rutherford might be willing to serve, and Freeman will be an asset to any organization claiming his support. Anderson seems to be a decent fellow, and I daresay Grant and Donohue have a few ideas about how to manage matters in this village."

"They don't own land," Purvis retorted. "You can buy them gamekeeper's certificates, and they'll make all manner of new friends when they have legal game to hand out, but that won't qualify them for the council."

Ann grasped my scheme before the others did. "They will own land," she said, bestowing a luminous smile upon me. "Beautiful wooded acres. If they sell the deadfall in Town as firewood, that alone will bring in far more than the forty shillings that separates a voter from his poorer neighbor."

"Clever," Dunkeld muttered. "Land is land, and the rules are the rules."

Lady Violet smacked his arm. "It's brilliant. Unlike St. Sevier, who wants only to practice medicine, those families will husband their acres conscientiously. I daresay the new aldermen ought to pass an ordinance making cruelty to a hound a felony offense."

Noah Purvis shook his head. "A misdemeanor carrying a heavy fine and resulting in surrender of the victim. My boys would love a dog or two to play with."

The discussion continued, ranging from potential changes to St. Ivo's village ordinances, to what activities might replace the hound races as a means of raising municipal money, but my interest lay elsewhere. St. Ivo's would muddle on, I hoped with fewer symptoms of greed and mismanagement, and that was good.

I was more concerned with how Ann and I would muddle on. She seemed to sense that my contributions to the discussion were at an end and rose when Freeman had concluded an oration about meeting minutes and agendas.

"The day has been long," she said, "and challenging. Monsieur, if you would please see me and our guests back to Belle Terre, I'd appreciate it."

The appropriate rounds of bowing and curtseying followed, and Marigold Fletcher surprised me with a stout hug. The woman needed some meat on her bones, but she lacked nothing in the fierceness department. Perhaps Freeman might benefit from that fierceness, if he played his cards right.

We four bundled into the coach, and I realized that sitting across from Violet rather than beside her felt right. My place was beside Ann—and hers beside me, I hoped.

"That was brilliant," Violet said, "getting the damned races shut down without identifying a culprit. And that business with the watering can and the various drugs… I would never have puzzled it out."

"No," Dunkeld said, "you would not have, but you would have badgered St. Sevier until his medical mind and madame's astute nose got to the bottom of the puzzle. I have some ideas about how you might parcel out those wooded lots."

His lordship blathered on, probably out of kindness. I was weary in body and soul and not up to making conversation. Dunkeld managed to hold forth most of the way back to Belle Terre, though he might as well have been speaking in ancient Etruscan for all I grasped of his wisdom.

I was aware of only my wife, sitting beside me. Ann had faced her worst fear—a lot of half-inebriated men intent on violence—and bent the lot of them to her will. My presence in that situation had fortified her.

Was she up to the challenge of taking me into her bed? I yearned to be intimate with her, to regain my status as lover in addition to husband. Even more, I longed for her trust and respect. Those treasures were worth working for and waiting for, though I hoped that on this odd, difficult day, I had made some progress toward my goals.

"Let's have an informal supper on the terrace," Ann said. "The evening is mild, the view of the woods peaceful, and none of us is inclined to change into formal attire. Dunkeld, you have reached your quota for the day of maundering on about trees and coppicing and whatnot. We will discuss baby names over our meal and whether Hugh ought to build a surgery on the green, with a space for Miss Fletcher to set up an herbal shop."

We acceded to Ann's management, gratefully in my case. Ann went off to confer with

Cook, Violet repaired to her room to freshen up, and I was left with Dunkeld's brooding company over a predinner glass of sherry in the library.

"I've been thinking," Dunkeld said, "about your lady wife."

That made two of us. "My Ann is formidable, but she frightened me half to death today."

"Violet was itching to wade into the affray as well. I half suspected she shooed me away from the vicarage so she could bring a rearguard action on her own."

"But her ladyship is sensible, and thus she remained safely on the porch. She will marry you, Dunkeld."

His lordship's smile was sweet and a little befuddled. "Do ye promise?"

"She lacks confidence. I suspect once she's past the six months' mark, some of her old ghosts will fade. A child can survive birth at seven months, though that's certainly not ideal."

"Old ghosts are the very devil," Dunkeld said, downing his drink. "They leap from the shadows just when you think you've put them to rest."

With his usual blend of delicacy and deliberation, Dunkeld was working up to something. I sipped my drink, though strong spirits in my present condition were ill-advised. I was unaccountably weary and, without Ann in sight, also restless.

"Are you haunted by old ghosts?" I asked, simply to be polite.

"I'm Scottish. Ghosts are part of it, but I'm thinking more of your Ann."

"Out with it, Dunkeld."

"Violet says Ann could not have run from you in Spain."

I was in no mood to hear her ladyship's assessment of my marital past. "Ann slipped away, carrying little more than an extra cloak, a canteen, and spare stockings." She had taken only half our supply of coins, and I—greetings, ghosts—had not given chase.

"Violet is right. Ann loves you," Dunkeld said with all the considerable certainty of which he was capable. "Ann loves you with the sort of... Violet doesn't look at me the way Ann looks at you. The only reason I don't kill you is because I never saw Violet looking at you the way Ann does."

"*Au nom de Dieu, de quoi—*" I stopped and tried again, though Dunkeld could manage quite well in French. "In the name of God, what are you going on about?"

"Motive," Dunkeld said softly. "The ladies were right to focus on motive. Violet claims that Ann's motive was not to get away from you—it couldn't have been. Ann loved you then, she loves you now. One can hardly grasp two intelligent women both committing such folly where you are concerned. I comfort myself with the notion that Violet was recovering from a bad marriage, and you were a sensible mount after she'd taken a hard toss."

My tired mind did not have the strength to grapple with Dunkeld's theories, but my heart... My lonely, hopeful heart found something in his words and Violet's theories. Ann was reluctant to take me to her bed, which was understandable after years of separation.

But in Spain, we'd rubbed along quite well. Our marriage had been a growing source of wonder and gratitude to me. I had had every indication that my wife was increasingly fond of me, and my own sentiments had qualified as smitten. Not merely appreciative or cordial... smitten.

I would have died to protect Ann in the village, and I would have died to protect her in Spain.

A combination of dread and relief washed over me. *What had Ann done to protect me?*

Motive, Dunkeld had said. Focus on the motive, as Violet so easily did. I passed Dunkeld my drink. "Don't wait supper on us. Madame and I have matters to discuss."

"Listen more than you talk," he called after me. "My sister told me that, though it's a precept Clemmie honors in the breach."

I left him looking smug as he sipped my drink. Perhaps for Violet I had been a sensible mount—spare me equestrian analogies in matters of the heart—but for my wife, I wanted to be much more, and for more than the space of a few pleasant hacks.

I found Ann asleep beneath the covers of the vast bed she'd shared with me only once before. I peeled out of my clothing, washed what needed washing, and used her toothbrush and toothpowder. Then I joined my wife beneath the covers, took her in my arms, and prayed for inspiration.

CHAPTER FOURTEEN

ANN

One of the first demands I'd made of Hugh upon becoming his wife was cleanliness. In the infirmary, he was a fanatic for washing—his hands, his instruments, the linens. His patients had greater odds of survival, and he attributed that success largely to soap and water.

After an impossibly long day of fighting medical battles, he would stumble back to our tent, too tired to do more than pull off his boots and tumble onto his cot. Try as he might to wear the aprons of his trade, evidence of his daily struggles accompanied him from the infirmary.

As much to make a separation between his profession and his domicile as to spare my delicate senses, I'd insisted that he wash thoroughly upon leaving his patients. He'd acceded to my wishes, with the result that I learned to love the scent of his honeysuckle soap.

That was the fragrance of Hugh prepared to spend the rest of his day with me, Hugh close and clean.

Even as I drowsed on the monstrosity that was my bed, I knew whose weight dipped the mattress. I bundled close to Hugh's side, delighted to find that he wore only pajama trousers.

"*Est-ce que je t'ai réveillé, ma femme chérie?*"

"You did not wake me. I wasn't quite asleep." Hugh hadn't called me his darling wife in that tone for so long, not in any language. The words wedged into one of the many fractures in my heart. "Are Violet and Dunkeld pacing the terrace?"

Hugh moved, and at first I thought he was leaving the bed. He instead shifted to his side to face me.

"I do not care one wretched English farthing what those two are getting up to. They must muddle on as they see fit. I told them not to wait supper on us."

"I'm not so tired that I would neglect—"

Hugh traced the side of my cheek with one long finger. "I am tired, and I am famished for the company of my wife, but if you tell me to leave this bed, I will."

Ah, well. The day's challenges were not over. "I don't want you to leave."

"Which is different from wanting me to stay, Ann. Are old ghosts in this bed with us?"

His question was so gentle, so sad. I rolled to my back and blinked away the damnable urge to cry. "We aren't children, Hugh. I have regrets."

He propped his head on his elbow. "As do I. I should have followed you from camp. I am not much of a tracker, but I knew the countryside was dangerous. I knew that you hadn't taken more than a few necessities and that you were so damned pretty and stubborn... bad things could and did happen to you when you left me."

I could not lie to him, not now. "I knew the risks."

He slipped an arm around my neck and drew me gently into his embrace. "And you are my Ann, so practical and so fierce. You knew the risks, and you took them anyway. Who threatened you?"

How had he put this together? But then, I knew how. Hugh St. Sevier could listen to a man's heart, assess his breathing, take a good long look at him, ask a few questions, and pluck an accurate diagnosis from a few scraps of information. He excelled at solving puzzles, and I had given him enough pieces to form the picture.

I could distract him temporarily—I wanted to distract us both, badly—but the time had come for trust and truth.

"The men knew when you were in the infirmary," I said. "The other infantry wives tried to keep an eye on me, but they were busy women, and the men were determined."

"Not *the men*," Hugh said, his hand tracing a familiar pattern on my back. "You were spoken for, and according to the informal rules of camp life, that was that. They might have taunted and bullied you, but not to the point that you'd risk your life trying for the coast."

"Damn you." I could have withstood this interrogation had I been anywhere but mashed up against my husband's chest, his caresses bringing back dear memories I'd never thought to relive.

"Tell me who, Ann. The who is part of the why, and I must know why."

"I don't want you to know the why."

His hand on my back paused, then resumed its magic. "Because," he said, "you were not only seeing to your own safety. You were also—and most significantly—seeing to mine. You were to accede quietly to repeated rape, lest I meet with an accident some dark night, *non*?"

Hugh St. Sevier excelled at remaining calm and rational in the midst of tragedy. I'd watched him deliver babies from women who would not live to see the next morning, and his manner had remained as hopeful and constructive as if all were going swimmingly.

He'd explained to fallen soldiers that they would never see again, never dance again, never have children, and he made the awful seem bearable, somehow imparting courage along with bad news.

He was doing that now, willing courage into me, when all I wanted to do was pull the covers over my head and sleep forever.

"My guess," he said, tucking those covers around my shoulders, "is that Lieutenant Colonel Lord Aloysius Dunacre put this proposition to you. He hated me, and do you know why?"

"Because you were a volunteer, French, and a true gentleman, while he was a vile coward."

"So it was Dunacre."

Dunacre, assisted by a few of his toadies. "If it hadn't been him, then some other fine officer would have got around to threatening me once Dunacre let it be known the game was on. Apparently, a red-haired Scotswoman is more temptation than Britain's finest heroes can withstand."

"Bah. Those officers were petty thugs before they bought their colors, and wartime exacerbated their arrogance. Dunacre consulted me regarding his inability to sire children, and I told me that his own intemperance was likely to blame. My honesty made him my enemy, and he took his ire out on you. Did the colonel do more than threaten you, Ann?"

Tears coursed down my cheeks, and all those fractures in my heart coalesced into one, unbearable ache. "He got to me once. I fought him, until he promised he would kill you unless I co-operated. He said the other surgeons resented you, and your death could be blamed on the nearest drunken private. Nobody would care about finding the truth, and without a husband, I would become the camp whore I deserved to be. He meant it, Hugh. He absolutely meant it, and then... I wasn't sure..."

My husband took a proper hold of me and wrestled me over him. His arms came around me, and for the first time in years, I could hold him in return without a barge-load of deception between us.

"You can be sure, Ann: Fiona is our child and there's an end to it. Dunacre was sterile, thank God or the devil. He could wreak violence on your person, but he is not Fiona's father. He is nobody's father, and that is the least of the punishments he deserved."

I held on to my husband as if my happiness depended upon his words, because it absolutely did. "You're certain?"

"As certain as I can be about any medical matter, *mon couer*," Hugh said. "Besides, Fiona has my eyes and my mother's chin, so put your mind at ease. She is our daughter. Did you fear I would not believe you if you told me Dunacre had violated you?"

Hugh was so dear, so precious and brave to put that question to me. "I knew you *would* believe me."

"Ah." He kissed my temple. "I was quite the strutting cock then, wasn't I? The hotheaded Frenchman, out to take on the world. Dunacre was a commoner for all his courtesy title. He would have faced me on the field of honor and delighted to put a bullet through my heart."

"Yes, and nobody would have done a thing to hold him accountable for murder." Much less for rape. I waited, not sure what I wanted from Hugh or he from me. Dunacre, thank a merciful Deity, had fallen at Waterloo, and the rumor was, he'd taken an English bullet 'gone astray.'

Hugh's hands framed my face, compelling me to meet his gaze. "In the village today, *mon ange*, you were brave. You forced those pigheaded Englishmen to admit that their stupid hound races had spun beyond their control and become a bad notion indeed. You did this when I lacked the words and Dunkeld lacked the insights. I was proud of you, I am proud of you. *Comprenez-vous*?"

I nodded, for I could not speak. Hugh was apparently only getting started.

"When you traveled the length of Britain to find me, to confront the husband you thought dead, because that was the honorable course, you were courageous in a whole different way. I admired your courage then, even as I was dumbfounded by the miracle of finding you alive."

"I didn't want to hurt you," I managed, "but Fiona..."

"Fiona has your spirit," Hugh said. "She has admitted me into her affections because she has the courage to love and be loved. You gave her that. I don't know how, I don't know..."

He stopped and pressed his forehead to mine. "*Je suis en admiration devant toi, mon amour*. Awe and admiration for you fill me. When that putrid excuse for an officer cornered you between bad and worse choices, you found a way out for us both. You risked *your life* to keep me from being killed in cold blood, and you humble me with your bravery and generosity."

He went on in French, showering me with adoration in phrases I could only half translate. He kissed me, too, and I kissed him back with all the passion in me. Then we both fell silent, save for the language of love and pleasure.

I fell asleep in my husband's arms, exhausted, at peace, and grateful beyond words. A journey I'd started years ago in Spain was finally over, and I was safely returned to the arms of my beloved. We yet faced challenges—all marriages did—but I drifted into dreams, knowing Hugh and I would face those challenges together.

Lady Violet sat along the rail of the riding arena, looking serene and content as I put the mare through her paces. The air held more than a tang of autumn, and the undergrowth bordering the woods was brushed with bright reds and vivid yellows. We had, overnight, moved from late summer into early autumn.

As for Hugh and I... I had put him through his paces the previous night and again before breakfast. I was quite in charity with the world, and with my husband.

"Fiona," I called, "what do you think of her?"

Fiona sat beside Lady Violet, with an expression that reminded me of Noah Purvis assessing young stock. The gentlemen watched from the rail, though Hugh had offered to try the mare's paces for me before I climbed aboard.

"You should canter her the other direction," Fiona called. "Horses need equal exercise on both sides. Papa always canters Charlemagne both directions."

"My daughter is an equestrienne," Hugh said.

"She gets that from her mother," Dunkeld muttered, deepening his burr in an imitation of our blacksmith.

"I get it from myself," Fiona retorted, "and from Mama and Papa, both. We all love horses in my family."

"So do I," Lady Violet said, brushing the end of Fiona's braid across the child's nose. "Your mama's excellent seat makes me long for the saddle."

I circled the mare in an elegant pirouette. "You must not tease the gentlemen, my lady. Your longing to ride has them both looking terrified. This horse is an utter delight. Fiona, would you like to sit in the saddle at the walk after I do a bit more in the canter?"

Fiona bounded to her feet and was halfway up the fence rails before Hugh caught her about the middle.

"Patience, child. You cannot tell your mother to canter left and then bolt into the arena like a confused rabbit."

For form's sake, I made a few tidy circles at the canter. The mare was perfection, light to the aids, quiet, and athletic. She was everything wonderful on four hooves, or perhaps she reflected my sanguine mood.

I dismounted, lingering only a moment in Hugh's arms before he tossed Fiona into the saddle. He and Dunkeld undertook the complicated business of lecturing Fiona on every aspect of staying atop a standing horse, while I assumed the place beside Violet.

"Fiona must be a very patient child," Violet said, "to put up with both of them holding forth at once."

"She gets that from her mother." We exchanged smiles, and I marveled that Violet and I could share such a casual joke.

"You have monsieur sorted out, then?" her ladyship asked, and my marveling went in a different direction.

"When will you put Dunkeld out of his misery?"

"Touché. Your situation with St. Sevier is none of my business, I know, but you are both so clearly... at peace, happy, beyond happy. You took St. Ivo's hound races in hand, and that has somehow put matters between you and St. Sevier right."

"Matters between me and my husband were never far wrong." He'd understood why I'd left him in Spain, and more than that, he appreciated what had lain behind my choice. I wasn't about to air that linen with her ladyship. Not yet, maybe not ever.

"Minor misunderstandings," her ladyship said. "Dunkeld and I have had our share." Her voice was wistful as she watched Dunkeld shorten the sidesaddle's single stirrup to accommodate Fiona's small size.

"But you and the marquess are beyond that now," I observed. "You worry that if you lose this baby, he will regret marrying you. For his part, he fears that you will be the one saddled with regrets." I did not know Dunkeld well, but he struck me as uncomplicated. He loved and fought fiercely and from principle. He could laugh at himself, and he was at heart profoundly kind.

Also in love with her ladyship.

"I was Freddie Belmaine's disappointment of a wife," Violet said quietly. "I could never be disappointed in Dunkeld, but he..."

"We are none of us perfect, my lady, and that man is head over arse for you. You approach the time when your child can safely leave the womb, and you will soon be out of excuses. Trust him. Trust your heart."

She had no tart reply for me, and I realized how difficult her position had become. The one person she'd relied on earlier in life—her great friend, Sebastian MacHeath—had gone off to war in a fit of temper nobody had explained to her. She'd taken a husband like the dutiful daughter she'd tried to be, and that fellow had gone off to the brothels, the horse races, and the house parties in a fit of male stupidity, when his young wife had needed him badly.

Worse yet, Belmaine had gone off to claim his celestial wings before reaching the cordial accommodation phase of married life.

And then Hugh...

"Dunkeld loves you," I said again, not sure why I needed to emphasize the point. "He will never fail you, and that means, if you fail him, he will still love you. You will weather the difficulties as a couple."

The gentlemen were allowing Fiona to fit her hands around both reins as the mare toddled forth at a placid walk. Hugh paced beside the horse, while Dunkeld kept a hand on the bridle, and all the while, one or the other man offered a stream of instruction.

"You and Hugh are truly sorted out, aren't you? Both of you, together."

"You worry for him still. Does that bother you?"

"A little."

"Worry over him all you like. He is the father of your child and one of the most loyal friends you will ever have. He is also my beloved husband, and I flatter myself that my sentiments are returned. I wish I could sketch this."

"They make a wonderful picture, don't they? They won't let her fall..." Violet's breath caught, and she shaded her eyes. "Motherhood makes a watering pot of me. Do tears weigh eight pounds per gallon, do you think?"

"I think love is the dearest burden and the lightest joy. Have you had any distressing symptoms during your stay here, my lady?"

"A tendency to fret over nothing and a passing desire to tear off Dunkeld's clothes."

Ah, well, then. "I believe both are normal, given your situation, but indulging in the latter is ill-advised until well after the baby arrives. Three months at least."

"Drat the luck. I guess that leaves the fretting."

"And putting your feet up. How many years do you suppose it will be before they allow Fiona to steer that mare on her own?"

"Dunkeld wants to get her a pony. Does she have godparents?"

My answer was irrelevant. As I watched Dunkeld let go of the bridle, I realized Fiona had godparents, and that was a fine thing.

"You are truly at peace regarding my situation with Hugh?" I asked.

Fiona bounced a little in the saddle, and the mare obligingly stepped forth with one iota more energy, while Hugh continued to pace parallel to Fiona's knee.

"No," Violet said after a moment. "I am not merely at peace. I am happy for you, and for Hugh, and for Fiona. I'm not just saying that."

"Your days of just saying anything are probably gone forever. Mine certainly are, and good riddance. Any recurrence of troubling symptoms, my lady?" She hadn't exactly answered the question on my first try.

"For pity's sake, call me Violet, and no. Putting my feet up and impersonating a gouty dowager have yielded some benefits."

Her ladyship was also taking plenty of walks with Lord Dunkeld at her side, and she was free from the meddlesome attentions of family. The marquess was less fretful for having brought Violet to Belle Terre, and that, too, had doubtless contributed to her ladyship's wellbeing.

In some odd way, this visit had also been a tonic for me and Hugh.

"Have you set a date?" I asked.

Her gaze was on the trio in the arena. Dunkeld now walked ahead of the mare, but he faced backward, keeping Fiona in his sight at all times.

"Barring the unforeseen, we will marry thirty days hence," Lady Violet said. "Autumn is a beautiful season, and we ought to have Ashmore ready for company by then. Sebastian has a special license, and I..."

"Yes, my lady?"

"I have loved him since I first spotted him lounging in the boughs of one my favorite trees and he bade me to climb up and enjoy the view with him."

Her brothers would doubtless have told her girls weren't to climb trees at all, and her father would have lectured her endlessly about decorum and maintaining standards.

"Did you?"

"Of course, though Sebastian was perched a good fifteen feet higher than I'd ever dared climb. He was right though, the view was marvelous."

The view was marvelous indeed. "Are you trying to decide

whether to invite us to the wedding? You need not. You must do what you and Dunkeld think best." I could speak for Hugh to that extent. He would want Violet and her marquess to make of their wedding day what they pleased—as I did—and to blazes with maintaining standards.

"Sebastian and I are agreed that you and St. Sevier must be our honored guests. My brothers Mitchell and Felix will be on hand with their wives, but we also want our friends with us. We want... you. I know we're asking a lot, but as you said, I'm through with platitudes and pleasantries for the sake of propriety. Please say you'll come."

"We will come, and not for the sake of appearances. We will come to celebrate with you, and to keep your family from driving you to Bedlam."

"Thank you. Sebastian says we'll winter here in the south, so you'll probably be seeing more of us than you'd anticipated."

That announcement had the ring of a dignified apology, which was the outside of too much. Of course, Hugh and I would want to be nearby when the baby was born.

"Violet, cease fretting. I value my friends, few in number though they are. Do you suppose I will ever be allowed back on that mare?"

Hugh had taken a step away from the horse, and Fiona was actually steering her mount, who plodded along like the good-natured soul she clearly was.

"You have already got back on the horse, Ann St. Sevier. One knows the look and one rejoices at your good fortune."

"On second thought, perhaps you'd best decamp for Scotland at first light."

We both started laughing. Our menfolk smiled at us, and Fiona waved with one hand. Lady Violet was right, I had was back on the horse, and she had finally climbed the last of the distance needed to join her marquess.

The views were wonderful, and at that moment, life was wonderful. Violet and I and our dear fellows had more adventures in store, but that, as her ladyship would say, is a tale for another time.

Made in United States
North Haven, CT
01 July 2022

20837550R00137